"Would it be safe for me to assume that things aren't going as you'd planned?"

John asked, breaking the heavy silence between them.

The sarcasm in his voice changed Kathleen's frustration to anger. Clearly he thought she'd hoped for personal gain by her actions. "Contrary to my normal behavior, I had no plan," she replied coldly, turning to face him. "I acted on impulse to save your life. I don't know why. It was obviously a moment of insanity. If we live through this, I can promise you I shall never act on such an impulse again."

John regarded her with sarcastic amusement. No woman he knew could have handled herself with such assurance against Captain Thorton and his crew. No, this was not a woman who acted out of weakness. "I find it hard to believe you have an impulsive bone in your body."

Dear Reader,

Our titles for June include *The Lady and the Laird* by Maura Seger, a charming story of mischief and mayhem. Forced to occupy a crumbling Scottish castle for six months or lose her inheritance, Kaitlyn Sinclair is ill prepared for the devilment caused by the castle's former residents—one living and one long dead.

Those of you who have enjoyed Julie Tetel's previous novels will not be disappointed with *Sweet Suspicions,* her first book for Harlequin Historicals, an intriguing romance that pairs a well-connected yet penniless woman with a rich outcast of London society on a hunt to uncover the murderer in their midst.

The Claim is the first of two titles by Lucy Elliot involving the infamous Green Mountain Boys. When frontiersman Zeke Brownwell declares himself the owner of the very same land that citified Sarah Meade believes is hers, the sparks begin to fly.

Captive Kathleen James impetuously marries fellow prisoner John Ashford to save him from certain death in *Pirate Bride* by Elizabeth August. This tale of danger and adventure is the first historical for Harlequin by this popular contemporary author.

Four enticing stories from Harlequin Historicals to catch your fancy. We hope you enjoy them.

Sincerely,

The Editors

Pirate Bride

Elizabeth August

Harlequin Books

TORONTO • NEW YORK • LONDON
AMSTERDAM • PARIS • SYDNEY • HAMBURG
STOCKHOLM • ATHENS • TOKYO • MILAN
MADRID • WARSAW • BUDAPEST • AUCKLAND

Harlequin Historicals first edition June 1992

ISBN 0-373-28730-5

PIRATE BRIDE

ELIZABETH AUGUST

is a well-known name to readers of Silhouette Romances. Although she loves writing about contemporary heroes and heroines, she feels that romance is ageless and she cannot resist writing a historical once in a while.

Elizabeth lives in Delaware with her husband and three sons. And for those readers who are quick to recognize a writer's individual style, we should mention that Elizabeth has also written under the name Betsy Page.

To those lovers of history who are clever enough to
realize that romance is the spice of life

Chapter One

Off the Carolina coast, 1673

The *English Wench*, prized by her pirate crew for her speed and agility, had had no trouble overtaking the heavier merchant vessel. Being attacked by pirates was one of the hazards faced by those who sailed along the coast of the Carolinas in the year of the Lord 1673.

While the merchant vessel had attempted to position itself to use its cannons, the *English Wench* had drawn alongside. Using grappling hooks, the pirates had bound the two vessels together. Even before all the lines were secured, members of the band had leapt from their vessel to the deck of the merchant ship.

Kathleen had watched the battle through a spyglass from the bridge of the *English Wench*. Captain Thorton's ruthless pirates had won, but not easily. The captain of the merchant vessel and his officers had fought valiantly. Even the crew had put up more of a fight than was usual. These men did not commonly feel a sufficient loyalty to the owners of the vessel on which they sailed to risk their lives in battle. Then there had been the brown-haired man who now stood tall and proud, despite his wounds, among the

other prisoners. She judged his age to be near thirty. It was
not easy to decide his place. He had moved with the air of
one used to being in a position of authority. But he wore
no wig. Had he, it would have been a certain sign of rank.
However, it was his own natural hair that hung thick and
full past his shoulders. Very nice hair, too, she mused, a
rich brown like the shell of a hickory nut.

His clothing was well tailored and most definitely the
attire of a gentleman. But to her shock she had found her
mind going beyond the depth of her gaze. It was difficult
to determine the true figure of a man beneath his clothing, but his movements had been strong and lithe, and
Kathleen had found herself envisioning strong shoulders
and firm legs. Not at all the kind of thoughts for a modest
woman to be having, but then she had not lived in polite
or refined company for many years. A sudden concern that
some of the pirates' lusty nature had rubbed off onto her
caused a cold chill. Never!

Her mind returned to the business at hand. The battle
was over and the captain of the captured vessel was ordering the healthy prisoners to help the wounded members of
his crew. Meanwhile, standing slightly apart from the
others, the brown-haired swordsman was tying a makeshift bandage around his arm. A slicing blow from a sa-
ber had cut through his clothing to the flesh below. The
bleeding had slowed, however, indicating that the wound
was not deep. For a moment she wondered if he was one
of the owners of the vessel. But noticing that the captain
made no move to consult with him, she concluded that he
was merely a passenger.

Suddenly realizing how long she had allowed this particular man to occupy her attention, she frowned. "You're
wasting precious time," she berated herself aloud. Putting the spyglass aside, she left the bridge. As she crossed

the long plank now connecting the two ships, she tried not to think of the blood on the deck or the bodies of the dead and dying.

"I've lost a few of me men today," Captain Lawrence Thorton said, addressing the crew of the ship he had just captured. "If any of you lads are wanting to join me merry band, you're welcome. Just step forward. The rest of you will be set adrift with what remaining officers you have. If you're lucky, the sharks'll eat you 'afore the Indians get you." He laughed at his joke while Kathleen fought back a wave of nausea as she nearly tripped over a severed arm.

As distasteful as such expeditions were, she'd convinced Captain Thorton to allow her to board the captured ships. She'd led him to believe her motives were purely those of mercy toward the wounded. Since he hadn't a single merciful bone in his body, he found this amusing and did not stop her. In truth, while she did try to help the injured, especially those of the captured vessel, her real purpose was to find small weapons she could conceal in a pocket in her petticoat. She was determined that one day she would escape from Captain Thorton. And that day will be very soon, she promised herself as she knelt beside a corpse and guardedly took a dagger and its sheath from the corpse's belt.

Hearing a splash, she glanced toward the rail to find that Captain Thorton's men were already tossing the bodies of those who had died, both friend and foe alike, overboard to the waiting sharks. No formal ceremonies for these cutthroats. Cries for mercy suddenly filled the air as a badly wounded member of the merchant crew was flung overboard along with the dead. "He'd never of made it, mate," one of the two pirates explained with a gleeful grin when the captain of the merchant vessel protested.

Kathleen's stomach knotted as she heard the body hit the water. After eleven years of sailing with Captain Thorton, she should have grown used to his and his crew's callous disrespect for human life, but she hadn't.

About half of the remaining merchant crew accepted Captain Thorton's invitation to join him. This didn't surprise her. Joining the pirates provided them an opportunity to gain wealth they would never otherwise have. It also afforded them a much better chance of survival than being set adrift in an overcrowded lifeboat.

Hearing a groan, Kathleen turned to see one of Captain Thorton's men lying dazed on the deck not far from where she knelt. She knew that if he did not regain his senses by the time the "burial" crew found him, he, too, might be tossed to the sharks. Captain Thorton's crew operated on the principal of survival of the fittest, always keeping in mind that the fewer left to share the booty, the larger their portion of the prize.

A part of her was tempted to leave the man to his fate. He had certainly shown her no kindness. None of Captain Thorton's crew had. They leered at her and made crude remarks, and she knew that should Captain Thorton ever decide to relinquish his guardianship over her, each would be willing to use her foully. Still, she couldn't bring herself to let the man die. Rising, she crossed over to him and helped him to his feet.

He had a large bump on his head, but other than that, he was not injured. "If you want to live, stay on your feet," she instructed him firmly. She saw the glimmer of understanding in his eyes. Reaching out, he steadied himself against the mast.

Moving away from him, she continued around the deck. The blood again caused her stomach to churn. "You can be sick later," she reprimanded herself in a harsh whisper.

The time had come for the officers and those remaining with them to board their lifeboat. Despite the fact that their chances of survival were very slim, with all her heart she wished she could go with them. The passenger who had captured her attention during the battle was in the group. Without even thinking, she moved closer until she found herself beside him. He was taller than she had first thought. Her slender five-foot-six-inch frame did not quite reach his chin. And he was even more muscular than she had judged from a distance. His shoulders were broad and his abdomen was firm and flat. While his manner was that of one ready to accept his fate, she noted that the muscles of his legs were flexed like those of an animal prepared to defend itself. Her gaze traveled to his hands. The palms were callused. He dressed like a gentleman, but clearly he was no man of leisure.

As if he suddenly felt her studying him, he turned and looked down at her.

His features were strong but blended well into a face that could be considered ruggedly handsome. His eyes were a deep brown, a shade darker than his hair. When they first settled on Kathleen, they showed surprise, then they became even darker with disapproval.

A pirate's whore, John thought to himself, as the shock of seeing a woman in the middle of this carnage wore off. He looked down at the fresh blood smeared across the back of one of her hands. He'd once heard that a bloodthirsty woman could be a thousand times more dangerous than a bloodthirsty man. Best to stand clear of this one, he decided, shifting his gaze back to his captors.

Kathleen's gray eyes flashed with proud defiance as she read the disdain in his features. Her head held high, she stepped away from the arrogant prisoner as Mr. Louker, Captain Thorton's first mate, approached and ordered the group to begin their descent into the waiting lifeboat. Oh, how she wished she could go with them.

Suddenly Joseph Yates was at the brown-eyed prisoner's side. "He stays to pay for the death of me brother." Grabbing the man by his wounded arm, Joseph yanked him out of the line. His knife was already drawn to slit the prisoner's throat. As if her own death was being set in motion, a chill shook Kathleen. Without thinking, she raced across the deck and grabbed Joseph's arm before he could do his filthy deed.

"Your brother died in a fair fight," she insisted, her fingers digging into Joseph's arm as he tried to shake her free. Even as she fought for the prisoner, she did not understand why it was so important to her that he live. She told herself her concern was only because he was an innocent human being who did not deserve to die at the hands of these cutthroats. "I was watching from the bridge of the *English Wench*."

"How me brother died is of no importance. He's dead and I'll have me revenge." Joseph's eyes glistened with hatred as he gave a strong jerk that sent Kathleen sprawling onto the deck.

The woman's attempt to save his life startled John. But he had no time to wonder at her behavior. The pirate's struggle with her had drawn Joseph's attention away from his quarry. John was not one to allow an opportunity to go to waste. He captured the wrist of Joseph's knife-wielding hand in a viselike grip and twisted it hard. As Kathleen scrambled back to her feet, the bloody knife dropped to the deck.

"You're a dead man," Joseph spat at the prisoner, who now held him captive.

"You cannot kill him without the captain's permission," Kathleen warned Joseph harshly. It was the direst threat she could muster. "Or you'll pay with your life."

Joseph greeted her warning with a self-righteous scowl. "He killed me brother. I've got a right—"

"You should listen to Kathleen," a male voice cautioned from behind her.

Glancing over her shoulder Kathleen saw Captain Thorton approaching them. He looked older than his forty-five years. The ocean winds and his own innate cruelty had etched harsh lines into his features. His attire was that of a fancy English gentleman. There were polished buckles adorning his boots, a lace cravat at his throat and a heavy, full wig upon his head. He was only an inch taller than she but the cocked hat he wore, graced as it was with a plume, made him seem taller. His green silk waistcoat strained against his stomach, but she knew he was made more of muscle than fat. His dress and the manner in which he carried himself caused her to think of a strutting peacock, a very vicious, very deadly one.

"She knows better than any member of my crew what disobeying my orders can mean." While the captain spoke calmly, the threat in his voice caused Joseph to grow pale.

Satisfied he'd made his authority felt, Captain Thorton turned his attention to John, who was still holding Joseph's wrist. "Release him," he ordered.

For a moment, John stood defiantly. But he knew he was in no position to bargain. There was a ruthlessness in the captain's eyes that told him that even if he were to kill Joseph, the captain would not care. With a force that sent Joseph sprawling, John released the surly pirate.

Kathleen saw Captain Thorton's jaw twitch. He didn't like this prisoner.

Joseph grabbed his knife as he scrambled to his feet. "I want him," he said, his gaze fixed on John. "And I'm willing to give half me booty for him."

Kathleen saw the agreement in Captain Thorton's eyes and panic twisted her stomach. "Wait," she demanded before he could give his consent. Without thinking, she approached the captain and whispered in his ear.

"No!" he bellowed.

Kathleen stood numbly, wondering what insanity had guided her. She'd bided her time carefully for the past several months, pretending to have accepted her servitude at last. After her last attempted escape, she knew her life hung by only a spider's thread, and yet she was risking everything for a stranger who had shown her nothing but contempt. She glanced toward him.

John was puzzled and suspicious. What interest could this woman have in him? For the first time, he noted that she was agreeably fair to look at. Perhaps she had tired of her less-civil bedmates and wished one she thought would be gentler. His gaze roamed appraisingly over her. She had the kind of curves that could entice any man. He scowled at himself. She was a pirate whore. He should be repulsed by the idea of sharing her bed. However, if I must die, there could be worse ways to go, he mused philosophically.

Kathleen's attention had returned to Captain Thorton. There was the promise of punishment on his face. Still she couldn't bring herself to allow the brown-eyed man to die at Joseph's hands. "You made my mother a deathbed promise," she said, meeting the captain's gaze levelly. "She was looking at you and listening to that promise at the moment she drew her last breath. If you break it, may all the evils of the world be visited upon you."

Captain Thorton's hand came down hard against her cheek. "Never curse me, Kathleen!" he snarled.

Her head reeled and for a moment she almost lost her balance. But he'd hit her before, and instinct born of practice allowed her to resteady herself before she fell. The dark imprint of his hand showed vividly against her ivory skin, but she paid no heed. Her feet once again firmly planted, she stood glaring at him defiantly.

"You take back your request," he ordered. "Or I promise you, you'll regret this for what remains of your life."

But she had made her move. There was no turning back now. Kathleen faced him without flinching. She knew Captain Thorton well. While he feared no living being, he was superstitious and terrified of the wrath her mother's spirit might unleash upon him should he not keep his deathbed pledge. "I'll not."

His hand came up to strike her again and she steadied herself for the blow. But this time it didn't fall.

John would not let any woman, even a pirate's whore, be beaten because of him. In one swift movement he caught the captain's wrist before the second blow could be delivered.

"Let me kill him for you," Joseph pleaded gleefully, rushing forward to claim his revenge.

"No!" Kathleen could not explain the urgency she felt to save this man, but she could not deny it. Swift as a cat she moved to place herself between Joseph and the prisoner.

"Stop!" Lawrence Thorton ordered.

Glaring at Kathleen with a promise of death for her interference, Joseph obeyed.

There was vengeance in Captain Thorton's eyes as he turned his attention back to the prisoner. "Free my arm."

"If you hit the girl again, I'll break it," John promised as he slowly loosened his grip.

He has signed both our death warrants, Kathleen thought frantically. Captain Thorton would never stand for being threatened, especially in front of others. Even his fear of her mother's ghost might not be able to save them now.

"I'll give me entire booty for him," Joseph offered.

The men destined for the lifeboat had been watching the exchange in silence. Now the captain of the merchant vessel stepped forward. "You might do better to consider a ransom," he suggested, clearly trying to save the brown-eyed prisoner's life. "This man is Mr. Jonathan Ashford. He's nephew to the Earl of Wheaton on his mother's side, and rumor has it that the old earl is very fond of him."

A sudden spark of amusement showed in Captain Thorton's eyes. "So he has a bit of noble blood flowing through his veins, does he?" he muttered. Turning his attention back toward the prisoner, he grinned maliciously. "And do you have a pretty little wife at home who'll grieve if you don't return?"

Surprised by the question, John scowled. "My domestic life is none of your concern."

The captain's gaze narrowed threateningly. "Unless you wish to die this moment, you'll answer the question."

John's jaw tensed angrily at this invasion of his privacy. However, he decided it was not worth offering his life for. "I've no wife."

The grin on Lawrence Thorton's face grew even wider. "This situation requires a bit of thought."

"It's me right to claim revenge," Joseph insisted, obviously worried that he might be losing his quarry.

"You'll get your chance," Captain Thorton assured him. "In good time."

Joseph looked unconvinced while Kathleen grew more anxious. She didn't like it when the captain grinned like that. It usually meant he had thought of a very cruel joke to play, and blood was generally spilt as a result.

His expression becoming serious once again, Lawrence Thorton turned to his first mate. "Bind Mr. Ashford's hands. Then you may load the others in the boat and set them adrift. Mr. Ashford will be remaining with me on the *English Wench.*"

"Aye, Sir." Mr. Louker's eyes gleamed with anticipation. He, too, knew the captain's grin meant an evil game was being set in motion, and clearly he was looking forward to watching the players being manipulated.

While Mr. Louker bound John's hands, the captain turned to another member of his crew. "Find Mr. Barrows for me and have him come to my cabin," he ordered. Then he motioned for Kathleen and Mr. Ashford to follow him.

Mr. Barrows had earned the rank of officer on Captain Thorton's ship because he could read and write. As Kathleen crossed the plank behind the captain and Mr. Ashford, she wondered why he'd been summoned. Had Captain Thorton decided to grant her request? If so, she knew he'd come up with a plan to make her regret it.

Opening the door of his cabin, Captain Thorton stepped aside to allow Kathleen and Mr. Ashford to enter ahead of him. "Please seat yourselves." With the pistol in his hand, he indicated the two straight-backed chairs in front of the wide desk that occupied a quarter of the floor space in the cabin. After closing the door, he seated himself in his chair behind the desk and eyed Mr. Ashford levelly. "Joseph and two others are waiting outside. In the event you should foolishly attempt to escape, I've given them permission to kill you," he warned. Then turning to Kathleen, he smiled broadly. "I've decided to grant your request. After which you'll be getting what you deserve."

A cold shiver ran along Kathleen's spine, but she refused to let her fear show. He liked it when she was afraid and she wouldn't give him that satisfaction.

A knock upon the door broke the heavy silence that had descended over the room.

"Enter," Captain Thorton barked.

It was Mr. Barrows. "You wanted me, Captain?" he asked, performing a half bow to show deference.

Kathleen didn't like Franklin Barrows. He'd gleefully joined the captain's crew ten years ago when he was only seventeen and had quickly risen in rank. He was a sly, clever man who used deceit or whatever else was necessary to gain his ends. She placed him in the same category as one of the ship's rats. He even looked like one. He was slender with a narrow face, eyes too close to one another and rotting, pointed teeth.

"I wish you to pen a marriage contract between Miss Kathleen James and Mr. Jonathan Ashford. I'll tell you what to write. I want this to be legal." The captain rose and motioned for Mr. Barrows to take a seat in the chair behind the desk.

John sat rigidly. Marriage to this pirate wench? She had risked her life for him, but he was not certain that made it his duty to marry her.

Mr. Barrows didn't move. His eyes narrowed in anger and his jaw formed a rebellious line. "You promised Kathleen to me," he seethed.

Bile rose in Kathleen's throat. She would rather die than let Franklin Barrows touch her. "He had no right to promise me to anyone."

Ignoring her, Captain Thorton patted Mr. Barrows on the shoulder in a friendly fashion. "I made her mother a deathbed vow that I'd allow Kathleen to marry whom she pleased. She's chosen Mr. Ashford. So I shall have to allow her to wed him. However, she'll have but one night of wedded bliss. On the morrow, Mr. Ashford will face Joseph Yates in a battle to the death.'' Turning toward Kathleen, he said with mocking apology, ''I cannot in good conscience deny a request to avenge a brother's death.''

So that was his game. He was allowing the marriage in order to satisfy his obligation to the deathbed promise. Then he would make her a widow and under his absolute control. Kathleen met his smug grin with a coolness she didn't feel. ''You're assuming Joseph will win.''

''Joseph always wins,'' he reminded her.

Kathleen could not dispute this statement. Her gaze shifted to Mr. Ashford. But there has to be a first time for everything, she told herself hopefully, remembering how gallantly the man beside her had fought earlier today.

His attention returning to Mr. Barrows, the captain finished jovially, ''She might be a bit used, but once she's widowed, she's yours for the taking.''

''Her being a bit used don't bother me none,'' Mr. Barrows assured the captain, and seating himself, he waited with quill in hand.

''Your full name, sir,'' Captain Thorton demanded, leveling his pistol at John.

Ignoring the weapon, John turned to study Kathleen. She had risked a great deal on this play, and if it were not for her, he would be already dead. Although she was not the kind of woman he would ever have chosen to wed, at the moment he had no choice. He would go along with this marriage, but provided he got out of this alive, he would have it annulled immediately. No court in the land would hold him to it.

Despite Kathleen's determination to react to no man, John Ashford's gaze made her uneasy. Her jaw tightened in defiance and she met the suspicion in those dark eyes with quiet dignity.

"Your name, sir," the captain repeated, cocking the pistol threateningly.

"Jonathan Samuel Ashford," John said evenly, his gaze remaining on Kathleen. He could not guess her game. He did, however, suspect that she had used her body many a time to gain what she wanted. For the moment he would act the pawn, but only for the moment. She was going to discover that he was not easily reckoned with.

Kathleen felt John's eyes upon her as the captain dictated the document. Ignoring him, she kept her gaze locked on the porthole, trying to imagine herself in a lifeboat on her way to freedom. When the document was finished, Captain Thorton handed her the pen. Grudgingly she signed. Then it was Jonathan Ashford's turn.

Captain Thorton again cocked his pistol and aimed it at John's head. "Untie him," he ordered Mr. Barrows. When the prisoner's hands were free, Thorton gave him a choice. "You may sign the document or die now."

With an expression of disdain, John picked up the pen and scrawled his name.

The captain and Mr. Barrows signed as witnesses and the deed was done.

After folding the document, Captain Thorton performed a deep bow and extended it toward Kathleen. "Mistress Ashford," he said, addressing her with mock deference.

Her mouth forming a straight, tight line, she accepted the contract.

"Since you have so little time to spend together, I'm sure you'll want some privacy," he continued in a jesting manner. "Kathleen, you may escort your new husband to your cabin." Still smiling, he added, "And please don't take this as an insult to your womanly charms, but I'll be placing a guard outside the door in the event Mr. Ashford should have second thoughts."

Rewarding the captain with a hate-filled glare, Kathleen rose and led the way to her cabin. Stepping aside at the doorway, she motioned for Jonathan Ashford to enter ahead of her. After scowling once again at the captain, who was watching her with amusement from the doorway of his quarters, she entered her cabin and closed and bolted the door. For a long moment, she stood with her back toward her new husband. Through the years, she'd learned it was safest to keep her innermost thoughts hidden, and she needed time to get her frustration under control before she faced him.

Chapter Two

"Would it be safe for me to assume that things aren't going as you'd planned, Mistress Ashford?" John asked, breaking the heavy silence between them.

The sarcasm in his voice changed her frustration to anger. Clearly he thought she'd hoped for a personal gain by her actions. "Contrary to my normal behavior, I had no plan," she replied coldly, turning to face him. "I acted on impulse to save your life. I don't know why. It was obviously a moment of insanity. If we live through this, I can promise you, I shall never act on such an impulse again."

John regarded her with sarcastic amusement. No woman he knew could have handled herself with such assurance against Captain Thorton and his crew. No, this was not a woman who acted out of a weakness. "I find it hard to believe you have an impulsive bone in your body."

Kathleen glared at him. He honestly thought she had married him for some purpose of her own! Well, she would show him what she thought of this marriage! "Please allow me to pass," she requested stiffly.

He moved to one side. Still, the room was so narrow she was forced to brush against him as she made her way to the small table at the far end of the cabin. His body was as hard as granite but instead of the coldness she expected to feel, the contact sent a disturbing rush of heat coursing through her. Shaken, she made three attempts before she managed to light the candle on the table. Having lived under Captain Thorton's rule since she was ten, she'd learned to neither like nor trust men. However, although her reaction to Jonathan Ashford had been disturbing, it had not been negative. It had, in fact, carried a certain excitement.

I'm simply overwrought, she reasoned curtly. Lifting the marriage contract to the flame, she allowed it to catch fire. She held it until the flames grew too close to her fingers, then dropped it into the basin on the table and allowed it to burn until it was nothing but blackened ash. This task completed, she turned to face him. "That is the end of this farce of a marriage. If, by some miracle, you should survive the duel tomorrow and we should find a way to escape before the captain devises another plan to do away with us, then you shall go your way and I shall go mine, Mr. Ashford. And may we never meet again."

Leaning against the wall of the small cabin, he studied her grimly. Her behavior made no sense. She had risked her life and now she claimed she wanted no gain. Eventually, if they lived long enough, he would discover her game, he assured himself. Aloud he said, "You don't seem to have much trust in my ability to do battle."

Kathleen regarded him with equal grimness. "It will not be a gentlemanly confrontation like the ones with which you are familiar. It will be a cutthroat, no-holds-barred fight to the death."

"A wife should have more faith in her husband," he admonished dryly.

The reference to himself as her husband caused a chill of fear to sweep through her. Had he decided he didn't want to spend what could very easily be his last night on this earth in a bed alone? If he thought he could so easily claim husbandly prerogatives, he was in for a surprise. "You're *not* my husband," she declared tartly. "The contract exists no more. I'll never admit to it ever happening and no one will believe a band of pirates should they tell anyone of this." With the swiftness of a cat, she raised her skirt and drew a dagger from a sheath strapped against her leg. "No man is going to use me against my will."

Leaning against the wall, John studied the woman in front of him. Her ebony hair had been tightly braided and wound around her head in a harsh, spinsterly style. But in spite of this obvious attempt to make herself look older, he could see she was young, perhaps in her early twenties. Her skin was a milky ivory, her nose small and straight. Her lips were full and sensuous and she had the most interesting color of eyes. They seemed to change from a pale blue to a smoky gray depending on her mood. Again he noted her full figure with its narrow waist and pleasantly rounded hips . . . womanly curves that could easily stir a man's desire. But there was no softness about her. In spite of the heat he'd felt when she'd passed him in the narrow cabin, she reminded him of an iceberg in an ocean in winter or a tiger, he qualified, his gaze resting on the knife held at the ready in her hand. "I'd never take a woman who was unwilling," he assured her. "I like my pleasure to come gently and with ease."

Kathleen had been very aware of Mr. Ashford's inspection of her. His gaze had been guarded, preventing her from reading his assessment, but his assurance made it clear he found her undesirable. This was the way she wanted it between them. Still, she felt the sting of having been insulted. Purposely she did nothing to make herself attractive. It was safest that way, considering the company she was forced to keep. But she didn't like being made to feel as if she had no appeal.

"I'm glad we'll not have to fight one another," she said icily. "You'll need all of your strength for the morrow." Lifting her skirt, Kathleen resheathed her knife.

Her leg was shapely and, in spite of himself, John felt a stirring in his groin. Don't act the fool, he chided himself. You'd be better off with a rattlesnake in your bed.

For an instant, when she straightened and met her companion's gaze once again, Kathleen saw the flicker of heat in his eyes. Then it was gone, his manner again becoming cold and calculating. So he was not totally immune to her. However, it was equally obvious he wanted as little to do with her as possible. And I want as little to do with him, she assured herself.

"Tell me why you think I'll lose the duel tomorrow. And, please, be specific," he requested, determined to keep his mind from paths that could only lead to disaster. "I've found it always helps to know one's enemy."

Again a chill of fear shook Kathleen as she pictured his opponent. "Joseph Yates is taller than you and heavier by four stone. He's also used to fighting unfairly. He'll buy the help of others to assure a win."

"So I must guard my back as well," he muttered.

He shifted his shoulder and Kathleen saw him wince. "Joseph was not wounded today, either," she added anxiously. She had been so disconcerted by all that had happened, she'd almost forgotten that Mr. Ashford had received a gash from a sword. "Sit down and let me see your arm."

"'Tis only a flesh wound," he replied, refusing her aid. He wanted none of her ministerings. He was, after all, merely a mortal man, and the stirrings he'd felt when she'd passed him still lingered. Although this could easily be his last night on this earth, he did not want to do anything that he would regret should he live to see another.

Kathleen's frown deepened. He didn't want her even to touch him. Well, she wanted no contact between them either, but there was no choice. "My life, as much as yours, depends upon the outcome of tomorrow's battle. The cut must at the very least be cleaned."

"That will only open it and start the bleeding once again," he argued gruffly. In his mind's eye he had begun undressing her. You are letting this situation get the better of you, he cautioned himself.

"Then I'll cauterize it and you'll have an elegant scar some fine lady can swoon over," she returned bitingly. "Now sit!"

He moved his arm again and the pain shot through it. She was right. The wound did need some fixing. "Fine ladies are sometimes impressed by marks of battle," he conceded.

Kathleen experienced a sudden uncomfortable twinge in the pit of her stomach. Jealousy? Don't be ridiculous, she chided herself. Jonathan Ashford was a stranger who'd provided nothing but trouble for her since he'd entered her life, and she'd be glad to be rid of him. As far as she was concerned, he could have his fancy ladies. All she wanted was her freedom.

Kneeling, she opened a large trunk set against the wall near the table. Her father had built this trunk for her. To appease her mother, Captain Thorton had allowed Kathleen to keep it. What the captain didn't know was that the trunk had a false bottom. As a young girl, she'd hidden her childish treasures in it. Now she kept weapons and other supplies she hoped would one day allow her to gain her freedom. Moving the clothing aside, she lifted the bottom and took out a full bottle of brandy.

Rising, she turned back toward Mr. Ashford to find him sitting on the side of the bed removing the bandage. The lines of pain etched into his face told her the wound in his arm was more serious than he was willing to admit. As the bandage came off, the bleeding began anew.

Not wanting him to aggravate it further, she quickly moved to stand in front of him. "I'll remove your coat and shirt. Hold your arm as still as possible," she ordered.

John started to say he could remove his own clothing, but the words died in his throat. That would be foolish valor and he had always been a practical man. Nodding his agreement, he obeyed.

She saw him grimace again as she removed the waistcoat and was startled to feel his pain as her own. But it was not the empathetic pain that disturbed her. She was shaken by the curious sensation of warmth that was spreading through her. It was unlike anything she had ever experienced. Attempting to ignore it, she removed his shirt. His shoulders were as muscular as she had imagined when watching him from the bridge. His chest, hard and flat, was covered with curly dark hair. She had seen men's chests before. It was common for members of the pirate crew to remove their shirts during the heat of the day. But seeing them had never made her feel this way. The warmth became a heat, and when she touched his exposed flesh, a tingling excitement raced up her arm. 'Tis some form of insanity brought on by fear, she reasoned and forced herself to concentrate on his wound.

Get control of yourself man, John ordered as his mind again began to travel paths he wished to avoid. Here was a woman who was using him to gain her own ends. Admittedly she had placed herself in grave danger. But then, he reminded himself, she had placed herself in grave danger when she attached herself to this group of cutthroats.

He could not trust her and yet his body was as sensitive to her touch as a bat's eyes were to sunlight. I have been without a woman too long, he reasoned.

Beneath her fingers, Kathleen felt the muscles of his shoulder flex as if he found the contact uncomfortable, and a coldness swept through her. Clearly he considered the touch of someone as lowly as herself distasteful.

Concentrating her attention on the wound, she began to clean it with the brandy. The gash was deeper than she'd thought and would cause soreness for several days. The only saving grace was that it was not his sword arm. However, in a battle with Joseph Yates it was best if a man had both arms in good repair.

The brandy burned and John felt a cold sweat break out on his forehead from the pain. "I could use a bit of that internally," he said gruffly.

"You'll need a clear head," she replied, refusing his request. She had been concentrating on the wound. Glancing at his face, she saw the tightness of his jaw and paleness of his skin. "I suppose one swallow wouldn't cause any harm," she conceded, handing him the bottle.

He took a gulp, then handed the bottle back to her.

The wound was again bleeding freely by the time she finished cleaning it. From a petticoat, she tore a fresh bandage and bound his arm securely. "The pressure should stop the bleeding," she said. "It's an even cut. If it doesn't fester and you don't get killed tomorrow, it should heal well."

"How encouraging," he muttered, wishing she wouldn't sound quite so pessimistic even if she had good reason to be.

Kathleen considered telling him that she was merely being realistic, but held her tongue. He looked exhausted, and the lines of strain from his attempt to hide the pain her ministering had caused were etched deeply into his features. Despite his unfriendly manner toward her, she found herself wanting to comfort him. Her hand moved toward his face to stroke his jawline gently, but before the contact was made, she drew it back. He would not want her to touch him thusly and she needed no further evidence of his dislike.

Picking up his shirt, she helped him put it on again. Even while she tried not to feel it, a surge of heat again rushed through her when her fingers brushed against his skin. Men, she reminded herself curtly, were nothing but trouble. And this one in particular had brought her to the brink of disaster. "You rest," she said. "I'll go fetch us some dinner." But as she started toward the door, she stopped and from the pocket of her petticoat took out the small sheathed dagger she'd found this day. "Keep this hidden but close," she instructed, adding, "and you'd best rebolt this door after I've gone."

John remembered her confrontation with the captain. Clearly she was no longer in his good graces. It was possible the crew might decide the captain was no longer interested in protecting her. He found himself picturing her the prey of one of the pirates and a cold chill raced through him. The strength of his concern for her safety surprised him. 'Tis only because I owe her my life, at least for the moment, he told himself. He eased himself back into a sitting position, then began to rise. "If this ship is that unsafe, then you should not go out alone. I'll accompany you."

His unexpected show of protectiveness startled her. One moment Jonathan Ashford acted as if he couldn't bear her touch and in the next he was worried about her. He's probably clever enough to realize that any ally is better than none, she reasoned. "The ship is safe for me to wan-

der," she said. "'Tis you who are in danger. I don't want
to come back and find a dagger in your back. These are
not honorable men. If Joseph can gain his revenge without a fight, he will."

That any woman would feel she was safe to wander
among these cutthroats stunned him. But then she was
used to them. However, whether he liked it or not, he had
signed the wedding contract, and until it was officially annulled, she was his responsibility. "Still, I shall come," he
insisted.

Even if his motives were self-serving, it was a new and
curious experience to have someone want to protect her.
But in this instance it was also reckless, and she scowled at
his stubbornness. "No! You need to rest and rebuild your
strength to the fullest. If you appear on deck now, Joseph
may provoke an immediate duel and you'll not have a
chance. 'Tis both our fates you'll seal if you behave so
foolishly."

He hesitated. She was right about him not being strong
enough to face Joseph. He was already feeling dizzy and
he had not yet fully risen. Grudgingly, he reseated himself
on the bed. "You know better than I what can happen
aboard this ship."

Relieved that he had shown some sense and not persisted in being hardheaded, she reached for the latch.
"Remember to rebolt the door," she repeated over her
shoulder as she slipped outside.

In the corridor she discovered that Captain Thorton had
been true to his word and placed a guard near her door.
But while this meant that Mr. Ashford would be watched
closely for any attempt to escape, it did not mean that the
guard would prevent anyone from attempting to harm
him. Any of these pirates would quickly turn their backs
if offered money, and Joseph had already made it clear he

was willing to pay for the pleasure of cutting the prisoner's throat. She must hurry.

As she made her way to the galley, Mr. Barrows fell into step beside her. "I hope Mr. Ashford ain't being too rough on you, lass," he said with a rotten-toothed grin. "'Cause I wants to be the one to teach you just how submissive a wife should be."

Outwardly Kathleen gave no indication that his words had any effect on her, but inwardly she cringed at the very thought of Mr. Barrows touching her. Solemnly she promised herself she'd kill him before she would submit to him.

A few minutes later, as she carried the food back to the cabin, she scanned the horizon. The booty had been divided, and now the heavier merchant vessel was sailing southward, captained by Mr. Louker. The ship had been his reward for the many years of service he'd given Captain Thorton.

The *English Wench,* however, was heading west toward Hatteras. This was a busy shipping time. Winter would be setting in soon and ships like the one they'd captured today would be trying to reach Jamestown before the weather turned cold and the seas became dangerously rough. She knew Captain Thorton wanted to make one last capture before turning to the West Indies. He'd hide near one of the islands making up the archipelago along the Carolina mainland and then swoop down on a slower merchant vessel just as he'd done today.

"Greed's clouded the captain's mind. Been warning him we're in fur a blow," Kathleen heard an old sailor telling a younger member of the crew. "But he won't listen. It's me joints. They always knows."

"Looks clear to me," the younger man replied, obviously choosing to trust the captain over the old sailor's aches. "And one last prize'll give me enough to leave this life."

"If we stays out on these seas much longer, you'll not live to reap your rewards," the old sailor cautioned.

Shaking off the sense of foreboding the old man's words caused, Kathleen hurried back to her cabin. She had no time to worry about a possible storm. She had to concern herself with a more certain danger...the match tomorrow between Mr. Ashford and Joseph Yates.

Reaching her cabin, she knocked. "'Tis Kathleen," she called out. Immediately the bolt was thrown back and the door opened. She noticed that Mr. Ashford's good hand was behind his back. As soon as she was inside, he reached out to close the door and she saw that he was holding the dagger. At least he had sense enough to be cautious.

After he'd rebolted the door, she handed him his plate of food. "The cook's not very good but you should eat," she said. "You'll need your strength."

Nodding, he took the plate from her. He chided himself for the surge of relief he'd experienced when she'd made it back in fine shape. Why shouldn't she, he told himself. She was used to these kind of men. She knew how to handle them. He said nothing as they ate. But he could not stop from wondering how she had come to be aboard this vessel and why she was still here. When he finished, he set his plate aside and studied her in silence.

Mr. Ashford's scrutiny made Kathleen nervous, but years of practiced indifference came to her aid and she did not show it. She did, however, wonder what he was thinking. Probably something very unflattering, she decided.

Again John found himself remembering the entirety of their encounter. There had been something about a death-bed promise made to her mother. But surely Kathleen had not been so stupid as to think the captain could be trusted to give her fair treatment. "Have you ever considered attempting to escape?" he asked, breaking the silence between them.

Indignation that she would choose to submit to this life flashed in her eyes. "Of course, I've considered it," she replied. She didn't tell him of her failed attempts and the punishments she'd endured. She didn't want his sympathy. She wanted nothing from any man. "Tomorrow, if you lose, I'll take my chances with the sharks. If you win, hopefully we'll have time to devise a better plan."

John's jaw tightened with determination. "I intend to win."

It was not a boast. He had made a simple statement of fact. He had a strength about him that gave Kathleen hope, but the fates had turned against her too many times. "Your arm will stiffen if 'tis not exercised," she said worriedly.

He was sitting on the side of the bed and she moved her chair so that it was in front of him. Then, seating herself, she began to gently bend the arm.

A cold sweat broke out on his brow but he made no sound. She did not understand why she was so sensitive to his pain. Still, it hurt her to see him suffering. I do not enjoy seeing anyone suffer, she reasoned, forcing herself to continue. But that was not exactly true. She had enjoyed seeing Thomas get his fifty lashes when he'd been caught trying to rape her. He'd nearly killed her in the attempt and she'd had bruises for a month. But it had been worth it in the end. His punishment had kept the rest of the crew at bay.

"Enough!" John suddenly hissed through clenched teeth, deciding that it was better to risk a stiff arm than to fall unconscious on the floor.

Kathleen started to argue with him, then stopped herself. He needed rest as much as the arm needed to be flexed. "Sleep then," she ordered, moving the chair away from the bed and reseating herself.

In spite of the exhaustion he was feeling, John didn't lie down. Continuing to sit on the side of the bed, he regarded her grimly. He owed this pirate wench his life. Tomorrow they would both face their fates. He would not be so boorish as to take her bed. "We both need our rest. The bed is large enough for us to share."

Like two peas in a very tight pod, she mused. She knew he could not truly want such a close proximity between them, and then there was the way her traitorous body was reacting. Just touching him disturbed her. The thought of lying beside him unnerved her. "I'll sit," she said.

John rose to his feet. If he must die, he would die a gentleman. "If you won't share the bed, I'll sleep in the chair."

Men! Kathleen thought acidly. Good or bad, they were difficult. "Don't be ridiculous. You're the one who must fight tomorrow. If you sit in this chair all night, not only will your arm be stiff but so will every other muscle in your body."

"There is the chance that you must face the sharks tomorrow," he countered.

There was a determination in those dark eyes of his that told her arguing would be useless.

"I promise to behave in the most gentlemanly of ways," he assured her with a strong note of impatience.

Kathleen's back stiffened. He was again letting her know that he found her less than desirable. "In that case," she said with cool dignity, "I don't see any reason why we cannot share."

However, a few minutes later as they lay back to back on the narrow bed, Kathleen began to doubt her decision. Jonathan Ashford had left his coat off and she'd removed her petticoats, but other than that, they remained dressed. Yet she was as strongly aware of his body as if they'd both been naked. Closing her eyes, she tried to ignore his presence, but instead found herself wondering what it would feel like to be held in his arms.

For so many years the thought of being touched by any of the men who surrounded her had caused her to feel nauseated. Because of this, she had begun to believe she had grown immune to men in general. But clearly she was not immune to Mr. Ashford. A heat spread slowly through her until her whole body was warmed. The nipples of her breasts hardened and she felt a curling sensation deep within her. *Now is not the time to discover my feminine weaknesses*, she admonished herself curtly.

As John lay with the length of Kathleen's body pressed against him, he could feel the stirrings in his loins. This was not the time nor the place, and she was certainly not a female he should desire, he chided himself. *'Tis the specter of death so close by that has my body craving a last pleasurable experience*, he reasoned. Then he recalled the threat in her eyes when she had warned him not to touch her. She could be as deadly as Yates. Besides, he had not the strength.

As Kathleen continued to lie with her body pressed against Jonathan Ashford's, it occurred to her that she might very easily die on the morrow without ever knowing how it would feel to have these longings burning within her satisfied. These thoughts brought a mingling of excitement and fear. Too tense to relax, she shifted.

She is tempting fate, John thought. Her moving against him had caused his male need to grow stronger. He smiled dryly. He'd thought he was too tired but he had been wrong. He shifted also as he tried to put such thoughts out of his mind. Facing Joseph's knife was deadly enough; he did not want to face this female pirate's also.

Kathleen felt the shrug of his shoulders. The action reminded her of an attempt to send an offending insect on its way. Pride caused her body to stiffen. Better to die in ignorance than turn to a man who considered her no better than dirt beneath his feet.

Chapter Three

The next morning Kathleen experienced a curious awakening. Normally she entered each day apprehensive, wondering if this might be her last, or if there was yet another cruel twist of fate in store for her. But on this morning, she awoke feeling warm and safe. Her cheek rested against soft linen, while a strong arm along her back held her securely.

Arm! Her eyes popped open as a rush of memory destroyed the gentleness of her awakening. Her head was resting on Jonathan Ashford's chest, while her arm and hand lay casually upon his hard, flat abdomen. His uninjured arm was wrapped around her, and as the ship pitched, it tightened to keep her from hitting against the wall of the cabin.

They were lying together like two lovers. His breathing moved the muscles beneath her palm and warm currents washed over her. Doomed lovers, her inner voice qualified.

Raising herself on an elbow, she found herself gazing into a pair of unreadable brown eyes. Her face was so close to his she could feel his breath playing upon her skin. It was warm and tantalizing.

She had unbound her hair before she slept and it hung wild and free. Lifting his injured arm, John combed the ebony tresses back from her face with his fingers. She did look enticing.

His hand brushing against her cheek took Kathleen's breath away. Her tongue moved across her suddenly dry lips and she saw the brown of his eyes darken. A tremble shook her. Her blood seemed to warm as, deep within her, the embers of desire began to ignite once again. Lost in his gaze, she felt the rest of the world fade from her mind until it was as if only the two of them existed.

"You're a dangerous woman, Kathleen," he said gruffly. "Those smoke gray eyes of yours could cloud a man's mind and bend his will to yours." His jaw tightened with determined resistance.

His words caused a moment's elation, but it died quickly as she read the distaste in his eyes. Clearly he wanted no part of her. And I want no part of him, either, she asserted. But her body called her a liar. Furious with herself for this unfamiliar weakness she was experiencing, she wiggled free and off the foot of the bed. Finding her brush, she stood at the porthole brushing her hair and watching the waves lap at the side of the ship.

The old sailor had been right. A storm was surely brewing, but it was nothing compared to the storm raging within her. Jonathan Ashford had awakened yearnings she'd thought she'd never feel. But they were from two different worlds and he had no wish to invite her into his. Even if he did, I would never belong there, she reminded herself. If we should manage to escape, our paths will not cross again. Sternly she ordered herself to bury the stirrings. They would only bring her trouble and grief, and she'd had enough of both for many lifetimes. A coldness slowly spread through her. Feeling once again in control of her mind and her body, she turned to face her companion. He was sitting on the edge of the bed bending his arm slowly up and down at the elbow.

Laying her brush aside, Kathleen began to braid her hair. She saw the pain lines again etching themselves into his features and her own arm seemed to ache in response. "Be careful," she cautioned tersely. "It would be best not to start it bleeding again."

He nodded in agreement. Damn, why did she have to look so bloody inviting, he swore silently. He had the strongest urge to stop her from plaiting her hair. He wanted to see it once again flowing down her back. Then he would slowly undress her and . . . Stop this! he ordered himself. Rising, he moved toward the door. "I need some fresh air."

Kathleen had seen his jaw tense and his expression grow grim when he looked at her. What he wants is to be free of my company. Indignation brought a flush to her cheeks and she was tempted to allow him to wander on his own. But her rational side reminded her that their fates were tied. She must do all she could to keep him alive. "Wait," she ordered. "You'll need this." Pulling a man's heavy cloak from her trunk, she held it out to him. "It belonged to the captain of a vessel Captain Thorton took two years ago. When the fighting was done, he needed it no more and so I took it," she said in answer to the question in his eyes.

She was most definitely a pirate wench. "The spoils of battle," he muttered as he accepted it.

Disapproval of her behavior was in his voice as well as on his face. It cut at her deeply. Because of him she might very well end up in the belly of a shark before the sun set on this day, and yet he felt free to judge her harshly. Her hand fastened around his arm as he again reached for the bolt. "I've done what has been necessary to survive and I'll not apologize for myself. I've never killed another person and I've taken from corpses only what was essential." Releasing his arm, she walked with dignity back to the trunk.

He watched her in silence for a long moment. It was not his place to judge her. And although he considered it wise not to trust her, if it had not been for her, he would have already met his maker. "'Tis I who must apologize. You risked a great deal to give me this opportunity for life."

Glancing back toward him, she saw the distrust in his eyes before they again became unreadable. He might be grateful for this meager chance to live another day, but he was still suspicious of her motives in aiding him. Again she was tempted to allow him to face alone the danger waiting for him beyond the cabin door. But as angry as he made her, she couldn't bring herself to abandon him. She grabbed a smaller cloak from the trunk and left the cabin immediately behind him.

On the deck, he stood at the rail looking out at the horizon. "A storm is moving toward us," he observed.

Too angry to even want to look at him, Kathleen concentrated on the clouds in the distance. "If we're lucky it will cause the fight to be delayed and give you more time to rebuild your strength."

"I think not." Kathleen stiffened as she heard Captain Thorton's voice. "The wind has been good to us," the captain continued as he joined them. "We are safely in the sound and will be putting into a sheltered harbor before nightfall."

"Ain't gona be no safe harbor from this storm," the old sailor whose aches had been predicting the blow interjected from behind the captain.

Captain Thorton scowled with impatience. "Unless you're ready to live without a tongue, get out of my sight."

The old sailor shrugged as if to say he'd tried to warn him, then quickly scurried away before the captain could carry out his threat.

Turning his attention back to Kathleen, Captain Thorton smiled. "As I was saying, we cannot ignore a cry for revenge, especially when it has been a brother's blood that has been spilt. Since Mr. Ashford is already on deck, I'll have Yates sent for and we'll settle this matter now." His smile broadened. "I'll give you a moment alone to say your goodbyes."

Kathleen shivered as the captain left them. "I did not expect the time to come so soon."

John saw true fear in her eyes and an anxiety for her stirred within her. For both their sakes, he must win. "You could at least pretend you have some faith in me," he admonished, making an attempt at lightness.

Holding her cloak tightly around herself, as if it could protect her from the doom she sensed was near for both of them, she turned toward him. "Yates wields his sword like a woodsman wields an ax. He will not simply slice your arm, he'll sever it. If it should come to hand-to-hand combat, he'll kick, scratch and bite. He is incredibly strong. I have seen him break a man's neck as easily as a cook wrings that of a chicken."

A dry smile played at the corners of John's mouth. "You do paint a clear picture."

Looking up at him, she felt her jaw tremble. She didn't understand it. They had no bonds and he clearly wanted none. Yet she knew as surely as if it were written in blood that if he died a part of her would die also. "May luck be with you," she said, adding in lowered tones, "I'll guard your back as best I can."

"Mr. Ashford," Captain Thorton called.

Kathleen looked over her shoulder and saw the captain and Yates near the middle of the deck. The rest of the crew was gathering quickly on the perimeter. She saw Mr. Barrow grinning with anticipation and her stomach churned with revulsion.

John followed the direction of her gaze. Even a pirate whore deserved better than Mr. Barrow. His gaze returned to her. She was a delicious-looking prize. "A kiss for luck."

Startled, Kathleen suddenly found her chin being tilted upward and Jonathan Ashford's warm lips upon hers. It was only a momentary contact but every fiber of her being came alive.

John was not certain why he had kissed her. 'Twas merely an act of camaraderie, he reasoned. After all, they were in this together. But her lips had been much softer and much sweeter than he had anticipated. Perhaps he should have risked her knife. But 'twas too late for any regrets. "I'll do my best for you, Kate," he promised.

Chewing on the inside of her bottom lip, she watched him walk to meet his fate. The promise in those brown eyes filled her mind while the warmth of his mouth lingered on hers. He will do his best because his life also depends upon it, she told herself, determined to keep his manner toward her in the proper perspective. The kiss was merely a show of bravery.

Suddenly all thought of what had passed between them was pushed to the back of her mind as she saw Captain Thorton hand Mr. Ashford a sword and step aside. Immediately Kathleen began to scan the onlookers. It wasn't easy to keep her eyes from wandering back to the two men circling slowly, beginning to size one another up, but she knew to let her attention shift away from the crew could be a fatal mistake. Still, with Yates's first thrust, her gaze swung to the combatants. Yates was clumsy, while Jonathan Ashford moved with a quickness that gave her hope. As the sound of steel against steel rang in the air, she forced herself to again study the men gathered to watch.

Intent on killing his opponent with a single blow, Yates lunged at John with all of his strength. John sidestepped the blow. The force of his attack caused Yates to lose his balance. As Yates stumbled and fell to the deck, Kathleen spotted a gleam of metal across the circle, behind John's back. Without a second's hesitation, she grabbed the knife from the sheath of the man standing beside her and sent it flying. Narrowly missing John, it embedded itself in the shoulder of his unseen attacker just as the pirate lunged for John's back. The man fell backward with a cry of pain while Captain Thorton turned toward Kathleen, his expression one of murderous reprimand.

But before he could issue orders to have her held, she grabbed a second knife and a sword from another unsuspecting sailor. "'Twill be as fair a fight as is possible with this rabble in charge," she said, meeting the captain's angry gaze with equal hostility as she poised the knife for throwing and held the sword at the ready, challenging any man to touch her.

Yates was getting to his feet. For a moment she feared she might have distracted Mr. Ashford too greatly. But as the pirate lunged for him, John again stepped aside and Yates again fell onto the deck.

His two misses only served to anger Yates more. Snorting like a bull, he held his sword in both hands and swung. Kathleen's breath locked in her lungs as Mr. Ashford moved to avoid the blow, slipped and nearly lost his footing. She knew that if he fell it would be the end of him.

Yates was running at him again. Just in time John regained his footing and moved out of Yates's path. The crowd parted and Yates ran through, crashing into the rail. Thrown back by the strength of his own assault, he hit his head on a barrel and fell to the deck unconscious. Frantically, Kathleen searched the rest of the crew for signs that any of them might be considering helping Yates. He was a bully and not well liked. Several were laughing at his clumsiness, something they would not have dared to have done had he been conscious. But none made a move to harm Mr. Ashford. If Yates had paid any others for their help, they'd decided the risk was not worth the price.

"If you are a wise man, Mr. Ashford," Captain Thorton was saying, "you will kill Yates where he lies. He has sworn a blood oath to kill you and when he regains his senses he will surely attempt to keep that oath."

Kathleen waited, barely breathing. She knew the captain was right. But in her heart she didn't want to discover that Jonathan Ashford was as cold-blooded as the men who had surrounded her all these years.

John regarded the captain with disdain. "I'll not stoop to the level of a common murderer."

Amusement flickered in Captain Thorton's eyes, then it was replaced by a threat. "Lay down your sword," he ordered. "And rejoin your wife."

John's grip on his sword tightened.

"Lay down your sword or die now," the captain warned.

For a moment John considered taking on the whole crew. But he knew that would be insanity. As short as his battle with Yates had been, it had left him weak and shaky. With a scowl, he drove the end of the sword into the deck and walked toward Kathleen.

"You, too, will surrender your weapons," the captain addressed her.

Hatred threatened to consume Kathleen. The desire to send the knife into the captain's heart burned strongly.

He smiled as if he could read her thoughts and found them amusing. "If you should kill me, Kathleen, who will protect you from them?" He waved his hand toward the crew.

Reason was on his side, she conceded, but still she held the knife at the ready. The thread on which her life dangled was growing very thin. She read that in the captain's eyes. "And what assurance do I have that if I should surrender my weapons, you will not allow the crew to murder Mr. Ashford on the spot, thus putting me at your mercy?" she demanded.

Captain Thorton smiled as if he was enjoying this little game. "You have my word that both of you will have my protection, at least for the moment."

Knowing it would be disastrous to let the knife fly, Kathleen laid her weapons aside. However, despite the captain's assurance of protection, she remained uneasy. "'Twould be best if we go back to our cabin for now," she advised Mr. Ashford in lowered tones.

John had remained poised for battle during the exchange between Kathleen and the captain. Even now he remained prepared for combat. He, too, didn't trust Thorton. But he was near exhaustion and his arm ached. Nodding his agreement, he offered her his uninjured arm. It was the gentlemanly thing to do, he told himself refusing to admit that he looked forward to her touch.

Kathleen was sure he was merely being polite, but she accepted for appearance' sake. Still, she felt like a true lady as he led her toward their cabin. 'Tis only a moment's fantasy, she warned herself, do not let it go to your head.

Back in their cabin, Kathleen closed and bolted the door, then, leaning against it, drew her first deep breath in minutes.

"Thank you," John said, breaking the silence between them. "'Twas a lucky throw of the knife for me."

Kathleen's gaze narrowed. He gave her no credit for anything. "Luck had nothing to do with it." Still smarting from his earlier condemning manner, she heard herself adding, "I've had to work to survive. While your fancy ladies were learning to do their delicate needle art, I was learning how to handle a gun, a sword and a knife. I suppose these are not ladylike skills, but they were necessary." Furious that she again was attempting to justify herself to this man, she stalked over to the porthole and stared out.

John studied her straight, proudly held back. He owed her his life not once but twice now. Perhaps even a third time—it was possible the captain had been considering having him killed when Yates had not done the job. "I did not mean that as a condemnation," he said apologetically.

Kathleen was angry with herself for overreacting. For as long as she could remember she had practiced showing no response to anything any man had said or done to her. But with this man that control seemed to have vanished. He made her feel vulnerable and she didn't like it.

In spite of his efforts to forget, John was remembering the softness of her lips and the sweet taste of her mouth. Bedding this particular pirate wench might be an experience to be savored, he mused. Before the thought was thoroughly finished, he reminded himself of her ability with a knife. Then again, perhaps not, he decided. "Do you know what will happen now?" he asked.

She sensed him watching her but she did not turn around. Looking at him caused her to experience a weakness she did not wish to feel. "No," she answered honestly. "But whatever Captain Thorton decides to do, we shall not enjoy it. He has a cruel streak that runs very deep." Black memories caused her to shiver. She pulled her cloak more tightly around her.

John continued to study her thoughtfully. His common sense warned him to be careful, but a part of him was beginning to want to trust her. "Since we're so soon to face our fates, satisfy my curiosity. Tell me how you came to be aboard this vessel, Kate."

This time Kathleen did turn to face him, her chin tilted upward with dignity. "My name is Kathleen."

His mouth formed a thoughtful pout. "No, you are definitely a Kate. I'm sure Sir William Shakespeare would agree."

Kathleen frowned in confusion. "I know nothing of this Sir William Shakespeare. Was his Kate held by pirates also?"

"No, she was merely strong-willed," he answered, his gaze traveling along the fine line of her neck to the smooth roundness of her bosom. Berating himself, he forced his attention back to her face.

"And I suppose you prefer women with weak wills who would swoon in your arms the moment there is any small threat of trouble," she returned icily, then wished she'd said nothing. The kind of woman he preferred was none of her concern.

His gaze narrowed. Their lives were in grave peril. This was no time for gentlemanly niceties. "What I prefer is a woman I can trust. How did you come to be aboard this vessel?"

Kathleen glared at him. There was no denying the challenge in his voice that suggested he thought her being aboard Captain Thorton's ship might be of her own doing.

Her back straightened with pride. "It was eleven years ago, when I was ten years of age. My parents were servants of a wealthy merchant who had holdings in the Bahamas. The merchant and his wife were on their way to England for a visit and had taken my parents and me along to see to their needs. Captain Thorton captured their ship. My mother was very beautiful. The moment the captain saw her, he wanted her. He killed my father and made her a widow. Then he drew up a marriage contract to make her his wife. She would have died rather than have agreed to such a match, but he was clever. He'd kept me alive to use to coerce my mother into obeying him. For nine years she endured him."

Kathleen paused and drew an angry breath. She'd never had anyone to tell this story to and now that she had begun, she could not stop. It was as if it had been held in too long and would not be held in any longer. In a voice filled with venom and frustration, she continued grimly, "I wanted her to try to escape but she was too afraid of the captain. And I could not leave her. She was weak and fragile, and needed me to care for her.

"When she died I thought Captain Thorton would simply kill me. I did not want to consider what other fates he might devise. He'd always hated me. I was a reminder that the woman he loved had never loved him. But with her dying breath my mother made him promise not to kill me or misuse me and to allow me to marry whom I pleased. I knew he would not go against a deathbed promise and for a short while I held hope that he'd simply free me. But instead he chose to torment me by keeping me aboard his vessel.

"For the past two years I have lived with the threat that he might die and leave me to the mercy of his crew. This amuses him. And now I have given him the opportunity to carry my torture even further. At this moment he is certainly plotting your death so that I will be at his mercy. Escape is the only solution." Her mouth formed a hard, straight line. "My other attempts have failed. This will be my final one. I would have preferred to have more of an advantage."

John did not doubt that she was telling him the truth. He had gravely misjudged her. She had lived through hell and deserved a chance for a good life. "I'm not usually considered a liability by those in need of assistance."

Kathleen saw the sympathy in his eyes and again her back straightened. She did not want his pity. Her gaze shifted to his shoulders and her body remembered the strong feel of him beside her when they had lain together. Despite her determination to never rely on any man, she was forced to admit that having him by her side gave her courage. Still, her pride refused to allow her to forget the truth of their association. "I'm grateful to have you beside me, even if you are only here because you were unfortunate enough to have killed Joseph Yates's brother."

John bowed low. "You saved my life and now it is my turn to save yours."

A bitter smile curled Kathleen's lips. "You sound so certain of yourself. I wish I had your confidence."

His brown eyes narrowed with resolve. "Where there's life there's hope, Kate."

"I've often told myself that," she admitted tiredly. "But the captain always seemed to win and ..."

The rest of her sentence was lost as the ship yawed strongly. Losing her footing, she fell forward. Two strong arms caught her, and together she and Jonathan Ashford fell onto the bed. His hold on her tightened as the sea continued to toss the ship wildly. The bowl and pitcher from the table crashed to the floor and her trunk slid into the far wall.

All around them whatever was not pegged to the floor was rolling and crashing around the room, but Kathleen barely noticed. Her whole awareness was focused on Jonathan Ashford. Without her petticoats, there was little between them. The strong musculature of his thighs burned their imprint into hers. The ship lurched hard once again and John rolled. Now he was on top of her. Her legs had parted and he lay between them.

John's breathing grew ragged. He fought to control himself. This was not the time for lusting. But the feel of her beneath him ignited a passion that threatened to consume him.

Kathleen was aware of his growing hardness. She had always experienced an acrid distaste when members of Captain Thorton's crew had taunted her, brushing up against her in the passageway, forcing her to feel their manliness. But she felt no distaste now. Instead there was a longing within her as if she was possessed by a desperate need that wished to be fulfilled.

The rocking of the ship moved their bodies in a wild rhythmic dance. He burned to know the full feel of her. Lifting his head he looked down into her face. Her eyes were a coal gray and foggy with desire. He knew he could take her this minute and there would be no threat of a knife.

Kathleen saw her awakened desire mirrored in John's eyes and she offered no resistance. She could not. His movement against her was driving all thought from her mind. She wanted to scream out at the pure pleasure of it. Her legs parted farther, inviting the full feel of him.

Damn the clothing between them, John cursed mentally. His tongue gently licked the throbbing pulse in her neck. He could feel the hardened nipples of her breasts crushed against his chest. She was ready for him. Her body was begging for him.

Suddenly the ship pitched even more violently. Now was not the time to let lust rule his mind. "I do not think we have reached a sheltered harbor," he said gruffly.

"No," she agreed, fighting for rational thought.

John forced himself to think beyond the enticing feel of her body. "This ship could sink."

"It could," she confirmed. The realization that they might drown caused a cold wave of reality to wash over her.

"If we do not act now, we could find ourselves in a watery grave," he said. He kissed her swelled breasts through the fabric of her dress as his hands moved possessively to her hips. "And I would very much regret not having the opportunity to know you more fully."

"I would regret that, too," she admitted huskily, then flushed with embarrassment when she realized the wantonness of this confession.

A smile played at the corners of his mouth and a promise shone in his eyes as he raised himself from her. "I hope you can swim."

Her body felt rudely abandoned. But her embarrassment at her forwardness was greater. "Like a fish," she assured him, already regretting her behavior. She could not believe she had responded so wantonly. Giving in to this desire for him was only going to lead to trouble. Every instinct she had told her that.

Balancing himself against the side of the cabin, he helped her to her feet. Clumsily she made her way to the trunk. Lifting the false bottom, she took out four more knives. Two had sheaths. Handing one in a sheath and one without to Mr. Ashford, she said, "Tie one on and carry the other." Then, fighting down a sudden flush of embarrassment, she ordered, "Turn around, I must change. This dress will only pull me under."

"I'm your husband, Kate," he declared, his eyes still dark with desire. "I plan to see a great deal more of you." His words stunned him. He had never lusted for a woman so strongly that it took away his reason. Yet here he was declaring that he intended to honor this marriage.

Her muscles tensed. She couldn't let him see her. "Please turn around," she ordered once again.

With a shake of his head to indicate he didn't understand her, he obeyed. But what he truly didn't understand was himself. It had not been his plan to remain bound to this woman. However, she had saved his life at the risk of her own, he reminded himself. If they lived through this he would keep her. She deserved a good life. Besides, considering his body's response to her, having her for a wife would be no great burden.

Quickly, Kathleen stripped off her dress and the confining undergarments beneath. They would only add more weight when wet. This was a time to think of survival and not decency, she reasoned. Quickly, she pulled on a pair of men's breeches and a loose tunic shirt. The knife she always wore tied around her thigh she moved to her calf and hid beneath her stocking. Then, finding an oilskin bag, she stuffed a small metal box containing pieces of flint inside, along with a change of clothing and the two cloaks. When the bag was secured, she tied the sheathed knife she had recently taken out of the trunk at her waist and picked up the remaining weapon. "I'm ready," she said with a confidence she didn't feel.

John unbolted the door. Luck was with them for the moment. The corridor was empty. Clearly the storm had forced the captain to require the aid of all members of the crew.

Out on deck, Kathleen found herself pelted by rain coming down so thick it was hard to see. From somewhere in the distance, she heard Captain Thorton shouting orders. She held her knife at the ready in case she and Mr. Ashford were spotted, but the crew were too busy trying to keep the ship from capsizing to worry about the two of them. Grabbing a bundle of rope, she motioned for Mr. Ashford to follow her. Carefully, they made their way to where several barrels were tied to the deckhouse. "Whether the ship weathers the storm or not, this will probably be our only chance for escape," she said in a whisper, fighting down a rush of fear. The angry sea was terrifying but she knew they had more of a chance for survival in it than on the ship. In firmer tones, she ordered, "Fix two loops of rope around one of the barrels as handholds for yourself, and best tie your boots to the barrel, too. They could drag you down." As she spoke she was already fastening the oilskin bag along with her shoes to a barrel. "We'll wait out the storm for as long as possible with the hope that the ship will be driven toward land. Then we'll throw the barrels overboard and go in after them. Hopefully they'll remain sealed and act as buoys."

Her plan was as good as any, John decided and nodded his consent.

They had finished tying their ropes and were huddled against the wall of the deckhouse when their luck took a turn for the worse. "What's going on here?" a voice suddenly demanded.

Looking up, Kathleen saw Mr. Barrows standing in front of her.

"You and Mr. Ashford wouldn't be planning to try to escape, would you now? 'Twould break me heart," he said with exaggerated grief. He started to beckon to a couple crew members who were working nearby. But before he could shout to get their attention, John delivered a blow to Mr. Barrow's jaw that sent the man senseless to the deck.

"What the devil?" another crewman demanded as he suddenly came around the side of the deckhouse and almost fell over Mr. Barrow's inert body.

Kathleen recognized him as the stunned man she'd helped the day before.

"Have you found trouble, Royd?" a second crewman yelled from only a few feet away.

For a moment the man stood there indecisively, then he yelled back, "Mr. Barrows seems to have tripped and knocked himself unconscious. Best I drag him below deck before he gets washed over." Stooping to get a grip on Mr. Barrows, he said to Kathleen, "We're even now. You best be gone when I get back or I'll slit your throat meself."

"We've no choice. We can't wait any longer," she informed Jonathan Ashford as Royd dragged Mr. Barrows away. "He means what he says."

"I could tell that." Moving quickly, he tossed her barrel overboard. "See you on shore," he said, and picking her up, tossed her in after it.

As she hit the water, the sea seemed to grab and try to pull her down. It was all Kathleen could do to keep her head above the waves. At least she need not worry about the sharks, she told herself philosophically. They would have gone deep beneath this turbulent surface to find calmer water. In the dim light that managed to filter through the storm, she saw her barrel. It took nearly every ounce of energy she had to fight her way to it. Entwining her hands in the ropes, she took several gasps of breath, then looked around for Mr. Ashford. A large wave carried her upward and she saw him. He'd found his barrel, too. They had a chance.

With the next wave, she saw that he was closer. The salty water stung her eyes and her arms felt as if they were going to be ripped from their sockets. But we're in the sound, she told herself. There was land on either side. She'd not give up now.

Her body went from cold to numb, but still she clung to the barrel. Night fell and she could no longer see Mr. Ashford, but just knowing she was not alone in these murky waters seemed to help. Her arms and hands began to lose all feeling. Afraid she would no longer be able to hold on to the ropes, she twisted them around her wrists even more securely and prayed they would not come loose. "You've lived through worse than this," she told herself when her strength threatened to fail her.

Desperately she clung to consciousness, but the struggle was difficult. Her mind became a blur and reality mingled with old nightmares.

Her legs hit something hard and she envisioned herself being swallowed by a whale. A biblical ending, she thought, half-amused at the idea. In the next instant her torso as well was lying upon something rough but solid. The buoyant feeling of being tossed on the waves gave way to an incredible heaviness. Vaguely she realized she was on land. Still attached to the barrel, she pushed it and herself in a snakelike motion farther away from the raging sea. Trembling in the icy air, she worked her hands free from the ropes and tried to rise, but her legs had no strength. "So cold," she murmured to the wind whipping around her. "So cold." Then darkness closed over her mind and she gave up the struggle.

Chapter Four

Kathleen was shivering so hard she thought her bones might snap. Her mind was groggy and her eyelids were too heavy to open. She could hear the storm but it wasn't reaching her. Curled into a tight bundle, she was aware of two strong arms holding her securely.

Still not fully conscious, her worst fears assailed her. Had she been recaptured? Had Captain Thorton given her to Mr. Barrows? With a strength born of terror, she started to struggle. But there was no room. Her elbows and one knee scraped against rough wood.

"Kate, be still," John ordered gruffly. "There is very little room in here."

"Mr. Ashford?" Immediately Kathleen's body stilled. She opened her eyes but saw only blackness.

Relief spread through John. When he had first found her, he'd thought she was dead. Then he'd detected shallow breathing. But for several hours now she'd remained unconscious and he had feared for her life. "I think 'tis time for you to start calling me John," he said, his arms tightening around her even more as she began to shiver from the cold. "Welcome back to the land of the living."

"I feel more as if I'm in a hovel in Hades except it's so cold," she muttered through chattering teeth. An edge of panic entered her voice as her nightmares returned. "Where are we? Have we been recaptured and thrown into the hold?"

"No, we haven't been recaptured," he assured her. "We're in the hollow of a tree. I've pulled a thicket of bushes in front of the opening, and if we're lucky they'll stay in place until the storm passes."

Becoming more cognizant of her surroundings, Kathleen realized that he was holding her on his lap with his arms and legs forming a cocoon around her. In spite of her coldness, embarrassment brought a faint flush to her skin. "You must be very uncomfortable."

"Only when you struggle," he replied.

"I'm sorry," she apologized. The heat of his body acted like a magnet and she curled up more tightly against him.

He found it incredulous that under these circumstances she could still feel so good in his arms. "Are you getting warmer?" he asked worriedly.

"Yes," she answered shakily. But even to herself she refused to admit just how much warmer she felt simply knowing it was his arms around her. She recalled his declaration that he was her husband, but that had been said in a moment of lust. She guessed he regretted it or, most likely, had forgotten it. And so would she. Still, she could not forget the fierce desire he had awakened within her. You must, she ordered herself. She tried to turn her mind away from him, but her life had been so filled with fear and the struggle for survival for so many years, she had no pleasant memories to escape into. With a will she could not control, her thoughts returned to the man who held her and she realized that she knew practically nothing about him.

Curiosity was not ladylike, but then neither was sitting wrapped in a man's arms inside the trunk of a hollow tree.

If conversation could take her mind off her body's wanton reactions toward her companion, then the social amenities meant nothing to her. "Were you on your way to Virginia?" she asked.

"Yes, I've a plantation on the Rappahannock River," he answered, wondering if he would ever see it again. Determination tightened his jaw. Both he and Kathleen would see it.

Kathleen pictured him astride his horse, overseeing his land. But the peaceful image was disrupted by vivid memories of him in battle against the pirate crew and then against Yates. "You fight like a soldier, not a farmer," she mused, then bit her lip when she realized she'd spoken aloud.

"My father was a soldier." John smiled with pride at the memory of Martin Ashford dressed to do battle for the king. "It was he who taught me to handle a weapon. He fought beside Charles I, and for his bravery, the king granted him land in Virginia. When Charles was defeated and beheaded, my father refused to remain in England. So he bid the country of his birth a farewell and brought my mother and me to the colonies."

"It's clear from your voice that you admire him," she said, wondering what life would have been like for her if Captain Thorton had not intervened and killed her father.

"Admired," he corrected with gruff sadness. "He died fighting the Dutch during an attempt by them to gain control of the James River."

Kathleen laid her hand upon his. "I'm sorry."

"He died in battle. It was a fitting end and the way he wanted it." Drawing a terse breath, he added, "I, however, would prefer to die of old age in a comfortable bed."

"Right now, I'd settle for the comfortable bed," she muttered.

The thought brought a pleasant picture to mind and John ran his hand along the length of her calf. "I was thinking the same myself."

A surge of heat swept through her. Wanton wench, she scolded herself. "I did not mean that the way you took it. What I said on the ship was due to a momentary lapse brought on by my fear. If you are a true gentleman, you will forget it."

The rejection in her voice stung. He'd not force himself on any woman. "I'll not hold you to anything you've said in the past, but don't begrudge me my flights of fancy. I must have something to see me through this night," he said dryly.

Curled up against him, Kathleen had to admit that it wasn't a bad dream to concentrate upon. "You may think what you will as long as you realize 'tis merely a fantasy," she stated as much for herself as for him, adding tersely, "I'll not allow myself to be used by any man simply for his pleasure."

In spite of her weakened condition, he heard the threat in her voice and recalled her ability with a knife. "I'll keep that in mind," he promised, adding to himself that it was just as well that he had not claimed husbandly prerogatives. She would not fit easily into his household. 'Tis never good for a man to let lust rule his brain, he admonished himself. He would return to his original plan and have this marriage annulled as quickly as possible.

With the bargain struck, Kathleen was suddenly afraid of where the fantasy might carry her. She fought against it taking over her mind. Trying not to think of her companion at all, she closed her eyes and fell into a restless sleep.

The next time she awoke it was to the sound of her name being spoken in a demanding tone.

"The rain has ceased," John informed her when she finally managed to open her eyes. "We must move."

Her body was throbbing with pain. "I'm not certain I can," she said shakily.

"Then this will surely be our grave," he replied matter-of-factly. "And someday someone will come along and find us like this...two skeletons locked in each other's arms. No doubt they'll think we were lovers who died of exposure while fleeing from some hideous danger. Poets will write sonnets about us...

'Twas in the fall of seventy-three,
Two lovers did hide from what dangers there be,
Tucked inside a tree so cramped
They could not move from the cold and damp.
So there they remained for all to see,
Locked together through eternity
In the hollowed trunk of that grand ol' tree."

Kathleen rewarded him with a reproving grimace. "Did anyone ever tell you, Mr. Ashford, that you've a very unusual sense of humor and you're not a very good poet?"

Amusement flickered in the dark depths of his eyes, then his expression became serious. "I got us in here, Kate, but now my arms and legs are numb, too. If we're going to get out, you're going to have to help."

There was a strength about him that gave Kathleen a renewed determination to survive. The opening of their hollow tree was in front of her. Saying a silent prayer that there was no one lurking outside waiting for them, she forced her legs to straighten and kicked at the protective curtain of brush. Enough fell away so that she could see the woods beyond. Then, twisting so that she was on her

hands and knees, she scooted out of the enclosure backward.

She tried to stand but her legs were still too numb. Sitting on the wet ground, she rubbed them vigorously as
John eased himself out of the tree.

He, too, was forced to rub some life back into his legs
before he could stand. Then, rising cautiously as if he
feared being the target of a pirate's knife, he looked
around. "Do you think Captain Thorton will send someone to search for us?" he asked in lowered tones.

"I don't know," she answered honestly. "If his ship was
badly damaged he'll be too concerned with repairing it to
think of us. If it was not, we can always hope he'll assume
we drowned. We were a problem to him and he should be
glad to be rid of us. But if he thought he could find me, he
might try. He did enjoy tormenting me." This thought gave
Kathleen the will to rise. Her feet felt as if tiny needles were
pricking them, but she ignored this discomfort. It was minor compared to what Captain Thorton would do to her
if he should catch her again.

A chill wind whipped around them. Reaching back into
the hollow trunk, John pulled out her shoes and his boots,
then the bundle with the extra clothing. "You'd better
change," he ordered.

Kathleen did not argue. Not only did she feel immod-
estly exposed in the man's clothing, but the material was
still damp and felt as if it were turning to ice on her body.
With fingers that refused to work properly, she fumbled
with the knots holding the oilskin bundle closed. After
what seemed like an eternity, they finally gave. But as she
reached inside, she frowned. "These clothes are wet, too."

"Then you may as well stay dressed as you are," he said,
adding tersely, "But even wet, the cloaks will help fight the
wind." Kneeling beside her, he pulled them out of the bag.

He placed one around Kathleen's shoulders and one around his own. After which he pulled on his boots, then rose and looked around once again. Reaching back into the hollow of the tree, he pulled out two pieces of flint and the small metal box in which they had been housed. "The flint has dried fairly well, but I suggest we move farther inland before we make camp for the night. I hid the barrels and the storm will have obliterated any sign of my footprints. If the captain should send men looking for us, they'll not know where we came ashore. That should make their search much more difficult. Still, I'd like to put a bit more distance between us and the water before we light a fire."

Kathleen nodded her agreement. As quickly as possible she put on her shoes. Then, saying a silent prayer that the captain would be too busy to concern himself with finding her, she followed John deeper into the woods.

As the day lengthened, each step became torture. The cold and exhaustion numbed her mind until coherent thought no longer existed. The world became a blur of pain. But the will to survive carried her onward. They walked for hours until, through the tops of the trees, she could see that the sun was descending in the western sky. Suddenly losing her footing, Kathleen stumbled and fell. Though she tried to bite it back, a strangled cry of agony escaped.

"Are you injured?" John demanded tersely, hurrying to her and kneeling beside her. He knew he had been setting a difficult pace but he had no desire for them to be recaptured.

Lifting her hand, she saw a minor gash. "Yes." She smiled dryly. "'Tis lucky, I'm too cold to bleed." She tried to lift herself, but her legs remained buckled beneath her. "I cannot go any farther," she said with apology.

Touching her face, he frowned anxiously. Her skin felt like ice. For a moment he considered carrying her, but he was too tired. Rising, he surveyed their surroundings. "On the other side of this gully, a large tree has fallen, bringing the full circle of its roots with it. I can build a shelter there." He held his hands out to her. "Come along."

She knew he had to be as exhausted as she was. "I can make it that far on my own," she said, determined not to be a burden.

"We'll make it together," he replied, capturing her hands in his and pulling her to her feet. Admittedly she was not his vision of what a woman should be. Still he admired her. "You've proven to be a most valuable companion," he said. "I would not want to lose you now."

His words brought a surge of warmth that gave her legs the strength to carry her across the gully and to the trunk of the fallen tree.

John had salvaged the rope from the barrels, and while she rested, he gathered sturdy poles for the framework of a lean-to.

Kathleen thought she might never move again, then she saw his grimace of pain. Her gaze narrowed on his arm. A redness had begun to stain his shirt and she knew his wound was bleeding once again. "You must stop and let me rebandage your arm," she demanded.

He glanced at it and frowned at the sight of the fresh blood. He was almost afraid to stop for fear that he would not have the strength to finish, but he knew that an untreated wound could prove to be dangerous. "You're right," he agreed. He joined her as she again opened the oilskin bag.

Kathleen pulled out a petticoat, then ripped a strip of cloth from around the bottom. Next she helped him out of his shirt and unwrapped his arm. To her relief, the bleeding was only minor. "It would seem that your swim did it no good, but no harm either." She frowned anxiously as she began to bind the strip of petticoat around his arm. "There may be salt left in this cloth by the seawater. That will cause your wound to sting." She knew her prediction was right when she saw his jaw twitch with discomfort. But he made no sound. "At least the fresh bandage is cleaner than the other and will stop the bleeding," she said as she finished and helped him back into his shirt.

The concern he saw on her face pleased him. His more cynical side was quick to point out that she must realize she was safer with a companion than alone in these woods. Still, the pleasure remained. He rose and gave her a low formal bow. "I shall be forever grateful to your healing touch." Upon a sudden urge, he captured her hand and placed a kiss upon it in the manner of a cavalier. Her skin was cold as ice. Fear for her again filled him. Quickly he released her and returned to building their shelter.

The feel of his lips lingered tantalizingly upon Kathleen's skin. The sudden wish that he would hold her threatened to overwhelm her. I must not give in to this weakness, she warned herself. As tired as she was, she could also not sit any longer while he worked. "I can help," she insisted, shoving the petticoat back into the oilskin packet and rising also.

He started to insist that she rest, but realized that sitting would only increase her chill. "We must hope we are far enough away from any searchers and chance a fire. If we do not get warm soon, we will surely become ill. Try to find some dry wood." He frowned. There were other dangers he would rather not mention yet, but she needed to be warned. "It would be wise not to wander too far. And do not approach any strangers until we've had time to observe them. There are some unsavory types who have escaped to the Carolinas to avoid prosecution." His frown deepened. "Also, you must be wary of the Indians. They have little love for the colonists."

"'Twould seem 'tis not a great deal safer here than on Captain Thorton's ship," she muttered. Then she smiled. "Still, I am grateful to be here." She did not add that his presence gave her the strength to believe they would reach safety. That would be admitting too much.

It had not rained all day and the top layer of pine needles that blanketed the ground was dry. Kathleen gathered a large quantity of those to use as kindling. To her delight, she also found some large pieces of wood that had begun to dry reasonably well.

Returning to the fallen tree, she discovered their shelter well underway. John had used the huge circle of roots as the back of the lean-to. His cloak was the roof. "My dress," she gasped as she recognized the material he'd tied to the poles to make the upper half of the left wall.

"'Tis as good a way as any to dry it," he said, continuing to pile brush and branches against the skeleton of their shelter wherever he had no cloth to guard against the wind.

Biting back any further protest, Kathleen laid her wood down.

"You can clear a spot for our fire right about here." He drew a circle with the toe of his boot in the center of the entrance to the lean-to.

While she cleared the patch of ground, he finished the sides of their shelter, then went to find more wood. When an area wide enough was prepared, she made a pyramid with the dry needles. Saying a prayer, she struck the flint he'd given her. It took several tries but finally a whiff of smoke began to trail upward. She waited until the needles were safely flaming, then began adding the driest pieces of wood.

Dusk had fallen and she hoped that the smoke would blend into the night mists enough so that if there were any pirates, hostile Indians or unsavory colonists nearby they would not notice it.

As she sat huddled, her arms wrapped around her legs and her head resting on her knees, the fire began to warm her. "Think pleasant thoughts," she ordered herself, attempting to escape from the fears that taunted her. John's image came into her mind. He is an unacceptable topic, she admonished herself. Still, his image lingered. She recalled the excitement of the feel of him upon her as they were tossed about in the storm-ravaged ship and a heat unrelated to the fire stirred within her.

"A penny for your thoughts."

She jerked her head up to see John adding a large armload of wood to the stack she had collected. "I was wondering what it will be like to be in the company of civilized people once again," she replied. This was not entirely a lie, she reasoned. This thought had been lingering somewhere in the back of her mind.

John suddenly thought of his mother, Lady Margaret. She was a woman who greatly valued her station in life and held no sympathy or respect for anyone she considered beneath her. There were others like her as well. A strong surge of protectiveness toward Kathleen swept over him. He would not allow people like that to hurt her. He would do all in his power to see that she was treated with kindness. He owed her that much. "You will enjoy it," he promised. Then, smiling as the flames flickered strongly, he sat down beside her. "I never knew a fire could feel so good."

"Nor I," she agreed as she carefully added more wood, and tried not to think of his nearness.

"I've hung the rest of the clothing from the bundle over the trunk to dry," he informed her, stretching his hands out over the flames. "And I think the weather is warming again."

Kathleen knew that at this time of year, the weather could be as warm as spring or cold as winter and could change as quickly as a thief changed his tale. "I hope you're right," she said, then flushed when her stomach growled loudly.

John had told himself to keep his distance, but he could not stop himself from reaching toward her and combing a stray strand of hair from her cheek. "We'll find more substantial food tomorrow," he said. He nodded toward the makeshift bag at the back of the lean-to. "There are some nuts left."

She glanced back at the small stash of food they had gathered during their trek. But his touch had made her forget her hunger. "I must look a mess," she muttered self-consciously, then was shocked by how feminine that sounded. For years she had not concerned herself with her looks expect to make herself as unappealing as possible.

"A very becoming mess," he assured her. He'd meant it merely as a gallantry, but in truth, even in such disarray, he found her attractive. Against his will, he recalled the tantalizing feel of her as she'd lain beneath him.

Kathleen looked up into his face. The fire danced in the dark depths of his eyes and she wondered how his lips would taste. They'll taste like trouble, delicious trouble, but trouble nonetheless, her instincts warned.

John called himself a fool. He told himself that this adventure had tainted his reason. Still, he could not resist her. "Kate?" He spoke her name softly.

The question in his voice sent a tremor of desire through her. *If you surrender to these urges, you will live to regret it*, she warned herself.

He traced the line of her jaw with the tips of his fingers. The fire was warming her skin, causing it to feel soft and inviting. *'Tis dangerous ground on which you are treading*, he cautioned himself. But he paid no heed.

Stop this now, she ordered herself. *You do not need the kind of trouble he's offering!* "No," she said firmly, turning away from him.

Capturing her chin, he forced her to face him once again. He wanted her as he had wanted no other woman. "You're my wife, Kate, but I'll not force myself upon you," he said grimly. "I want you to come to me of your own free will." His words stunned him. Again he had declared her his wife. *'Twas perhaps a high price to pay for lust*, he mocked himself. But in the same breath he reasoned that there was honor involved also. He had signed the agreement and she had no one else to look after her.

Kathleen could not believe that he honestly wanted her for his wife. "I freed you," she reminded him stiffly.

He told himself to take this opportunity to escape the commitment, but instead he heard himself saying, "We signed a legal document. Its destruction does not make it less binding."

The realization of how much she wanted to be his wife frightened Kathleen, but she had her pride. And, she cautioned herself, *'twas most likely he would not want her once he saw all there was to see of her*. "I would never hold you to an agreement forced upon you as that one was. It was merely a ploy."

John's jaw tightened. Twice now, in less than the passing of a minute, she had rejected him. He felt like a fool. He was offering her an honorable alliance and yet she steadfastly refused. "As you wish," he said curtly. Abruptly he rose and went in search of more wood.

Alone by the fire, Kathleen pulled her cloak more tightly around herself. She had done the right thing. She had given him his freedom. And he had accepted it without any great struggle. He knows I could never have fit in with his family and friends, she thought. I would be an embarrassment to him. 'Tis the danger we are facing together that has my emotions stirred so violently. By the time we reach Jamestown, these feelings will fade. I will be free for the first time in my adult life and I shall revel in that freedom.

Having had this stern talk with herself, she tossed more wood on the fire, then lay down. Her stomach growled and she remembered the nuts stored at the back of the lean-to. But when she tried to rise, her body refused. Exhaustion won over hunger. She curled up near the fire and drifted into slumber.

John returned a little later with a fresh armload of wood. Dusk had fallen. He added more wood to the fire, then he also lay down in the shelter of the lean-to. His jaw formed a determined line as he ordered himself to ignore the woman beside him. He should be grateful to her for freeing him from so unsuitable a marriage, he reasoned. And I am, he declared silently. Determined that this would be the end of any thoughts of Kathleen other than to see her safely to Jamestown, he, too, slept.

Chapter Five

When Kathleen awoke the next morning she was alone. She knew that John had been there during the night. She'd wakened during the dark hours to find herself snuggled up against him. Quickly she'd moved away and put more wood on the fire. Those were the flames that must provide her with the warmth she needed. She dare not turn to the kind John could ignite.

But now he was gone and she felt more alone than she had ever felt in her life. "I am not alone, I am *free*." She scolded herself.

Sitting up, she looked out of the lean-to at the unfamiliar wilderness beyond. As John had predicted, the weather had warmed. A dry smile curled her lips. "And as long as Captain Thorton's men don't catch us, we aren't discovered by hostile Indians, we don't meet with any of the unsavory types who have come here to escape the law and we aren't eaten by wild beasts, I shall have a grand life." Suddenly her stomach growled and knotted. "And as long as we don't starve to death," she added, putting on her shoes.

Stepping out of the shelter, she surveyed their surroundings. She had no experience foraging for food. And even if she had it wouldn't have done any good here. The captain never allowed her on dry land except when he put in to port for the winter. And that was always on one of the islands in the Caribbean. The wild food available there was not the same as that found here in Carolina. While she pondered this dilemma, a small furry creature with a large bushy tail scurried past her.

Her mouth formed a speculative line. "I can watch him and gather whatever he eats. Or I could try to kill him and see how he tastes." Acting quickly, she drew her knife and let it fly. It missed by an inch. "Darn!" she hissed.

"Luckily for our stomachs, my fishing was more successful than your squirrel hunting," John said, coming up behind her.

She turned toward him. He was once again the brown-eyed stranger, distant and cold. She congratulated herself for having judged rightly. He was Mr. Jonathan Ashford, nephew of the Earl of Wheaton, wealthy landholder. And she, Kathleen James, had no place in his life. And he has no place in mine, she affirmed. "'Tis lucky," she agreed with matching coolness. But as he handed her one of the two cleaned fish he was carrying, she suddenly paled. "I thought we were a much greater distance from the sea."

"We are," he replied. "There's a stream to the north. I speared these there."

Kathleen drew a relieved breath and turned her attention back to her fish. It had been skewered on a stick.

"Hold it over the hottest part of the coals but not in them," John instructed. After leaning his roughly fashioned spear against the side of the lean-to, he seated himself across the fire from her and began to cook his fish. Concentrating on the fire and his cooking, he refused to think about how enticing she looked in the early morning light. Again he told himself that he was relieved to be freed of any obligation to her. Taking her home with him would only have brought trouble and he had no wish for that.

Kathleen tried to concentrate on her cooking, but the silence that hung between them grated on her nerves. For the first time since their association began, she found herself feeling like a burden placed upon him. "You must teach me how you caught these," she said stiffly, "so that I may help."

John nodded his consent. This attraction he felt toward her was unreasonably strong and he would prefer to keep a distance between them. But if they were to survive, it would take the efforts of both. "We will follow the stream. It will provide us with food and water. And it should eventually lead us to the James River."

And the James River will take us to Jamestown, she finished in her mind. She had heard the impatience in his voice. Clearly he would be glad to be rid of her. And I shall be glad to be rid of him, she decided.

"Save some of your fish for later," he directed as they began to eat.

It tasted so good and she was so hungry, it was difficult for Kathleen to obey, but she did. As soon as they had finished with their breakfast, John began taking their lean-to apart.

Glancing down at herself, Kathleen suddenly flushed with embarrassment at her attire. "I will change into my dress now," she said, beginning to unfasten it from the poles.

John's gaze traveled over her. He would prefer her in a dress, he decided. The man's breeches revealed too much of what he did not want to think of. Also, having carried her to the tree, he was aware that she wore no confining undergarments either. But that knowledge he tried not to consider. There was a need to be practical. "You will be able to travel more swiftly and you'll be less encumbered in the clothing you are wearing," he replied. "Besides, the journey will be through untrod wilderness. I doubt your dress will weather it well.''

Kathleen knew he was right. The loose tunic shirt she wore was much less confining and decidedly more comfortable than a corset and dress. Also, the breeches were less likely to catch on thorns and brush. Even more importantly, she did not wish to enter Jamestown in clothing that was no more than rags. Without any further discussion, she packed the dress away.

John set a moderate but steady pace as they followed the stream northward. When they first began, Kathleen thought he intended to ignore her completely. But several times he paused to warn her about a plant that could cause irritation if she were to brush against it. Also, on one occasion he spoke to her briefly when they stopped to snack on a few nuts and gather some to carry with them. Actually, she mused, that had not been a conversation but a discourse on his part concerning edible foods they should look for along their path. Other than those instances, there were no exchanges between them. Because we have nothing in common to talk about, she reasoned. Marriage to him would have been a bore, she added, refusing to allow herself to remember how exciting his touch had been.

By noon her legs ached, and she was glad when John announced they would take a longer break to have their meal and to rest. But as she began to sink to the ground, she saw him grimace. Her attention immediately went to his arm. He flexed it and grimaced again. "I must unwrap your arm and clean both the wound and the bandage," she said, moving toward him. She had no wish for any physical contact with him, but she was not willing to risk his getting an infection. I placed my life in jeopardy for him, she told herself. It would be a waste if I should allow him to die now that we are so close to freedom.

John had been trying to ignore her during their morning's trek. But he had not been entirely successful. Once, he had made the mistake of allowing her to take the lead for a short while. The swing of her hips had tantalized him until he was thinking only of the feel of her beneath him once again. He had resumed the lead and kept it after that. Now as she approached, he saw a trickle of sweat run along her neck to the V opening of her shirt. When it continued downward, he had a strong desire to follow it with his tongue. "My arm is fine," he said, refusing her aid.

The rejection in his voice stung and the urge to leave him on his own was strong. But Kathleen couldn't make herself turn away. "If your arm should become infected, it will do neither of us any good." Then, because her pride refused to allow him to think for even a moment that his well-being was of a deep personal concern to her rather than merely a practical consideration, she added, "Together we have a much better chance of reaching safety."

John regarded her coolly. She was as he had first suspected, a woman who looked after herself, he mused dryly. However, she did have a point. "I suppose it should be cleaned," he conceded.

As he removed his shirt, Kathleen tried to concentrate on anything but the sight of him. You shall have to look at him to clean his arm, she admonished herself. Perhaps he won't seem as appealing as before, she thought hopefully. She allowed her gaze to move to him. A rush of heat swept through her. He's merely a man, she told herself. Other civilized men will look as good as him and cause me to feel these stirrings, she assured herself. Moving toward him, she removed the bandage from his arm.

The wound looked red and sore but not infected. As she washed it with water from the river, his muscles tensed against the pain. Immediately she felt a responding pain in her own arm. When the cleansing was finished, she opened the bag and ripped another strip from the petticoat inside. At this rate, I may be quite indecent beneath my dress, she thought wryly, again trying to turn her mind, at least for a moment, away from Jonathan Ashford.

But despite all of her efforts, she was strongly aware of the firm texture of his back and shoulders. Quickly, she rewrapped the arm with the dry bandage. Then she carried the soiled one down to the stream, rinsed it out thoroughly and hung it over a branch to dry.

"What are your plans for after we reach Jamestown?" John asked as she sat down to eat. He told himself he was only interested because he felt he must see her situated securely before he could return to his plantation.

"I shall find work and build a life for myself," she replied. "And I suppose you will be most anxious to return to your home," she added, assuring herself that once he was gone from her life, she would have no trouble forgetting him.

A grimness came over his features. "If it is still there for me to return to."

A sudden apprehension for him filled Kathleen. She wanted to be rid of him, but she did not wish him any evil. "Do you fear the Indians may have destroyed it?"

A cynical smile tilted one corner of his mouth. "I do not fear the destruction the Indians can do half as much as that which my mother can render."

Kathleen stared at him in confusion. "Your mother?"

"Whereas I love this land, she hates it. Because of that my father left his estate to me. Lady Margaret has the right to live with me and she receives a yearly allowance. If I should be judged dead, however, without any heirs, all goes to her. 'Tis likely she would sell my land and sail for England at the first opportunity." The cynical smile on his face deepened. "She had great hopes that her brother, the earl, would arrange a marriage for me that would be so enticing I would agree to sell my holdings here and return to England for good."

"But he found no match that enticed you so strongly?" The moment the words were out, Kathleen was furious with herself for asking. Jonathan Ashford's marriage was not her concern.

"There were possibilities," he admitted. "But I am a man who likes to think over a decision of such magnitude." At least, I used to be, he added to himself. The fact that he had been so ready to claim Kathleen as his wife still stunned him. It was a matter of honor, he reminded himself, and he had always been a man of honor.

The thought of him with his fancy ladies caused a tightening in Kathleen's stomach. He can have them. I will have my freedom, she told herself. But a restlessness had come over her and she had lost her taste for her food. "Perhaps we should be on our way," she suggested, rising and retrieving the drying bandage from the branch. "I would not want you to lose your land and find yourself again faced with a marriage contract that is not of your choosing."

"No, I would not want to face that twice in a lifetime," he agreed, rising also.

"He can have his fancy ladies and be welcome to them," Kathleen muttered. It was late afternoon and she was standing in the stream with her spear in her hand. Her shoes and stockings were safely dry onshore and her breeches were rolled up high enough to keep them out of the water.

She and John had been traveling steadily for a week now. During that time, he had taught her how to fish and how to build the lean-to. And she had told herself a mil-

lion times how happy she would be to reach Jamestown
and be free of him. But every time he was near, her heart
pounded faster, and when he would accidentally touch her,
a surge of heat would rush through her. Right at this moment, he was watching her from the top of the sloping in-
cline that led down to the bank of the stream. She felt his
gaze almost as if it were a physical contact and it was
causing her nerves to grow more on edge by the moment.

John's jaw was set in a terse line. A week ago, he'd assured himself that he would grow bored with Kathleen's
company quickly. By the time they reached Virginia soil,
he would be glad to be rid of her, he'd told himself over
and over. Thus far, however, that hadn't proven true. He'd
expected her to grow more haggard in appearance with
each passing day but instead this rugged life seemed to
agree with her. She was more beautiful than ever. As he
watched her, a frustration like none he'd ever known
flowed through him. He'd ordered himself to turn away
when she bared her legs, but the order had fallen on deaf
ears.

Kathleen tried to concentrate only on the fish swim-
ming in the pool of deep water in front of her and not on
the man watching from the shore. Spotting a large trout
coming toward her, she stood motionless until it was close.
Then in one swift motion, she speared it. But the fish was
larger than she had thought and her footing wasn't as
steady. Letting out a surprised yelp, she fell forward into
the deeper water.

John raced toward the bank, but before he reached the
stream, she had regained her footing. Abruptly, he came
to a halt. She was standing there proudly holding her spear
above her head with the fish still securely impaled. But it
wasn't the fish or the spear that held his attention. Her wet
clothing was clinging to every curve of her body. "She

would threaten even a saint's control," he growled under his breath.

Kathleen grinned proudly. The day had been warmer than usual and the water had felt refreshing. Even more, she had managed to salvage her spear and her catch. Combing her wet hair back from her face with the fingers of her free hand, she waded toward shore. But as she neared the bank, her pleasure faded. She had never seen John looking so angry, and she had no doubt that his anger was directed at her. Before she could even wonder what she had done to incur his wrath, he reached out for her hand and jerked her up onto the bank.

It was taking every ounce of John's control not to claim her as his wife and immediately consummate their marriage on that grassy slope. "Get out of that wet clothing," he ordered.

Kathleen looked down at herself. Even the nipples of her breasts, hardened by the unexpected plunge into the cold water, were well-defined by the clinging fabric. A flush of embarrassment spread over her. She thrust the spear into his hand, then strode quickly toward their camp. The urge to run was strong, but she was determined to maintain some dignity. She found her cloak and was swinging it around her shoulders to cover herself when suddenly it was torn from her grasp.

"That will only serve to dampen yet another garment," John snarled. He would have preferred to allow her to cover herself immediately, but he had to be practical. She would need the cloak to keep her warm when she slept. "You must take off your wet clothing, then wrap yourself in the cloak." His mind felt muddled from his battle for control. Standing behind her, his gaze traveled along the curve of her back to her waist then downward to the soft roundness of her hips. Impatience overwhelmed him.

Wanting only to get her covered by the cloak as quickly as possible, he grabbed the bottom of her tunic shirt and began to strip it from her.

"No!" Kathleen gasped, clutching at the fabric. But she knew she had spoken too late when she heard his harsh intake of breath. She stiffened defensively.

John stood frozen, staring at the thin white lines crisscrossing her back. "What the devil?" he muttered.

Kathleen jerked her shirt free from his hold. Pulling it down to cover herself once again, she turned to face him. Defiance flashed in her eyes. "'Twas a lesson taught by the captain. Twice before I tried to escape. The first time was soon after my mother's death and the specter of her ghost was still strong in his mind. That time, he gave me only two lashes. The second time, he reasoned that punishment for misbehavior did not count as treating me badly, so long as he did not kill me. That time he determined to teach me a lesson I would not forget." Her body stiffened as she recalled the anger on the captain's face. He had beaten her until her back was raw and bleeding. "But he could not make me cry for mercy," she said softly, more to herself than to the man in front of her. It had been a matter of pride and she had been willing to pay the price to win. And she had won. Nearly at the cost of her life, but that didn't matter.

"The captain needs a lesson taught to him," John declared, promising himself that if his and Thorton's paths should ever cross again, he would teach him one the man would never forget.

The note of sympathy in his voice caused Kathleen's stomach to knot. She wanted no one's pity, especially his. "'Tis curious," she said, forcing an indifference into her voice. "On men scars are considered a mark of honor. On women they are an imperfection."

"Imperfection is not a word I would use to describe your body," John replied, his gaze traveling over her form, rekindling the desire he was trying so hard to control.

There was a heat in his eyes that caused a hard warm knot to form in her abdomen. Her heart began to beat faster. The thought, that in his own way John Ashford could be as dangerous as Captain Thorton, flashed through her mind. "I am already beginning to dry," she said, turning abruptly away from him. "I will go hunt for wood. By the time I return, I'm sure I shall be completely dry once again."

John ordered himself to let her leave, but instead his hand closed around her arm. "You could catch a chill," he said curtly. He had meant only to stop her, but his muscles were tense from his struggle to restrain himself and she was swung around by the force of his grasp. His leg brushed against hers and the fire he had been trying to control blazed. "Damn you, Kate," he snarled, his mouth claiming hers even as he cursed her for this weakness she caused in him.

A heat surged through her. Grudgingly, she could not deny that she had hungered for his kiss. But she would not allow herself to be taken in anger. Her body stiffened for battle.

Furious with himself, John lifted his head. Still, his hand remained firmly around her arm. "You are my wife, Kate. 'Tis my right to bed you," he growled. He'd claimed her yet again! He could barely believe his own ears. He was allowing lust to completely rule his reason.

"Even if the contract we signed were binding, I would not allow you to misuse me," she replied defiantly. "No man shall ever have that right."

He had misjudged her, he thought dryly. She was a hundred times more dangerous than any human or beast he had yet encountered. "I have no intention of misusing you," he assured her. He had never taken a woman against her will and he would not start now, he promised himself. He commanded himself to release her and forget this folly. But even as he freed her arm, his other hand moved caressingly along the curves of her body. "There are many," he said coaxing, "who find mating a pleasure."

The trail of his touch sent rivulets of excitement coursing through her. Kathleen knew she should move away from him, but never had anything tantalized her so.

John studied her narrowly. He had freed her but she had not stepped away from him. 'Twould be wise of me to step away from her, he advised himself. But before this thought was even completed, his fingers entwined in her hair and he claimed her mouth once again.

You are a fool if you allow this to go any further, Kathleen warned herself. Her hands came up to push him away. But his kiss had become more playful than demanding. He was teasing her lips with his tongue. It tickled and yet excited her at the same time. Her will to fight him weakened even more. "There is the chance we may die tomorrow," she heard herself saying against his lips. "'Twould not be fair for me to leave this world without experiencing some of its pleasures."

"'Twould not be fair," he agreed.

The beard he had been forced to grow for lack of a razor brushed her neck as he trailed kisses downward. It was a deliciously rough sensation.

"'Tis definitely time to remove your wet clothing," he said, beginning to ease her tunic upward.

As the garment was drawn over her head, then discarded, her teeth closed over her bottom lip to hide the sudden embarrassment of being so exposed. Then he smiled, his eyes dark with passion. Cupping a breast, he greeted it with his tongue. Ecstasy so intense her breath locked in her lungs vanquished her embarrassment.

John had been trying for days not to think of how touching her would feel. Now he ridiculed himself for ever thinking he could have imagined how very intoxicating her body could be. Move slowly, he ordered himself. But it was not easy. This hunger he had for her was potent. Carefully he removed her breeches, greeting the newly exposed flesh with kisses.

Kathleen had never believed any man's touch could be so enjoyable. A tremor of pleasure swept through her. Suddenly his clothing seemed like a horrible barrier.

"Now you must allow me to disrobe you," she heard herself saying and was amazed at her forwardness.

He hated to leave the taste of her, but he could not resist this invitation. Rising, he stood in front of her.

The shirt she had removed before. That she discarded quickly. Unable to resist the temptation, she combed her fingers through the crisp dark hair that formed a V on his chest. She felt his breathing become ragged and a sense of womanly power came over her. She grinned. "'Tis fun."

'Tis heaven and hell, John corrected mentally, fighting the urge to claim her then and there. He knew she would not be ready yet.

"You must sit," she instructed. When he raised a questioning eyebrow, she added, "Your boots must be removed next."

Relief washed over him. A short reprieve from her touch would be of great aid to his control, he told himself. But as he seated himself on a nearby boulder, he mocked himself for that notion. Just the sight of her made him ache to possess her. She reminded him of a wood nymph. Her dark hair cascaded over her ivory skin and the firm curves of her body were as femininely enticing as any artist could have envisioned.

Kathleen could not believe her own actions. She had spent so many years keeping herself fully covered at all times. Now here she was taking off a man's boots without a stitch of clothing on her back. She glanced up at John. Well, he did seem to be enjoying the view, she noted with satisfaction.

After his boots came his stockings. And now it was time for his breeches.

"One moment," he said, stopping her before she could work loose the fastenings. They had no bed but he could provide better than the mere rough soil for them to lay upon. He rose from the boulder, quickly found his cloak and spread it out upon the ground. "'Tis always best to think ahead," he remarked.

Her gaze traveled over him and she noted his growing readiness. "'Tis not too far ahead," she observed.

"Not too far," he conceded.

A wave of apprehension suddenly washed over her. It mingled with the excitement that stirred within her.

John saw her sudden anxiety. He did not have the strength to allow her to turn away from him now. "You will enjoy me as much as I shall enjoy you," he promised, gently pulling her to him. He fitted her against him, then with firm command began massaging and caressing her.

Kathleen gasped as the fires of reawakened passion threatened to consume her. Her need to know him fully was so strong it was a physical pain. Her hands sought the fastenings of his breeches. "We must rid ourselves of this barrier," she insisted.

Triumph flowed through John. "Yes, we must," he agreed.

The sight of his maleness shook her but she was beyond fear. As they lay down on the cloak, her legs parted with welcome.

As he entered her and met the maidenhead, John had the urge to cry out from sheer exultation. He had not truly believed no man had ever known her before. But here was proof that he was the first, and it gave him a sense of power like none he had ever known before. He waited a moment for her to get used to the feel of him, then he drove hard and fast, breaking the barrier quickly.

Kathleen had not expected pain. A surprised cry broke from her lips and her body suddenly wanted to withdraw.

"The pain is over now," John soothed gruffly. "'Twill be only pleasure ahead." Slowly he began to move within her while his mouth teased and played over her lips, shoulders and neck.

Kathleen felt herself being drawn back into a world of enchanting sensations. The memory of the pain vanished. All she felt was pleasure and the desire to return to him what he was giving her. She dug her fingers into him, holding him more firmly to her as she added her own strength to the union.

Her mind seemed to spin dizzily. When she thought she could feel no greater rapture, her body seemed suddenly to ignite. A burst of wild uninhibited ecstasy shook every fiber of her being and she cried out from the sheer pleasure of it.

"I never knew a woman could feel as good as you," John confessed in a low growl, shocked by how much his own enjoyment was increased by her pleasure. Then all thought vanished as he joined her in the pulsing release of their passion.

For several minutes afterwards, John lay holding her molded to him, until their bodies relaxed fully and their breathing became more normal. He had thought that once he possessed her this lust he felt for her would lessen, but it seemed to have grown stronger. The urge to claim her once again began to grow within him. Control yourself, sir, he commanded himself. She was new to this. It would not do to be too demanding. She stirred in his arms and the feel of her against him threatened to weaken his resolve. "I must gather wood before dark," he said, abruptly releasing her and then rising.

Kathleen drew the cloak around her as she watched him dress quickly and then leave. Clearly, he was already regretting having seduced her, she decided. No doubt the pleasure was not as great as he had hoped. "And it was probably only so great for me because of the newness," she muttered, rising and pulling on her still-damp clothing. Retrieving her spear, she headed for the stream. "Another man's bed will be just as pleasurable," she assured herself.

By the time John returned to camp she had speared two fresh fish for dinner. While he cleaned and skewered them, she built a fire. They had said little to one another since his return and she wondered if he meant to remain silent all evening. 'Twould be their usual way, she reminded herself.

During his foraging for wood, John had reached a decision. As they sat down to cook their fish, he regarded her levelly. "We shall go directly to my home," he said with authority. "In the eyes of God as well as the law, we are now married."

Kathleen's stomach knotted. 'Twas duty that caused him to say that. He did not truly want her. "Many a man has bedded a woman he did not wed. You have no obligation to me."

Why he should even want her amazed him. She rejected him at every turn. "I did not think my lovemaking was that distasteful to you," he said. "Or have you decided that you wish to try a variety of men before settling on one?"

She glared at him. "You know your lovemaking was not distasteful. And I do not desire a variety of men. I simply do not wish to harness you with a wife you do not want." She drew a terse breath. "I have spent too much of my life in the company of those who would dance upon my grave. I wish to spend the rest of what time is left me among those who desire my company."

"I desire your company," John assured her. In truth, he wished he did not desire it so much. He hated the thought of a woman having such a hold over him. Still, she would serve a practical purpose in his life, he reasoned. Aloud he said, "And 'tis time I began producing heirs. I am offering you a home and family, Kate."

"'Tis all I've ever wanted," she replied. She had hoped also for a man who would love her, but one could not have everything one hoped for, she told herself.

"Then 'tis settled." His eyes darkened with passion. "Eat hearty," he ordered. "I have plans for an active evening."

Immediately, the embers of desire began to glow within her. He might not love her but he was an excellent lover. 'Twas a good compromise, she decided. As long as she did not wish for more or learn to care too deeply for him, she could have a full and happy life.

And that night she could find no reason to regret her decision, as she lay exhausted but satiated from his lovemaking.

* * *

"There is one matter I should mention to you," John said, breaking into her thoughts.

I knew there must be a catch to this somewhere, she mused to herself, turning toward him.

"If anything should happen to me, Kate," he continued, "don't bury me with my boots on."

She frowned at him in puzzlement.

Rewarding her dubious stare with a grin, he picked up one of his boots. With a knife he pried out a corner nail from the heel, then gave the heel a twist. It opened, and in the light from the fire, she saw that it had been hollowed out. Inside was a store of gold coins.

"My father taught me never to go anywhere without some hidden gold to fall back upon," John explained, resetting the heel in place.

Kathleen smiled with approval. "Your father was a wise man."

"In many ways," he agreed. But not in his choice of a wife, he thought to himself as he lay back down. And I hope I have not played the fool either, he added.

Chapter Six

Dark storm clouds threatening to bring the first staying snow hung low in the sky the afternoon they rode down the long tree-lined lane to Ashford Hall. It was the end of their journey and Kathleen knew she should be feeling relieved. Instead, a foreboding filled her.

This uneasiness she had been feeling had begun days earlier with the hiring of their horses. When they had reached the James River, she had changed into her dress before they approached the cabin from where they hired a boat to take them to the nearest plantation on the other side. Thus, when they had been received at the manor house, she had looked unkempt due to their long and dangerous journey, but not unsuited to be the wife of a gentleman like Mr. Jonathan Ashford.

John had refused the master's invitation to a meal and lodgings for the night. This Kathleen understood. He felt an urgency to return home and reestablish his authority over his lands. And, in truth, she had not minded. The house had been large and intimidating. And although her mother had taught her manners, she was not certain she remembered all that was proper for her to do.

At John's request, they had gone immediately to the stables. When they had reached the James River and he had informed Kathleen that, with luck, they would be making this last leg of their journey on horseback, she had not thought of this as luck. She'd quickly explained that her experience with horses was limited to observing them from a distance. But he'd countered by assuring her that she would enjoy learning to ride.

As they neared the stables and she saw the groomsman leading their beasts forward, Kathleen had to admit the animals were handsome and it would be nice to have these sturdy-looking creatures do the walking for her. But when the groomsman had begun to saddle the horses, Kathleen had taken one look at the sidesaddle being fastened upon her mount and balked. "I do not believe I can remain seated on that," she'd said.

"I will teach you," John had replied.

But Kathleen remembered as a young child seeing the elder daughter of her parents' master being carried back to the house. The girl's neck had been broken in a fall from a saddle such as this one. And, Kathleen promised herself, she had not survived Captain Thorton so that she could endanger herself in such a manner. "If I am to ride this beast," she said, "I will have a saddle that allows me to wrap both legs around it's belly."

A flash of amusement had appeared in John's eyes. "'Tis a more secure seating that way," he'd said with a wink, and she'd known he was not thinking of the horse. A flush, due more to a pleasure that they should have this private joke between them than to embarrassment, had appeared on her neck. In return, her eyes had flashed a saucy rebuke. He'd grinned, knowing she had caught his dual meaning. Then he'd turned to the master of the house. "On this, I must bow to my wife. We have a long and rough ride ahead of us. A man's saddle would be safer and more practical."

The master had been polite, but Kathleen had seen the disapproval in his eyes and in those of the grooms. Then there had been the maid who had been sent by the mistress with a basket of food for Kathleen and John. Shock followed by horror had shown on her face when she saw Kathleen mounted with her legs straddling the horse's back.

As they had ridden away from the plantation, John had told her that he was pleased she had chosen a more practical saddle. But she was sure that deep inside he had to be embarrassed to have a wife who was so ill equipped in the ways of his class.

Now, as Ashford Hall loomed in front of her, her insecurities grew a hundredfold. It was a magnificent house, much more elegant than that from which they had secured the horses. It was two stories, built of brick, with diamond-shaped chimneys. The kitchen house was larger than most of the cabins in which she and John had found shelter during the last days of their ride. To her left, she saw a series of single-storied buildings, which she guessed were servants' quarters. The thought that she did not belong here flashed through her mind.

"Mr. Ashford!" A man who looked to be in his mid-fifties, dressed in the formal attire of a high-ranking servant, came out to greet them as they dismounted. "We'd heard you were taken prisoner by pirates and didn't hold much hope of ever seeing you again," he said, coming to a halt in front of John and bowing low in greeting. "'Tis good to have you home, sir."

"'Tis good to be home, Quinn," John replied with a smile. Then his expression became stern. "Where is my mother?"

"She's in her sitting room, sir. She'll be so happy to see you." Quinn's eyes traveled to Kathleen, but in the manner of a good servant, he said nothing.

Leaving Quinn with orders to see that the horses were cared for, John tucked Kathleen's hand firmly through his arm and led her into the house. Crossing the large entrance hall, they passed through a long parlor. "These are my mother's rooms to do with as she pleases," he explained as they walked. "The rest of the house will become your domain."

Cold fear swept over Kathleen. "My mother told me of her duties in a large household and of those of the mistress, but I've had no experience in these matters."

He gave her an encouraging smile. "My mother will instruct you. You're a fast learner. I've no doubt you'll succeed very well."

Kathleen had her doubts but she had no time to voice them. They had come to a halt in front of a door and John was knocking upon it.

A uniformed maid opened the door. "Mr. Ashford," she gasped.

"I hope you're not going to faint, Sally," he said with a kind smile, his hand going out to steady the woman.

"John?" a second woman's voice demanded curtly, as the maid flushed and, remembering her station, dropped a low curtsy.

Looking to where the second voice had come from, Kathleen saw a woman she judged to be in her late forties or early fifties. The woman had been working on a canvas of needlepoint. For a moment, she appeared stunned, as if she could not believe her eyes. Then, pushing the stand holding her sewing aside with little regard for its safety, she rose abruptly and came toward them. She was slender, and in her heeled shoes, nearly as tall as John. Her graying hair was styled most elegantly, having been braided in the back and wound into a knot fastened against her head, while the front and sides were a mass of corkscrew curls. Her dress was black with only an emerald brooch fastened at her neck to give color. She moved with an authority and grace that left no doubt in Kathleen's mind that this was John's mother.

"Fetch some tea," the woman ordered the maid, adding a wave of her hand to scurry the servant along. "And close the door when you leave."

"Yes, m'lady." The maid curtsied and was gone before Kathleen could blink. Clearly, John's mother ran a very tight ship.

"I've prayed every day for your safe return," Lady Margaret was saying as she reached her son and gave him a welcoming hug. "After Captain Howle and his men were rescued and safely brought to Jamestown, the good captain came to see me personally. He told me of your being taken hostage by those horrible pirates. I have been frantic with fear that I would never see you again." Continuing to clutch his shoulders as if she were afraid he might disappear if she let go, she looked up at him and breathed a heavy sigh. "If only I hadn't been ill when you sailed for England. I would have gone with you and insisted that we remain and never come back to this horrid place where people must fear daily for their safety."

"This horrid place is my home," he replied with a scowl.

She flushed slightly, then waved away his harsh remark. "Let us not argue on this happy occasion."

"Let us not," he agreed.

As if only then realizing that Kathleen was present, Lady Margaret released her son and turned toward his companion. As her eyes traveled over Kathleen's much-worn, dirt-splattered attire, her nose crinkled in distaste. Then, remembering her manners, her face became a mask of cool politeness. "I don't believe we've been introduced."

"Mother," John said very formally, "I would like to present my wife, Kathleen. Kathleen, this is my mother, Lady Margaret Ashford."

As Kathleen performed a nervous curtsy, Lady Margaret's hands went to cover her heart, as if this news threatened to kill her. "Your wife?" she demanded in total disbelief. The cool mask of politeness vanished as her gaze raked Kathleen, this time clearly making an even less-flattering appraisal. Suddenly a look of horror spread over her face. "This cannot be! The captain mentioned a dark-haired pirate wench who tried to save your life. Surely you've not married her for her simple act of humanity?"

John again scowled at his mother. "Kathleen was being held a prisoner aboard the ship, and you should be honored to accept her as your daughter-in-law. I would not be alive today if she had not intervened on my behalf."

"I'd have thought a thank-you and a handsome monetary reward would have been adequate," Lady Margaret replied snappishly.

Kathleen had watched the exchange in silence. Clearly Lady Margaret considered her totally unsuitable to be John's wife. And she could not dispute the woman's opinion. Nor could she dispute the woman's belief that gratitude had played a large part in causing John to declare her his wife. The notion stung. Her back stiffened. He had allowed gratitude and honor to bind him to her. Well, she owed him a debt of gratitude also and she had as much honor as he. "'Tis my opinion that we're not legally bound," she said levelly.

John jerked around to look at her. He had thought this matter was settled. "The hell we aren't," he growled, furious that she would deny him yet again.

"Let the girl speak," Lady Margaret demanded, her gaze fixed on Kathleen with interest. "Explain yourself, Kathleen."

"The contract was signed under duress. It has been destroyed and the two witnesses cannot be counted as honorable men," Kathleen said simply.

Lady Margaret turned her attention to her son. "Is what she says true?"

John's face was a study in controlled anger. "I will speak to my wife alone," he said tersely. Taking Kathleen by the arm, he practically dragged her from the room. He did not understand what was going on in her mind, but he'd pledged himself to her and he was a man who stood by his word.

Maintaining his hold, he continued through the parlor, causing Sally, who was returning with a huge tray of tea and cakes, to jump out of their way, nearly spilling the contents of her tray.

Kathleen felt the maid's eyes on her as John guided her across the wide entranceway and into the other wing. The pace he set required Kathleen to trot to keep up with him. Entering a room that was clearly a man's study, he kicked the door closed behind them. As it slammed shut, he came to an abrupt halt. Still holding on to her arm, he glared down at her. "I thought you were enjoying being my wife."

"You have been a most pleasurable companion," she admitted. "But 'tis clear to me that I don't belong here. Your mother strongly disapproves of our union, and I cannot help but believe that in your soul you would not choose me as a wife if you were given a free choice." Her jaw tightened with pride. "I've lived too long among those who wished me no good. I've a need to find a place where I'm wanted and people wish me happiness."

John's anger lessened. He could not fault her reasoning. "You are wanted here," he said harshly. How great a truth that was stunned him. "And I wish you happiness," he added. A part of him wondered if he was being unfair to her. Lady Margaret could prove difficult. But he could provide Kathleen with a much better life than most men, he argued. Besides, 'twas too late for questions. "I have committed myself to you. You are my wife," he said. Impatience flickered in his eyes. "However, since you've expressed doubts about the legitimacy of our marriage and have placed those doubts in my mother's mind, a wedding will be required. You'll be introduced to the staff as my betrothed. As soon as it can be arranged, you and I will be wed here by a proper authority." Having issued this ultimatum, he strode toward the door. Now it was time to explain to Lady Margaret what he expected of her. His jaw settled into a grim line as he left the room. Why couldn't women be the obedient creatures they were supposed to be? he mused.

Kathleen stood quietly. When he'd said he wanted her there, hope had swept through her. "You idiot," she mocked herself. "You thought that he might be going to declare that he cared for you." Until this moment she had not allowed such thoughts to come to the front of her mind. She had expended a great deal of energy reminding herself that this union was based solely on honor and practicality. He had said he required a wife to produce heirs.

She paced across the room to stare out the window. But she had done what she most wanted not to do. She had begun to care very deeply for him. In truth, she had fallen in love with him. "'Tis not unreasonable," she murmured, attempting to justify this weakness. "He is, after all, an admirable man." A smile teased a corner of her mouth as she recalled their lovemaking. "In all ways," she added.

Her jaw firmed. And there was the hope that he could learn to care for her. Had he himself not said that where there was life there was hope? She had braved Captain Thorton, she could brave Lady Margaret. Her back stiffened with resolve. She could even learn to manage this house as a true mistress should. If these things would cause him to learn to care for her, 'twould be worth any anguish she might suffer.

A knock on the door interrupted her thoughts. Reacting on instinct, she crossed the room and opened it. Quinn was standing on the other side. The spasm of shock that appeared on his face was enough to tell her that she had not behaved properly. The woman who would be mistress of this house would never have opened the door herself, she scolded mentally. She should have called out, "Enter," and allowed him to come to her. In future, I must think before I act, she commanded herself.

His manner once again staid, Quinn performed a polite bow. "Mr. Ashford has asked me to escort you to your room. If you'll follow me, miss," he requested.

Kathleen noted that, like all good servants, Quinn hid his emotions well. But her survival had demanded that she learn to read even the smallest nuances of expression and she saw the shadow of disapproval in his eyes. Clearly he agreed with Lady Margaret that John should have made a much more suitable match.

Well, I shall prove them both wrong, she declared as she followed him back to the main entrance hall. From there, they ascended a wide curved stairway to the second floor. Turning toward the back of the house, he led her to the farthest door. "These will be your rooms," he said with a dignified bow as he opened the door and stepped aside to allow her to enter a very elegantly furnished sitting room. Crossing the room, he opened a door leading into a bedroom. "And Nancy is to be your maid."

As Kathleen passed him and entered the second room, she saw a pretty, slightly plump redhead in her late teens, dressed in maid's attire. The girl was kneeling by the fire, watching over a kettle of heating water.

"Welcome, miss," she greeted Kathleen, rising quickly and dropping a deep curtsy.

"You mind your manners, girl, and don't prattle on as you usually do downstairs," Quinn instructed Nancy sternly from the doorway. "I'm sure Miss James will not want to be bothered with a constant stream of chatter."

Maintaining a prim demeanor, Nancy dropped a second curtsy in his direction. "Yes, sir."

Turning back to Kathleen, Quinn said, "If you desire anything at all, just send Nancy for it or pull the cord beside your bed or the one in your sitting room."

"Thank you," Kathleen replied, breathing a mental sigh of relief as the staid butler performed a final bow and left, closing the door behind himself.

"Yes, Mr. Quinn. Thank you, Mr. Quinn," Nancy muttered sarcastically at the closed door. Then, turning toward Kathleen, she flushed a bit at her less than respectful manner toward the butler. "He can be a wee bit overbearing sometimes," she explained defensively. "Came from England with Mr. Ashford's father and Lady Margaret, he did. Used to serve her ladyship's family before her ladyship married. He's always talking about the fine parties the old earl used to give and all the fine china and linens they stored in their pantry, and he treats me as if I wouldn't have been good enough to clean out the pigsty."

Kathleen guessed that cleaning out the pigsty was where Quinn thought she belonged, too.

"He's right about one thing though, miss." In the wink of an eye, Nancy's manner suddenly changed from one of righteous indignation to friendly sympathy. "I do prattle on a bit too much. You look exhausted. Mr. Ashford said you might be wanting a bath after a journey such as the one you've endured." She nodded toward the tub that had been placed near the hearth. "Then we'll get you into some fresh clothing."

Looking down at her dirty, worn dress, Kathleen again felt out of place in this house. Then she thought of John and her resolve to belong here returned. "I am afraid these are the only clothes I have," she said with a scowl of frustration.

"That was right stupid of me." Nancy frowned at her own thickheadedness. "I guess you wouldn't have time to pack a valise when you're escaping from a band of pirates." Her frown disappeared as quickly as it had come and she smiled brightly. "Don't you worry none, miss. I've a shift you can borrow for now, and by morning, I'll have that what you're wearing cleaned and mended. I'm right handy with a needle. I'm hoping to open my own seamstress shop in Jamestown when I've finished serving my indenture." Then, frowning, she shook her head. "There I go, prattling again, and you lookin' as if you're ready to collapse. You just sit a bit, miss, and I'll go fetch the shift. Then I'll pour your bath." Suddenly remembering her place, Nancy dropped a quick curtsy. "If that's all right with you, miss."

"Yes, thank you very much," Kathleen replied gratefully.

Smiling brightly, Nancy moved toward the door. "Won't be but a minute or two," she promised over her shoulder as she left.

A small smile tilted the corners of Kathleen's mouth as the door closed behind the girl. It was clear that Quinn had tried hard to teach Nancy to be a proper servant. It was equally clear that he'd failed miserably. Which suits me just fine, she affirmed. Despite her resolve, a female version of Quinn, disapproving of her behind the polite facade of a helpful servant, would have been more than she could bear.

But the smile faded as she surveyed the room. The chairs, the tables, even the porcelain figurines on the mantel were all of the finest quality. Then there was the bed. It was a large four-postered affair with a canopy that matched the comforter covering the mattress. After first rubbing her hand on her dress, she pushed on the comforter to test the firmness of the mattress beneath. Gasping at the softness she encountered, she lifted the coverlet. There were fine Holland sheets below, and pressing again, she realized that they covered a feather mattress. After so many years aboard Captain Thorton's ship, she could not help but be overwhelmed by such luxury. Smoothing the comforter back in place, she moved away from the bed.

As tired as she was, she could not bring herself to sit upon any of the available seats for fear her dusty, travel-worn clothing might soil them.

Noticing a door on the far side of the hearth, she crossed to it and carefully turned the latch. It was locked. Her instinctual need, born during her years of captivity, to know her surroundings as well as possible in the event of danger, were too strong to resist. Kneeling, she peeked through the keyhole but could see only a chair, rug and a bit of richly textured curtain hanging beside a window. None of these helped her determine the use of the room.

Feeling suddenly embarrassed that she'd been peeking through keyholes in John's home, she rose and crossed the room to gaze outside. Below her, she saw a box maze and a rose garden. Beyond that was an orchard and then the river.

Her uneasiness returned. John's home was much more grand than she had imagined. Tersely, she paced back to where the tub sat, partially filled with water. This waiting was wearing on her nerves. "It cannot do any harm for me to see to my own bath," she muttered. Her smile returned. Nancy would not judge her harshly. Removing the cloak she was wearing, she laid it carefully on the floor. Next came her shoes and dress. She was standing in her underclothing pouring the water into the tub when a knock sounded on the door. "Enter," she called, assuming it was the redhead.

"You shall have to exercise a great deal more prudence in the future," a familiar male voice cautioned dryly.

Looking up, she was met by John's dark gaze as he entered and closed the door behind him. "I thought you were Nancy," she explained stiffly. She knew it was improper for him to be there. Yet it took all of her control not to move toward him and invite him to stay. "She went to fetch a shift to loan me until I can arrange for clothing of my own."

John had paced outside for several minutes before entering. He was angry with Kate and had ordered himself to ignore her for a while. Also, for appearance' sake, he knew he should not go into her rooms. Yet he had not been able to stop himself. He had felt curiously alone since parting with her. 'Tis only because I have grown so used to her constant companionship, he reasoned. "I was thinking of your clothing situation also," he said coolly. Moving toward the bed, he tossed the bundle he had been carrying onto it. "I brought you one of my shirts in which to sleep and one of my mother's shawls to keep you warm when you are not in bed. Tomorrow we shall order material for new clothing for you.''

''Thank you,'' Kathleen replied, displeased with herself for having caused this chill between them.

He told himself to leave before he scandalized them both, but she looked so damned enticing. The urge to bathe her himself was strong. But she had robbed him of that freedom. Frustration mingled with his anger. ''For a woman who does not consider me her husband, you show very little modesty in front of me,'' he remarked caustically.

Clearly, he was furious with her for having robbed him of free access to her. Well, she wasn't happy about it, either. But what was done was done. ''I was trying to do what I felt was right,'' she replied in her defense. ''I told you the day I burned our marriage contract that I would never hold you to that document.''

He remembered that day well. Approaching her, he cupped her face in his hands. ''Don't you believe in the fates, Kathleen? They've thrown us together and whether 'tis for the best or for the worst, we are bound together now.''

His touch burned like fire while his words chilled her. They gave evidence that, despite his insistence to the contrary, he had grave doubts about the wisdom of their union. But even those doubts had not dampened his desire for her, she realized as she met his gaze. His eyes were dark with passion and her own need for him flamed within her. I can be the wife he requires, she assured herself.

''We should be together now,'' he said gruffly, ''sharing this bath, sharing the bed.''

With every fiber of her being Kathleen wished this could be so. She craved his touch, hungered for his kisses.

John's hands left her face to move along the curves of her body. He knew her well, and he felt her response beneath his palms and saw her eyes darken with invitation. He smiled a triumphant smile. "However, if I were to stay, my mother and all the servants would be scandalized. So we shall have to wait." Releasing her abruptly, he strode toward the door.

Kathleen had never felt so deserted. "That was cruel," she hissed.

"Perhaps in the future you will not be so quick to deny me as your husband," he replied and stalked out of the room. The moment he closed the door behind him, he regretted his behavior. He had let his anger and frustration rule him. A gleam sparked in his eyes. He would make it up to her.

Kathleen was furious. But she would forgive him this small act of revenge. She was as frustrated by the situation she had created as was he. A sudden smile played at the corners of her mouth. Actually, it was nice to know that he craved her company enough to be so enraged by having been deprived of it. If his lust was that strong, there was surely a chance it could turn to love.

Chapter Seven

A short knock sounded on the door and for an instant Kathleen thought John might have returned.

"It's just me, miss," Nancy announced cheerfully, entering before Kathleen even had a chance to respond. Then, seeing Kathleen by the tub with the water jug in her hand, she frowned. "You shouldn't be doing that, miss. That's my duty." Hurriedly Nancy crossed the room to lay the shift on the bed, but froze in mid-motion when she saw the clothing John had brought. "Now where'd these come from?" she muttered.

"John... Mr. Ashford sent them," Kathleen answered. "He knew I'd been forced to flee with only the clothes on my back."

Nancy drew a wistful sigh. "You're a very lucky woman. Mr. Ashford will make a fine husband." A thoughtful frown suddenly wrinkled her brow. "Though I don't know about having her ladyship as a mother-in-law. She's got a right nasty streak in her." Her hand suddenly covered her mouth as she realized what she'd said and she flushed scarlet. "Please don't pay me any mind, miss. I'm sure you and Lady Margaret will get along just fine." Then, quickly laying the shift aside, she hurried to the tub and took command of pouring the water.

I'm not so certain of that, Kathleen thought, recalling her meeting with Lady Margaret. But in all fairness, she couldn't fault her ladyship. It was only right that a mother should want the best for her son.

"Now let me help you finish undressing," Nancy was saying, bringing Kathleen back to the immediate present.

Kathleen took a step away. She didn't want the girl to see her scars. "I'm really not used to being waited upon," she said in dismissal. "I can finish my bath alone now."

Looking taken aback, Nancy chewed on her bottom lip. "I'm so sorry, miss, if I've made you angry. I confess I do talk a bit too much. Me mum was always upbraiding me for it. But I can't seem to stop."

"I don't mind your talking," Kathleen assured her, not wanting to hurt the girl's feelings. "I simply prefer to bathe in private. If you could simply take my dress and cloak and begin cleaning them, I would be most grateful."

Nancy looked perplexed. "But what about your underclothing?"

"If you'll wait in the sitting room, I'll hand them out to you," Kathleen replied.

Nancy's smile returned as if she suddenly understood. "One of me sisters was shy like that. I'll wait in the sitting room, miss."

Alone in the bedroom, Kathleen quickly removed the remainder of her clothing. The knife she had worn tied to her thigh, she tucked under a pillow on the bed. Then, after bundling the clothing, she used the door as a screen. Opening it just far enough to get the bundle out, she handed the clothing to Nancy.

Reclosing the door, she hurried back across the room to the warmth of the fire and the bath. The hot water felt soothing, but not as soothing as John's touch, she thought. "I've really got to stop thinking about him so much," she admonished herself. "I'm beginning to think like a love-sick cow."

But then I am in love with him, she admitted once again a little later. She had finished her bath and was standing beside the bed. From the bundle he had tossed upon the coverlet, she had extracted his shirt. Just holding it against her made him feel close. The temptation to put it on was great but Nancy had provided her with a woman's shift to wear, and Kathleen wanted to behave as properly as possible. Folding John's shirt carefully, she put it in the chest by the wall and then dressed herself. She was sitting in front of the fire in the shift and shawl, drying her hair, when Nancy returned.

"I'll just put this screen here for a moment, miss," the girl said, moving a large hinged screen so that it blocked Kathleen from the view of anyone coming into the room. "Then David and Adam can remove the tub."

Before Kathleen could even respond, the screen was in place. She heard Nancy issue an "All's clear," and guessed that was not how Quinn would have wished the maid to instruct the men that they could enter. Kathleen smiled. Nancy, she decided, was perfect for her.

As soon as the tub had been taken away and the door closed, Nancy removed the screen. "Good fortune must shine on you, miss," she said excitedly as she replaced the partition in the corner. "Just before we heard of Mr. Ashford's being taken prisoner, a new bundle of material had arrived for Lady Margaret. Of course, she had me put it away. She would wear only black all the time he was missing. Anyway, now she says you must have all of it for new dresses and petticoats and such. There's a right pretty calico print, some muslin and some very fine silk."

Kathleen was stunned. She'd been certain Lady Margaret would fight her presence in this house with every ounce of strength she had in her. A gift of any sort was unexpected, and yet her ladyship had given her one of great value. Material was always in short supply. "'Tis very kind of her, but I cannot accept all of it," she said, finding her voice.

Nancy shook her head. "You must. She insisted you was to have a complete wardrobe." A flush of embarrassment spread over the girl's face. "I feel just terrible about what I said about her ladyship earlier. I hope you won't hold it against me."

"No, of course not. But you should guard your tongue more closely in the future," Kathleen instructed, reciting another lesson she had learned upon Captain Thorton's ship. Her cynical side was quick to point out that Lady Margaret's charity was most likely due to the fact that her ladyship didn't want her son's fiancée to appear in public in rags. However, this charitable act on Lady Margaret's part gave Kathleen hope that perhaps everything would work out all right after all.

Nancy looked properly chastised. "Yes, miss," she said with a quick curtsy. Then her face brightened again. "If you'll permit me to take a few measurements, I can get started on your new clothes this very night."

Kathleen readily consented. Once she looked more presentable, 'twould be easier to win her acceptance here, she reasoned.

"I'm right sorry I can't have your old dress cleaned and mended by suppertime," Nancy apologized as she finished. "I'm afraid you're going to be confined to this room for the evening. But the cook, Mistress Oats, and a right fine cook she is, is making you up a delicious supper tray. Whenever you're ready to eat you just let me know."

"I could eat at this moment," Kathleen replied, the mention of food threatening to cause her stomach to growl.

To her delight, within a very few minutes she was sitting down eating hungrily. She'd never known food could taste so good. The only thing she regretted was not being able to share this meal with John. As delicious as each morsel tasted and as famished as she was, she still missed his presence.

She'd just finished a last little bit of cheese when a knock sounded on the door. Assuming it was Nancy coming to take away the tray, she remained relaxed as she called out, "You may enter."

But when the door was opened, it was Lady Margaret who appeared.

Instantly, Kathleen was on her feet. As the woman closed the door, then turned and approached, Kathleen dropped into a low curtsy. "Please accept my gratitude for your generous gift of the material," she said.

"You are most welcome," Lady Margaret replied with a kindly smile. Motioning toward the chair Kathleen had been occupying, she said, "Please, do sit down. I know you must be tired from your arduous journey."

There was nothing hostile in her ladyship's manner. Yet, as Kathleen lowered herself into her chair, her body tensed as if for battle. *I am too used to being constantly on my guard*, she chided herself as Lady Margaret seated herself in the twin chair on the opposite side of the hearth. Still Kathleen did not relax. She could not forget her ladyship's first reaction to the news of her son's marriage.

As if able to read Kathleen's thoughts, Lady Margaret said apologetically, "I have come to beg your forgiveness for my rude behavior upon your arrival."

Both shocked and pleased, Kathleen smiled self-consciously. "I cannot fault you for wanting what is best for your son."

"Thank you." Lady Margaret smiled with relief. Then, her voice taking on a sympathetic note, she said, "My son tells me your parents were servants and both died aboard the pirate ship. He has also informed me that you have no family to notify of your survival?"

Although Lady Margaret's manner remained polite, even conciliatory, Kathleen's guard increased. Perhaps the woman was being too kind. Kathleen wasn't quite certain what caused her to feel threatened. But she had learned to trust her instincts. Besides, it did not seem likely to her that Lady Margaret would accept her so easily. John was a man of position, and it would only be natural for his mother to object to his marriage to a woman who was an orphan with no station at all in life. "There is no one," she confirmed.

"Well, you have a family now, my dear," Lady Margaret assured her. Then, covering a yawn with a lace-gloved hand, she rose. "Now, if you will excuse me, I must retire. It has been a very exciting day but a draining one as well."

Rising also, Kathleen curtsied low. She could hardly believe her good fortune. Her instincts had been wrong. Lady Margaret was actually willing to accept her as a daughter-in-law. "Thank you again for all your kindness," she said.

Nancy entered as Lady Margaret left. "Are you all right, miss?" she questioned anxiously, as soon as the door was closed.

"Of course, I am." Kathleen frowned impatiently at the girl. Clearly, Nancy's constant chatter had caused Lady Margaret to reprimand the girl and now Nancy had a distorted image of her ladyship's temper, Kathleen decided. "Lady Margaret was most gracious."

"You're right fortunate, miss." Nancy's voice held an edge of amazement. "Her ladyship does seem to have taken a liking to you."

"I really think you've judged her much too harshly," Kathleen reprimanded sternly. "She's your mistress and any punishment she might have inflicted upon you was merely as a lesson to teach you proper decorum."

"Yes, miss," Nancy replied grudgingly, picking up the dinner tray. In the formal tones of a servant, she added, "I'll be back to warm your bed momentarily, miss."

Kathleen frowned at herself. She'd not meant to hurt the girl's feelings. "I do appreciate all of the kindness you've shown me today," she said in gentler tones.

Nancy's smile returned. "Thank you, miss," she said. She looked as if she wanted to say more. Then, obviously thinking better of it, she bit down on her bottom lip as if this was necessary to keep her mouth shut and carried the tray out of the room.

An hour later Kathleen could still not believe her good fortune as she lay in the warmed bed covered with a heavy comforter to ward off the chill of the winter night. It was like a fantasy. The only thing necessary to make it complete was John lying beside her.

Suddenly her body tensed. A key had turned in the lock of the door beside the fireplace. Her hand closed over the knife beneath her pillow. Silently, she scooted out of the bed. But as the door opened and she saw her late-night caller in the light of the candle he carried, she drew a shaky breath and slid the knife back into it's hiding place. "You nearly scared me to death," she scolded as she grabbed up the shawl and wrapped it around herself.

Relocking the door, John sat the candle on the table. "I came to apologize for my boorish behavior this afternoon," he said, moving toward her with purpose.

She could feel the heat of his eyes upon her as if it were a physical force. The thought that she should show some restraint crossed her mind. Immediately she brushed it away. She wanted to win, not to wage battle with him. "Your apology is accepted," she replied, her body already aching for him to touch her.

John could barely believe his ears. He'd expected her to be furious with him. "I am glad to hear that," he said honestly.

Suddenly remembering that she was in a proper home and that proper decorum was expected of her, Kathleen frowned. "Won't it cause a great deal of gossip to have your rooms right next to mine?"

John smiled. In this matter he had been wise enough to think ahead. "My rooms are across the hall." He glanced toward the door through which he'd entered. "That is the music room." Then, turning back toward her, his jaw formed a determined line as he reached her. "I'll do what I can to keep the servants from gossiping, but I'll not spend my first night in a decent bed alone."

The fire within her grew hotter. "'Twould be a shame to waste such luxury," she conceded. "I've given you your chance to escape from this alliance and you did not take it. I'll not deny you your husbandly rights." Going up on tiptoe, she kissed his neck, then began to work the fastenings of his clothing loose.

I could get very used to this more docile Kate, he thought. He smiled with pleasure as she freed him from his shirt and ran her hands over his bare chest. Capturing her by the wrists, he nipped the tips of her fingers.

Tremors of heated excitement raced through her, but when she tried to free her hands to continue their task, he held her firmly.

John did not want to halt her, but he had come with another purpose this night also. "There's one small matter of business I must attend to before this goes any further," he said.

She frowned disgruntledly as he left her. Perhaps she had forgiven him too readily.

John retrieved his candle, then went into the sitting room. A few moments later, he returned with paper, a quill pen and an inkwell. Approaching her again, he knelt in front of her. "Place your foot on the paper," he directed.

The quill tickled as he drew an outline of her foot. She wiggled her toes in protest.

"Hold still," he demanded. Unable to resist a small taste of her sweet-smelling skin, he nipped her ankle as a warning for her to behave. "If you don't stand quietly, you'll end up with shoes big enough to fit an elephant," he cautioned.

Shoes. For years now her shoes had come from captured trunks and had either been too big or too small. To have shoes that actually fit would be a new experience. But the feel of his teeth as they lightly raked her skin had sent a tingle of excitement up her leg, causing her impatience for his touch to grow even stronger. "'Tis you who should be behaving," she scolded.

He smiled at the slight catch in her voice. It told him that she desired him as much as he desired her. That pleased him greatly.

As Kathleen watched him circle her ankle and the lower portion of her leg with a piece of string and then relay the circles onto the paper, she began to frown. While he calmly worked in a businesslike manner, his touch was igniting fires of passion in her so intense she could barely stand. Yet he seemed unaffected. 'Tis dangerous to feel so weak toward him, she cautioned herself. But her body paid no heed.

His task completed, John set the papers and ink aside. It had not been easy concentrating on his mission. But now 'twas time to concentrate on his wife. He blew out the candle and let the light from the moon illuminate the room. Then, to apologize for his harsher treatment earlier, he kissed her on the ankle where he had nipped it. "For being so cooperative," he said, against her skin.

Kathleen could not stop a gasp of delight as the heat from his lips spread along her leg.

Pleased, John placed a hand on either ankle and began an upward journey, carrying her shift as he went. Slowly, possessively his hands moved along the curves of her body. At her hips he paused to caress their firm roundness. "You feel like silk," he said huskily, kissing her thigh.

"And you have a very tantalizing touch," she returned, her voice barely audible as her breathing became ragged with desire.

He smiled crookedly. Standing, he again began to carry the shift upward. "I've found that 'tis always safest to have a full view of whatever I am touching," he said, as he freed her completely from the shift.

Moving more closely against him, she luxuriated in the feel of his hair-roughened chest against her softer skin. "Whatever my master desires," she replied, determined to please him so greatly he would never regret having honored their contract. As her hands massaged his back, she trailed kisses along his neck.

The fires of passion raged within John. "He desires you," he stated tersely. Hating to release her for even a moment, he forced himself to. Impatiently, he threw the covers back, then lifted her onto the bed and recovered her with the bedclothes.

She watched with eager longing as he finished undressing. When he joined her under the covers, she moved without hesitation into his arms.

"I'd planned to make you pay for your disclaimer of me," he confessed against her skin as he tasted her neck, then moved lower to let his tongue explore her already hardened nipples.

His hands again caressed her hips, then moved to her thighs. She groaned with pleasure as they sought an even more intimate contact. "I'm glad you did not," she gasped, her fingers curling into his hair and her body arching against him.

"But I do not plan to let you off entirely," he warned. "You're going to have to work for your pleasure this night." As he spoke, he shifted onto his back, bringing her with him.

Knowing what he wanted, she smiled playfully. Then, kissing the hollow of his neck, she mounted him. She had wanted to set a slow pace to prolong their lovemaking for as long as possible, but her desire was too strong. She moved with a hunger that brought a deep laugh of pleasure from him. Then his breathing too became ragged and his hands captured her hips with possessive ardor as their bodies blazed with the fulfillment of joined passion.

Lady Margaret paced angrily around her sitting room, a much-read letter held tightly to her bosom. Quinn was there also, standing with the proud rigidity of a good and proper servant.

"We cannot allow this union between my son and that…that woman," her ladyship was saying for the tenth time. Each time it had come out with stronger conviction.

"Yes, m'lady," Quinn answered with sincerity as he had each time before.

Lady Margaret stopped her pacing and faced Quinn with a determined gleam in her eyes. "He is bound to her by honor, so we must discredit her. We must place her in a position where he will not feel honor-bound to continue with this ludicrous marriage. We must find a way of proving to him that she is totally unacceptable as his wife."

Quinn coughed quietly.

Lady Margaret scowled at him. He always coughed that way when he had something he thought he should say but knew she wouldn't like hearing it. "All right, what is it?" she demanded irritably.

"I have seen the way Mr. John looks at her, m'lady. 'Tis more than honor that binds him to her. He feels an attraction for her," Quinn replied.

The scowl on Lady Margaret's face grew more intense. "She's an attractive woman and probably very experienced in pleasing men. After all, she did survive several years aboard that ship, and I don't for one moment believe that story she told John. What he feels for her is purely lust. It will not last. If we allow this marriage, when he comes to his senses—and I don't doubt that that will happen swiftly after the vows are said—he'll regret his actions. And we shall all suffer together except for Miss James, who will have acquired a station in life much higher than she could ever deserve."

Quinn nodded his agreement. "But we'll need time to devise a plan and Mr. John has already sent for Reverend Vales."

"Without John's knowledge, I sent a message along also." A smile of triumph momentarily replaced Lady Margaret's scowl. "I have explained the circumstances of this marriage to the reverend and I feel certain he'll understand my wish that it not take place. Considering the amount of money I've given him for his church here, he should bend to my wishes even more fully than he does to God's. I expect we'll hear that the good reverend is ailing and will not be able to travel for several weeks.''

Quinn continued to look worried. "What if Mr. John should decide to take himself and Miss James to see the reverend? Or what if he hears from others that the reverend is actually in good health?''

"The reverend won't mind taking to his bed for a while. He doesn't relish the winter weather." A wicked gleam sparkled in Lady Margaret's eyes. "Besides, I'm certain he'll be grateful for the chance to spend extra time under the covers with that new wife of his. He'll say that he fears he may be contagious and does not want to subject any of his congregation to a possible threat of illness. Since he rides the circuit and his congregations don't see him save once every four weeks, this will be no great burden to anyone. It will simply mean that the lay members will have an extra Sabbath on which to orate." A cynical smile curled her lips. "For some this will be a boon. I've heard it hinted that Arthur Wiggins actually resents giving up the pulpit to the Reverend Vales.''

Quinn smiled. "You've thought of everything, m'lady.''

"Not everything." The scowl had returned to Lady Margaret's face. "I've not yet come up with a plan to rid us of Miss James.''

"You will, m'lady," Quinn said with admiration. "You will.''

Lady Margaret's smile returned. "Yes, most certainly, I shall." She looked at the letter she had clutched in her hands. "There is too much at stake for us to fail.''

Chapter Eight

Kathleen awoke alone the next morning. Sometime in the very small hours of the night, John had left her to return to his own quarters. But the memory of his lovemaking lingered, bringing a soft smile to her lips.

Leaving the bed, she slipped into her shift. The room was frigid and she was tempted to climb back into the warm bed. On the pirate ship she had spent her days much as she pleased. But she knew that wouldn't be proper here. Breakfast would soon be served downstairs and she would be expected to be there, providing Nancy had gotten her dress mended and cleaned. She rang for the maid, then lit a new fire in the fireplace. The wood had just begun to blaze when there was a knock on her door. This was followed by the sound of the latch being tried without success.

"'Tis me, miss," she heard Nancy calling softly from the other side.

Quickly, Kathleen unlocked the door.

Nancy gave a shiver as she entered. "I'd have had the fire going before you awoke, miss, so's you wouldn't have to leave your bed with the room still being so cold," the maid said with apology, "but your door was bolted."

Crossing the room, she laid the clothing she'd been carrying on a chair.

"'Tis a habit I developed on board Captain Thorton's ship," Kathleen explained, adding to herself that it was a habit she planned to keep until she and John were officially wed. She didn't want anyone disturbing them unexpectedly.

Nancy shuddered. "I can understand that, miss. It must've been a horrible experience being captured and having both your parents killed. Those pirates are right heathen, I've been told. Lucky you had Mr. Ashford to save you."

Clearly the servants assumed she'd spent only a short while aboard the ship, and that was fine with Kathleen. She knew they would believe the worst if they knew she had spent eleven years in the company of Captain Thorton and his men. "Yes, I was very lucky Mr. Ashford was there," she replied.

Nancy's smile returned. "I've got your dress into wearable condition, miss, and the rest of your clothes is cleaned and pressed. I had to put a few patches on the dress but it should hold you in good stead until I can get your first new one finished. Soon as I've helped you into it and seen to any other of your needs, I'll be getting back to my sewing."

Again Kathleen remembered her scars. "I am most anxious to have my new clothing," she said. "I can manage on my own. You must get back to your needle as quickly as possible."

"I'd be pleased to help you, miss," Nancy offered hesitantly. Obviously she'd been instructed to assist her new mistress. But it was equally obvious she remembered Kathleen's shyness of the night before.

"No, thank you," Kathleen replied kindly but firmly.

Nancy smiled with understanding. "Then I'll be getting back to my sewing. Breakfast is being served in the dining room." Dropping a quick curtsy, she left.

Kathleen's stomach growled. Well, it had been an active night, she reminded herself. Confessing to herself that, as hungry as she was, she was even more anxious to see John than to eat, she dressed hurriedly, then went downstairs.

John watched her as she entered the dining room. Memories of the night before filled his mind. He would like to have spent the entire day with her, but that was not possible. He had duties he must see to. It had been many months since he had personally inspected his holdings. "I've a great deal of business I must attend to," he informed her as she joined him and Lady Margaret at the breakfast table. "And my mother tells me that she must pay a duty call on an ailing neighbor. I'm afraid you will be on your own for most of the day."

"But before I leave I shall introduce you to the staff," Lady Margaret interjected with a kindly smile. "They'll see to your every need."

John was the only person she required to see to any of her needs, Kathleen thought, and she caught the glint in his eyes that said the same idea had passed through his mind. Fighting down a pleased flush, she directed her attention toward Lady Margaret and politely thanked her.

With Lady Margaret in charge, meeting the staff was a strictly formal affair. Her ladyship had them all gather in the large entrance hall and form a line in order of their rank. Then she proceeded down the line, with Kathleen beside her. Pausing before each servant, she informed Kathleen of the person's name and duties. There was nothing personal in Lady Margaret's manner toward her staff. In turn, Kathleen noticed that they seemed to hold her ladyship in awe and, in the case of the upstairs and downstairs maids, she even sensed a touch of fear.

"You mustn't smile so much," Lady Margaret cautioned Kathleen when the servants had been dismissed. "They'll begin to think you want to be their friend and you'll lose their respect and your authority."

"I cannot see that a little kindness could be that hurtful," Kathleen replied in her defense.

Lady Margaret sighed. "You've much to learn, my dear."

Kathleen felt like a pupil who had just failed a crucial test. She didn't honestly see the harm in a smile, but she was determined to be a good wife to John and that meant behaving as a proper mistress of his house should behave. "Yes, m'lady," she said respectfully.

Lady Margaret continued to regard Kathleen uncertainly. "Now I'm afraid I must leave you to your own devices."

Kathleen had the feeling that Lady Margaret was fearful that upon her return she would find her house a shambles. Kathleen's back stiffened with pride. She might not have been brought up as a lady of station, but she was not a savage.

Then Lady Margaret smiled sweetly. "I do hope you won't get bored. I feel quite guilty leaving you on your own."

Kathleen chided herself curtly. She was too defensive. She had misjudged the expression on Lady Margaret's face. "I shall be fine," she said with assurance.

Lady Margaret took Kathleen's hand and patted it gently. "You must spend the day resting. I'm certain your adventures have left you fatigued." Then, bidding Kathleen goodbye, Lady Margaret moved sedately toward her quarters to prepare herself for her journey.

Back in her room, Kathleen tried to rest, but she wasn't really tired. She felt full of life. The fates were truly shining upon her. Pacing the floor, she paused by the window to watch Lady Margaret, with two men servants in escort, ride away. Then, unable to stand this idleness for one moment longer, she went in search of Nancy.

"I'll fetch her, miss," Janet, the downstairs maid said when Kathleen asked where Nancy might be found. "She's in her quarters sewing."

"Please, just show me to her quarters," Kathleen requested.

The girl looked a bit dubious but did as she was requested.

"Miss Kathleen?" Surprise followed by shock registered on Nancy's face when she opened her door to discover Kathleen there. Then, remembering her manners, she dropped a quick curtsy.

Out of the corner of her eye, Kathleen noticed Janet lingering a few feet away, obviously curious as to why the master's future bride would venture into the servants' quarters. Well, it wasn't totally unheard of to have the mistress of a fine house pay a call upon a servant, she reasoned. It was many years ago, but she remembered that during the times the fever came and afflicted so many, the mistress for whom her parents worked would come into the servants' rooms and personally care for those who were ill. "May I come in?" she asked.

"Of course, miss." Nancy stepped quickly aside.

Kathleen entered, closing the door behind her. "I was wondering how your work on the dresses is proceeding?"

"I've just begun to piece the first bodice together," Nancy replied, picking up the piece to show to Kathleen.

"I've done a bit of sewing myself," Kathleen said, getting to the real object of her visit. "I thought I would offer my services and together we could have the dresses done in half the time.''

Nancy looked doubtful. "I don't know if Lady Margaret would approve of you being here."

Kathleen had promised herself that she would do nothing to embarrass John, but he was a practical man. He would surely agree that two hands could finish a job more quickly than one. As for Lady Margaret... "Surely she cannot object to my helping," she reasoned aloud. "She more than anyone else in this household must want me to look presentable as quickly as possible."

Bowing to this logic, Nancy smiled brightly. "I always like a bit of company while I work."

All morning they sewed, and Kathleen felt a great sense of accomplishment as the dress began to take form.

At the noonday meal, when John asked her how she was spending her day, she simply said she was keeping busy acquainting herself with his home. She didn't mention the sewing because she wanted to surprise him. She had great hopes of being able to wear one of her new dresses that evening at dinner.

Returning to Nancy's room, she found her maid looking a bit puzzled.

"I had a most curious conversation with Mr. Quinn in the kitchen," Nancy said, as Kathleen sat down and picked up her needle and thread. "He asked me if I'd been serving you properly. Then he began listing my duties, as if he were afraid I couldn't remember them." Nancy gave a shrug. "'Course I guess I can't blame him. I haven't always lived up to his expectations in the past." She breathed a heavy sigh. "I don't believe anyone could live up to his expectations."

Then the puzzlement returned to her face. "Anyways, I was real nervous, and when he asked me if I'd started your fire, I confessed that I didn't. I ain't never been any good at lying. But I was quick to explain about how you'd learned to lock your door when you was being held prisoner by those pirates. I figured that wouldn't hold no salt with him, but instead of upbraiding me, he just shrugs his shoulders and says, 'We are merely servants. If our masters and mistresses have their little quirks, we must respect them.' Then he asks me about did I see after your things properly and make certain you was getting everything you wanted. I assured him that you was."

Nancy's voice lowered conspiratorially. "I didn't say nothing about you liking to dress yourself, though. Figured that wasn't any of his business." A twinkle entered her eyes. "And I didn't mention that knife you keep under your pillow, either. If I'd been captured by pirates, I'd probably learn a habit like that, too."

"I appreciate your discretion," Kathleen said. She guessed that the knowledge of the knife would cause gossip or at least a few raised eyebrows. Still, she had no intention of giving it up.

Nancy smiled brightly. "Anyways, then he tells me that I'm to see that you are well served or he'll have my hide."

Kathleen guessed that the haughty Quinn's concern for her was on orders from either John or Lady Margaret. Still, he appeared to be obeying them with relish. Perhaps fitting into John's life was going to be a great deal easier than she thought.

Lady Margaret returned home late in the afternoon. Ringing for Quinn, she paced in her sitting room until he arrived. "Well, how did Miss James spend the day?" she demanded as soon as he had entered and closed the door securely.

Quinn's eyes glistened with malicious amusement. "She spent the day in Nancy's room sewing. They were even heard giggling and laughing."

"The servants' quarters is where she belongs," Lady Margaret spat out, but she was pleased with this news.

"She also set her own fire this morning," he added.

Lady Margaret frowned thoughtfully. "'Tis not unheard-of, but still, that knowledge may prove useful as well."

It wasn't easy, but Kathleen and Nancy managed to get the dress done by dinnertime.

It was not a fancy dress, but it was new, and Kathleen felt triumphant as she entered the dining room.

"You look very lovely this evening," John greeted her with approval.

"The material did work up nicely for you," Lady Margaret agreed as John waved Quinn aside and seated Kathleen at the table himself. Then, her voice taking on a motherly but reprimanding tone, she said, "However, 'tis not proper for the future mistress of this house to spend her day in the servants' quarters, giggling and laughing with her maid."

A flush of embarrassment began to creep upward from Kathleen's neck to her face. Lady Margaret made her actions during the day sound vulgar. And she had spoken in front of witnesses. Kathleen's back stiffened, certain the two maids waiting table and Quinn, who had remained by the door, were all mentally condemning her as well. "I was simply helping Nancy with the sewing. I did not relish sitting idly," she explained in her defense.

"My dear, you must understand you have a position to maintain," Lady Margaret pointed out. The disapproval in her voice grew even stronger as she added, "What you do reflects upon John and myself."

John frowned. His mother was right. But he could not blame Kathleen. She had never been taught proper decorum. He should not have left her to her own devices.

Kathleen saw John's frown. She could face the disapproval of all of the others with her head held high, but his caused a sharp pain of anguish. And she had to admit that her reasoning could have been faulty. "I'm truly sorry," she said contritely. "I never meant to cause you or John any embarrassment. I was trying to be practical. I wished my dress done so that I could be more presentable, and it occurred to me that four hands could do the job faster than two."

An edge of venom crept into Lady Margaret's voice. "I do hope you can learn to control yourself in the future and think before you act."

The thought that she would never fit into John's world suddenly flashed through Kathleen's mind. Her gaze shifted to her food. I should never have come here, she berated herself.

John scowled at his mother. "You're being much too hard on Kathleen. What she did was improper, but it was not done out of malice. In truth, there is a certain logic to her thinking."

Kathleen glanced toward him. He was defending her. Her resolve returned. She would be the wife he required. Silently, she vowed never again to do anything to embarrass him.

Her son's defense of Kathleen irked Lady Margaret, and her control on her temper slipped. "No, it was done out of stupidity and lack of training." She caught herself just before she added that Kathleen didn't belong among civilized people.

But Kathleen saw the flicker of malice in the woman's eyes and called herself a fool. Lady Margaret's show of kindness had been only that—a show. Clearly her ladyship still disapproved of her strongly. Another truth dawned on Kathleen. Quinn hadn't been concerned about her well-being. He'd been spying for Lady Margaret.

"Mother!" John's voice carried a terse warning. He'd known his mother would not accept Kathleen easily. But he had chosen to honor this marriage and he expected her to respect his decision.

Lady Margaret drew a calming breath. The malice was well hidden when she met her son's gaze. "I realize we're in the wilds, but I should like to think that the proprieties of social behavior are not going to be totally overlooked. Perhaps you could request that Kathleen consult with me before she takes any future actions."

Amusement at the thought of Kathleen consulting anyone regarding her every move glistened in John's eyes. But, he conceded, a compromise had to be made. The amusement was gone when he turned to his mother. "Kathleen's survival has depended on her free spirit. I could not in good conscience require that she shackle it so completely as to have to ask permission for her every movement. However, I will suggest that when she has a question as to what is proper and what is not, she may consult either you or myself."

Lady Margaret's mouth formed a petulant pout. "Perhaps I'm asking too much to try to maintain a civilized decorum in this hateful wilderness."

"You're being overly dramatic, Mother," John replied dryly. "And as I informed you upon my return, if you find living in the colonies so despicable, your brother begs you to come live with him."

A martyred smile played across Lady Margaret's face. "My duty lies with you, my son."

As he had on many occasions before, John found himself wishing she did not feel so. "I want you to be happy, Mother," he replied with an impatient scowl. "There's no reason for you to sacrifice yourself for me. I'll have Kathleen to look after me."

Disdain mingled with self-pity on Lady Margaret's features. "If you're ordering me to leave to make room for your wife, then I shall go."

The scowl on John's face deepened. He had promised his father that he would always look after his mother, but she could be most trying at times. "I'm not ordering you to leave," he said in pacifying tones. "This is your home. I merely want you to be happy."

"I am happy when I'm with you," she replied. Then, expelling a deep sigh, she said weakly, "This unpleasantness has been too much for me. My appetite is gone. If you'll excuse me."

John nodded and Quinn quickly came to draw back Lady Margaret's chair.

Watching the older woman leave on the arm of one of the maids, Kathleen marveled at Lady Margaret's ability to manipulate the situation. She had begun as the accuser, and when that ploy had turned sour, she had made herself the wronged martyr. Even her walk carried a message. She moved more slowly than usual and her shoulders were slightly stooped, as if this exchange with her son had truly taken a physical toll upon her.

"I want to apologize for my mother," John said when Lady Margaret had left.

Kathleen wanted to hate the woman. Lady Margaret had tried to humiliate her and make her seem unworthy in John's eyes. But in fairness she could not entirely fault her.

"'Tis only natural that your mother should want you to make the best match possible. I cannot blame her for not accepting me readily," she said levelly.

John smiled with relief and surprise. His Kate was showing a great deal more tolerance then he had thought she possessed. This match was working out even better than he had hoped. "I appreciate your indulgence. I'm afraid she can be a bit difficult, but I'm certain she will come to accept you in time."

Kathleen wasn't so certain of that, but for John's sake she was willing to make the effort to befriend his mother or, at the very least, reach a truce with her. And, she vowed, for John's sake she would learn the rules of proper decorum. "Would it be proper if Nancy were to come to my sitting room and we sewed there?" she asked, trying to find a way she could continue to help with the sewing without causing John or his mother any further embarrassment.

"I believe that would be fitting," he conceded. Lowering his head toward hers so that only she could hear his next words, he added, "As long as you do not work late into the night."

Kathleen read the message in his eyes—her nights were to belong to him. "We will not," she promised.

Chapter Nine

The next morning as she sat sewing with Nancy, a soft smile played across Kathleen's face. It was memories of the night before, not Nancy's chatter, that put it there. Her promise to John was going to be very easy to keep. The smile straightened into a worried line. But she was not so certain about her ability to keep her promise to herself to make peace with Lady Margaret.

A knock suddenly sounded on her door. As if her thoughts had been able to conjure up the object of her worries, Lady Margaret flung the door open before Nancy had a chance to rise. Her gaze was dark with accusation as it raked over the two women sitting sewing. "I cannot believe this!" she seethed, striding toward them. Pointing a finger at Nancy, she ordered, "Get out this minute!"

Nancy looked to Kathleen in stunned surprise. Recovering from her own shock, Kathleen nodded for the girl to obey.

"And close the door behind you," Lady Margaret instructed sharply as Nancy scurried past her. Her gaze leveled on Kathleen, she added, "I want a few words in private with Miss James."

Maintaining an outward calm, Kathleen rose and performed a polite curtsy. "And what do you wish to speak to me about?'' she asked, her hopes of a peace between them growing dimmer with each passing moment.

Lady Margaret stood with her hands on her hips, glaring at Kathleen. ''I thought it was agreed that you would seek my permission before you acted in any way.''

Kathleen's jaw tensed. She was willing to be cooperative, but she would not subjugate herself to anyone. ''We agreed that I would seek yours or John's advice before I acted,'' she corrected.

Lady Margaret stamped her foot. ''I am appalled by your attitude. I've allowed you into my home and yet you dare to disobey me.''

Kathleen could not believe her ears nor her eyes. The woman was throwing a childish tantrum and trying to bully her. ''I've not disobeyed anyone.''

Lady Margaret's eyes gleamed with hatred. ''It was agreed by both my son and myself that it was improper for you to cavort with your maid.''

''I was not cavorting with Nancy,'' Kathleen replied, continuing to keep her voice calm in spite of her desire to tell the woman how absurd she thought her behavior was. ''We were sewing and with John's permission.''

Lady Margaret drew a deep breath, reminding Kathleen of a fire-breathing dragon preparing to burn it's victim with one huge blast. ''This is even worse than I thought. You have subverted my son's sense of propriety. But I suppose he does find it easier to give in to your demands than fight you. You common people are well-known for your thickheadedness.''

''This had nothing to do with thickheadedness,'' Kathleen replied curtly. ''It has to do with practicality. I have almost nothing to wear. My assisting Nancy with the sewing provides me with clothing more quickly.''

"You may do as you please about this matter," Lady Margaret replied haughtily. "I wash my hands of it. But mark my words, you'll never marry my son. I will see to that." Having made this pronouncement, the woman strode to the door. Her skirt swished as she jerked it open. After passing through, she slammed it closed.

A cold chill ran along Kathleen's spine. She'd survived Captain Thorton, but she was not certain she had the strength to again endure the company of someone who hated her. Her need to see John overwhelmed her. She found him in his study, but he was not alone.

The door to the room was open a crack. From within, Kathleen heard Lady Margaret saying in a shrill whine, "She spoke to me with such disrespect. You cannot possibly marry her. She was vulgar. She even swore."

Furious that the woman would lie so outrageously, Kathleen started to enter, but came to an abrupt halt when she heard John saying, "You must understand that Kathleen has lived a difficult life. You should show her some charity."

Kathleen's cheeks flushed red. Did John actually believe she had behaved in the manner his mother described?

"Show charity to a woman who will bring shame and ridicule to our family name?" Lady Margaret demanded sarcastically. "Never!"

Kathleen knocked sharply, then entered. Facing Lady Margaret, she said curtly, "I did not behave disrespectfully toward you."

"There! You see?" Lady Margaret pointed an accusatory finger at Kathleen. "She has no honor. She behaves vulgarly toward me and then has the nerve to call me a liar to my face."

John frowned impatiently. He admired his father, save in one respect, he mused. His father had spoilt his mother by giving in to her tantrums and her petty grievances. That came from caring too much for a woman, something he had no intention of allowing himself to do. He crossed the room to stand beside the open door. "Mother, you will leave us," he ordered.

"You're a fool if you believe her," Lady Margaret spat. Over her shoulder, she tossed Kathleen a hate-filled glare as she obeyed her son.

"I was not vulgar toward your mother," Kathleen said as soon as the door was closed and she and John were alone.

He shrugged to indicate that the accusation was inconsequential. "You do not have to defend yourself to me. I know that my mother can be difficult and I know that you are a woman of spirit. 'Tis that spirit that saved my life and 'tis that spirit that has convinced me you're the perfect wife for a man with my aims. I want to carve a place for myself here in the colonies and for that I need a woman by my side with the courage, will and cunning to survive, a woman who will bear me children with those same qualities."

His words cut like a knife. He believed his mother's lies! "I may not have been brought up in a fine house, but my mother was, and she taught me to be polite under the most difficult of circumstances," she said with cold control. "I did not behave like a common trollop toward your mother and I'll not remain where people think that of me." Brushing past him, she stalked out of the room. Tears burned at the back of her eyes as she walked swiftly toward her rooms. Anger and hurt mingled within her. He thought her vulgar and base but was willing to overlook those faults to breed her spirit into his children, she fumed. Well, he could find himself another brood mare.

"Women!" John muttered, standing alone in his study. They were the most unreasonable creatures.

Entering her sitting rooms, Kathleen found Nancy gathering up the pieces of the dress on which they had been working. "I thought I would take this to my room and finish it, miss," the girl said shakily, obviously still unnerved by her brief encounter with Lady Margaret.

"Leave everything and go. You may come back later for your things," Kathleen ordered grimly. She did not wish to waste even a moment making her exit from this house.

"Are you all right, miss?" Nancy asked worriedly. "You look a bit pale. I could fetch you some tea."

"I don't want any tea. I want you to leave," Kathleen repeated as she strode toward her bedroom, unfastening her dress as she went. She would change into the clothing she'd worn upon her arrival and take with her only what she'd arrived with. She wanted nothing from the Ashfords, either Lady Margaret or her son.

Continuing to ignore Kathleen's command, Nancy followed her. "I know Lady Margaret can be a bit trying, miss. I'm still a bit uneasy myself, but..."

Kathleen's patience had reached an end. She was about to scream at the maid when the door of the sitting room opened and Nancy stopped with a gasp in midsentence as John entered.

"I wish to speak to Miss James alone," John said to Nancy in dismissal as he crossed the sitting room and entered the bedroom.

Rushing to place herself in front of Kathleen, Nancy shielded her mistress with her body. "She's not decent and it ain't decent of you to come unannounced into her rooms."

"I will decide what is decent or not decent in my house," he replied angrily. "Be off with you, girl!"

Nancy glanced worriedly over her shoulder at Kathleen. Clearly she was torn between the duty she felt toward her current mistress and incurring the wrath of her master.

"Leave us," Kathleen ordered. She didn't wish to face John again, but since she must, she would do it with dignity and not hide behind her maid.

Still looking uncertain, Nancy dropped a quick curtsy and left the room.

The moment Nancy was through the door, John closed it, locked it and pocketed the key. Then, turning toward Kathleen, he demanded grimly, "I want to know what you're planning." That was a stupid request, he chided himself. He'd read her intent upon her face when she'd left his study. And for a moment he'd considered allowing her to go. With her gone, his life could return to a reasonable state of peace. But almost immediately, he'd discarded this notion. He was a man who did not turn his back on his obligations. Grudgingly, he also admitted that the thought of life without Kate caused a sense of emptiness within him.

"I'm leaving," she answered, continuing to unfasten her dress. John had seen her in much less and she was not willing to let anything, even his presence, slow down her departure.

Approaching her, his hands closed around her upper arms. "No, you're not. You're my wife, Kate, and you'll remain beside me."

She stiffened with pride. "I am sure you can find someone else who will fit your requirements as a wife and suit your mother much better than I."

"I don't care to suit my mother," he said gruffly. "And I could not find another who would fit my requirements as fully as you." His gaze burned into her. "Your spirit is stronger than most. But even more, you please me, Kate, more than I thought any woman could please a man. And you cannot deny that I please you, too." John's jaw tensed. He'd admitted aloud what he had not even wanted to admit to himself... that she stood above other women in his mind.

You please me because I love you, she thought bitterly. But you don't love me. Aloud she said, "You're speaking only of lust and that cannot last forever. Beyond our physical attraction we had only trust, and now we do not have even that. You believed your mother's lies."

The scowl on his face deepened. "I did not say I believed her. I know she has a tendency to exaggerate, and her idea of what is proper would make those in the king's court shudder. What I believed was that you had stood up to her, and I would never condemn you for that."

She felt herself weakening. Every instinct warned her that to stay could bring pain, but she loved him and was not yet ready to give up the hope that he could learn to love her. "I am not certain 'tis wise for us to remain together," she admitted aloud.

His gaze narrowed with determination. "Whether 'tis wise or not, Kate, we are bound together through eternity." His hands tightened around her arms, and pulling her up against him, he claimed her lips. A fleeting moment of guilt assailed him. He had never sought to possess another. He had never believed it right. But he wished to possess her. 'Tis for her own good, he reasoned. He could provide her with a pleasant life and protect her from harm as well, if not better, than most men.

His kiss spread fire through her and her body ached for him. 'Tis only trouble you are gaining by staying, she warned herself, but she refused to listen.

Lifting his head, John looked hard into her face. "If you attempt to leave, I'll have you brought back," he said in a voice that held no compromise.

"I'll not leave," she replied. At least, not this day, she added to herself.

His jaw relaxed and he released her. "I'll send Nancy back and the two of you can continue with your sewing." He started to move away, then, turning back, he captured her chin and tilted her face upward, kissing her again. "'Tis a shame we cannot spend the remainder of this morning in a much more enjoyable way," he said as he drew away from her. Then he grinned and added in a gruff but playful manner, "Once our vows are publicly said you will owe me a great deal of your time."

Kathleen's blood heated as she read the intent in his eyes. When he looked at her like that, she was tempted to forget proprieties entirely. But the vision of Quinn listening outside her door so that he could report to Lady Margaret quickly halted that thought. Entering into John's bantering mood, she curtsied completely to the floor as if he were of the highest royal rank. In a voice of sugared innocence, she said, "I shall be yours to command."

My life would be simpler if that were truly so, John mused, as he answered her curtsy with a bow and then left. But not nearly as interesting, his inner voice added, and to his surprise, he found himself agreeing.

Kathleen had just finished refastening her dress and gone back into the sitting room when Nancy returned.

Interest mingled with concern as the girl entered and curtsied. "Mr. Ashford sent me, miss," she said as if afraid this might not have been to Kathleen's liking.

"We'll return to our sewing," Kathleen directed, seating herself and finding her needle.

"Yes, miss." Nancy breathed a sigh of relief as she, too, seated herself and picked up the piece on which she had been working. "Been a right trying day fur you, miss, ain't it," she said sympathetically as they again began to sew.

Kathleen frowned. "I've had worse."

"I don't envy you having Lady Margaret as a mother-in-law," Nancy continued in the same sympathetic vein. "But don't you let her go getting between you and Mr. Ashford," Nancy said sternly.

If John learned to love her, only death would part them, Kathleen vowed. "If you wish to be of help to us," she said, "'twould be wise to guard your tongue around Mr. Quinn."

Nancy smiled and nodded. "Done figured that out for myself."

Chapter Ten

That evening Lady Margaret dined alone in her rooms, and the next morning she was not present at the breakfast table.

Feeling it was only polite to say something, Kathleen remarked to John, "I do hope your mother isn't ill."

He frowned impatiently. "My mother is brooding. When she can't have her way, she sits in her rooms and pouts. I've found it best to ignore her at these times. Conciliatory visits only encourage her. She'll eventually get bored and rejoin us."

Clearly, dealing with Lady Margaret was much like dealing with a spoiled child, Kathleen decided, and she said no more.

For two days peace reigned. Then, on the third day, Kathleen found Lady Margaret seated with John at the table when she entered the dining room for breakfast.

"My son feels that I'm a bit too demanding and take offense much too readily. Perhaps he's right," she addressed Kathleen self-consciously as Kathleen seated herself. "I hope you'll forgive me."

"Of course," Kathleen replied, but while she outwardly accepted the older woman's apology graciously, inwardly her guard remained high. She would not again be fooled by false kindnesses.

Lady Margaret ate demurely for a few minutes, then, setting her fork aside, she said, "Quinn, please leave us and make certain we're not disturbed." While Quinn obeyed, her gaze traveled from Kathleen to John, then back to Kathleen. "I hope the two of you won't be angry with me, because what I have to say is in all of our best interests."

Kathleen braced herself. Now that she knew Lady Margaret was against the marriage, she assumed that the woman had devised some new way to try to discredit her in John's eyes.

"Fairly soon, we'll be having callers," Lady Margaret continued in a reasonable tone. "They will discreetly, of course, inquire as to Miss James's background, and it has occurred to me that perhaps it would be prudent to tell the story a bit differently." Her gaze fixed on Kathleen and a sharp edge entered her voice. "Unless you have told Nancy all the facts of your adventure with the pirates."

"I've told no one anything," Kathleen assured her coolly.

"Good," her ladyship replied approvingly, and Kathleen experienced a flash of dry humor at the thought that she had actually done something the woman considered acceptable.

"It has occurred to me that we need only to switch the story around," Lady Margaret continued. "We can say that while John was being held prisoner on Captain Thorton's ship, the pirates attacked the ship on which you were sailing with your parents. While the pirates were busy fighting the crew of your vessel, John managed to break his bonds and join in the fight. Your parents had already been killed, and knowing what the pirates would do to you, John grabbed you and together you dove overboard, more willing to take your chances in the sea than on board the captive ship."

Lady Margaret smiled triumphantly as she finished. When neither John nor Kathleen spoke immediately, she said in a coaxing voice, "Considering the reputation of the pirates, 'twill be difficult for anyone to believe that a woman as pretty as Kathleen could survive even a short while aboard the vessel without..." she paused as if she found it difficult to choose the right word "...without being misused."

Kathleen flushed scarlet with anger. Lady Margaret was implying that John was a fool to believe in her innocence. However, she had to admit Lady Margaret had made a valid point. Vividly she recalled John's original attitude toward her. And she herself had avoided correcting Nancy's version for this same reason.

"Kathleen's story is the truth," John said firmly.

"Of course, it is," Lady Margaret hastened to agree. But Kathleen caught the glint of disappointment in the woman's eyes and knew that her ladyship had hoped to plant the seed of suspicion in John's mind. It would be humorous, she mused, if her ladyship's reasoning weren't so legitimate.

"I was merely pointing out what others might think," Lady Margaret continued. Her manner becoming conciliatory, she turned back toward Kathleen. "My version would also allow you to keep from tarnishing your mother's memory. If you tell the truth, you will have to explain how she 'bargained' for your safety."

Kathleen had to admit that Lady Margaret had truly hit a delicate spot. Her mother had done what had to be done to save her daughter's life, and Kathleen did not want her memory tainted by whispers behind ladies' fans. "Perhaps you're right about this," she agreed. Turning to John she said, "I do not relish practicing a deceit. But maybe it would be for the best. People will suspect my innocence, and I don't want my mother's name bandied about. She was a good woman who did what she did to save my life."

John looked skeptical. "And what if someone asks about the woman Captain Howle mentioned seeing on the pirate ship?" he questioned.

"No one will connect her to Kathleen once I've finished training Kathleen to behave like a lady," Lady Margaret proclaimed with confidence.

"If Kathleen wants to go along with this story, I will bow to her wishes," John conceded. He also did not relish living with a lie. However, in this instance it would do less harm than the truth.

Lady Margaret smiled happily. "Then we shall start our lessons this morning."

"You will also acquaint Kathleen with the management of this house," John ordered.

For an instant, Kathleen saw the look of hatred flash again in Lady Margaret's eyes, then the woman lowered her head toward her son in a condescending manner. "Of course. Once you're married she will be mistress of Ashford Hall. Now if you will be so kind as to ring for Quinn, I would like some fresh tea."

By late morning Kathleen was in grave pain.

"No, no, no! You must never slouch," Lady Margaret was berating her. "And you must always hold your cup level. If that cup had any liquid in it, it would be all over your dress and the rug!"

Kathleen frowned down at the empty cup in her hand. This had all been much easier when she and her mother had used make-believe plates on the pirate ship. Her mother also hadn't made her sit rigidly for four hours. Kathleen knew Lady Margaret had offered these lessons as a way of ensuring that Kathleen would not embarrass her when friends called for tea. Now she suspected that Lady Margaret had an ulterior motive... she was trying to see how much agony Kathleen could endure before she balked. Then Lady Margaret would claim she had been uncooperative. Well, I've endured worse than this, Kathleen thought grimly, determined not to give in. A muscle knotted in her back and she shifted her shoulders in an effort to straighten it.

"And you must never squirm," Lady Margaret reprimanded, not allowing even the smallest movement to get by without a biting remark. "People will have the impression that you're either nervous or bored, and neither is acceptable. You must appear relaxed and at ease at all times."

That's a little hard when I'm forced to sit like a wooden soldier, Kathleen commented to herself. Aloud, she said, "Yes, m'lady."

Lady Margaret frowned and shook her head in dismay. "This is going to take quite a bit more work than I thought."

Kathleen knew she had done well. She also knew from the gleam of pleasure in Lady Margaret's eyes that her ladyship was enjoying meting out this torture.

Lady Margaret glanced at the clock on the mantelpiece. "I am exhausted," she proclaimed, as if she had been the one enduring the physical punishment. "We shall stop for now and resume later this afternoon. Perhaps around three. You can practice pouring the tea, and then at teatime you may pour and serve. I shall have to write and tell all our friends we're having a bout of the fever so none will invite themselves over for several weeks."

Inside, Kathleen was furious. Outside she presented the picture of subdued calm. "Yes, m'lady," she said, rising and performing the necessary curtsy.

Shaking her head as if to say she felt it was going to be impossible to create a truly civilized person out of Kathleen, Lady Margaret turned and moved gracefully out of the room.

Watching her leave, Kathleen was tempted to throw the cup she was still holding at her. But first I have to pry my fingers loose, she mused. She had been willing her hand to unbend, but it was so stiff it obeyed only with concerted effort. Finally, as her fingers released their hold, she set the cup on the tray and flexed them to make certain they still worked.

Facing the afternoon was not going to be easy, she admitted to herself as she went up to her room to rest a bit before lunch. But I will persevere, she promised herself, though she couldn't help feeling apprehensive. Lady Margaret had made learning the simple rituals of having tea a grueling torture session. What would it be like when her ladyship began to teach Kathleen how to run the house?

At luncheon, John asked how the lessons were progressing.

"Kathleen has a great deal to learn," Lady Margaret replied with a sigh. "A great deal."

John turned to Kathleen with concern. "I hope my mother isn't being too demanding."

Kathleen saw the sudden worry in Lady Margaret's eyes. "No, she is not," she assured him. "As she said, I've a lot to learn. But I learn quickly." This little test of endurance was between herself and Lady Margaret. She did not need John's help.

John's gaze shifted from one woman to the other. He sensed a battle of wills behind their polite masks. If this was so, there was no doubt in his mind that his Kate would win. Still, she had suffered enough at the hands of Captain Thorton. He did not wish to see her put to the test here, also. Turning to his mother, he said with a warning in his voice, "Kathleen does not need to learn everything within the space of one day."

Lady Margaret's gaze leveled on Kathleen. "You must be certain to tell me when you are tired."

Kathleen met the challenge in the woman's eyes. "Of course," she replied.

John watched the exchange with a frown but said no more. Women, he decided, lived by rules of their own that no man could ever comprehend.

However, following the meal, while Kathleen was occupied with Nancy, he went to his mother's rooms.

"And to what do I owe the pleasure of this visit?" Lady Margaret asked with a welcoming smile as he entered.

"I don't want these lessons you're giving Kathleen to be too strenuous. You'll keep your demands within reason and you'll limit the time of the sessions to a tolerable length," he ordered.

"Why the sly little cat," Lady Margaret mused sarcastically. "I suppose she has complained to you behind my back. How very ungallant of her. If she'd not such a cowardly soul, she would have faced me herself."

"There's nothing cowardly about Kathleen," he informed her curtly. "She has said nothing to me. But I know you. You'll try to break her will. In this instance, however, you will lose. Kathleen's will is stronger than any I've ever known."

Lady Margaret smiled acidly. "Then you should not worry about her."

"She has been through a great deal and I owe her much. I will not allow you to make her life unnecessarily difficult," he replied uncompromisingly.

The smile vanished. "Fair is fair," Lady Margaret replied with a flick of her hand, as if brushing away a disagreeable insect. "She has made my life unbearably difficult."

"It is you who have chosen to remain here in the colonies," John pointed out coldly. "Your brother has opened his home to you. At any time, you may return to England and live out your days in the style and comfort you so much desire."

Lady Margaret approached her son and cupped his face in her hands. "I cannot possibly go without you." She breathed a deep sigh, and the contents of the letter she had so recently received filled her mind. "I cannot understand how you can give up so much for this pirate wench. Surely there is an honorable solution to this dilemma that would free you from this alliance."

John's jaw hardened with resolve. "I am married to Kathleen, and the sooner you accept that, the sooner we can all learn to live in harmony together."

"I will never accept it," she hissed. "I cannot understand a code of honor that holds you to so unsuitable a marriage."

John scowled impatiently. "If it were not for Kathleen I would be dead. You should be grateful to her."

"If you insist on this marriage to her, you might as well be dead," Lady Margaret returned with venom. "I cannot believe you would give up so much for so little."

John regarded his mother with cool command. "If that is the way you feel, then I must insist you go to your brother. I'll not have this kind of hatred beneath my roof."

Lady Margaret's eyes rounded in horror. "Please, you cannot send me away," she pleaded, tears brimming in her eyes. "I'm only thinking of you and your happiness. Someday this honor and gratitude and pity you feel toward Kathleen will turn to bile within you and you will regret all you have sacrificed."

"Perhaps someday I will curse the fates that brought Kathleen and myself together," he admitted. "But what is done is done and we are bound." Then, his gaze narrowing upon his mother, he ordered, "And you will treat her well or you will find yourself on a ship heading for England."

Lady Margaret curtsied submissively toward her son. But as he left, she assured herself that what was done could be undone.

Kathleen was not looking forward to the afternoon session with Lady Margaret, but she was prepared to endure in silence whatever the woman meted out.

"It has occurred to me that we should work upon your story," Lady Margaret said, when she had Kathleen seated again with teacup in hand. "I shall play the part of Mistress Compton. She's the most ardent gossip in Virginia." Seating herself across from Kathleen, she leaned slightly forward, as if requiring an even closer inspection, and said, "You must tell me, dear, of your adventure with the pirates."

Kathleen closed her eyes for a moment to allow the story to form in her mind. On many days, during those long years aboard Captain Thorton's ship, she had kept her hopes of escape alive by creating fantasies of rescues. A soft smile played across her face. Now she had a hero to place at the center of her story.

"You must look me in the eye," Lady Margaret admonished. "And you must not smile. You must make people believe you were in danger."

Kathleen's smile vanished at the implication in Lady Margaret's voice that she'd had a jolly time aboard the ship and the danger would be merely another part of the lie. "I was visualizing my rescue," she said curtly.

"Yes, of course, you were," Lady Margaret replied, her honeyed tone calling Kathleen a liar.

Kathleen's temper flared. As anger flashed in her eyes, she saw a gleam spark in Lady Margaret's. She's baiting me, Kathleen realized. Well, she would not fall into that trap. She drew a calming breath as she brought her anger back under control. She even managed a polite smile as she said, "Shall I proceed?"

A shadow of disappointment passed over Lady Margaret's face. Then her expression again became one of a tutor who was worried that her pupil was not capable of learning even the smallest lesson and she said, "Yes, proceed."

"'Twas a horrid day," Kathleen began, her mind going back to the day the vessel upon which she and her parents had been sailing was attacked. Despite the passage of years, the memory remained vivid. A shudder shook her. "A cry was raised that sails had been spotted on the horizon. At that time we could not know if it was friend or foe. The ship was showing English colors, but our captain was a cautious man. He attempted to keep a distance. But Captain Thorton's ship was smaller and swifter. We were also laden with cargo. As the pirates drew near, they lowered the English colors and raised a flag of Captain Thorton's own design. 'Twas a gold dragon breathing fire and holding a sword in its forepaw."

"My dear, how very observant of you," Lady Margaret interrupted sharply.

Kathleen immediately saw her mistake. It would have been too great a distance for her to have seen the details of the flag. "I did not see it," she replied calmly. "I heard the first mate describe it to the captain."

"'Tis as good an answer as any," Lady Margaret conceded. "But perhaps you should leave out the part about the flag's design in the future."

Kathleen nodded. She had no desire to recall more than was necessary.

"Continue," Lady Margaret instructed.

"The captain ordered us all to our cabins." The real events that followed, her and her parents' capture, and her father's murder at the hands of Captain Thorton, flowed through Kathleen's mind and her stomach churned. Pushing them aside, she began the story she would tell any callers. "But my father knew how to use a sword and insisted upon remaining on deck. My mother and I returned to our cabin. There we loaded my father's pistol and waited. We heard the pirates boarding and the clash of swords. Frantic for my father's safety, my mother ordered me to remain in the cabin and, taking the pistol, she left. Unwilling to be left behind, I found a knife and followed. As I reached the deck, I saw my father lying dead." A hard knot formed in Kathleen's stomach as the sight filled her mind. "His throat was slashed," she said in a voice barely above a whisper.

"Very good," Lady Margaret complimented, her tone making it clear that she thought this was nothing more than playacting.

Ignoring her, Kathleen forced the painful image from her mind and returned to her story. "My mother was standing beside him. She aimed the pistol and shot the man who had murdered him. Then another shot was fired, and she slowly sank to the deck beside him. I saw a short man, dressed as fancy as a peacock, standing with pistol in hand. He laughed. I looked down and saw blood pooling on the bodice of my mother's dress. He had shot her through the heart."

Kathleen again paused as a fresh wave of pain washed over her. In her mind's eye, she was again at her mother's bedside. "Even for you, my heart cannot endure that man any longer," her mother had said in a voice weakened with fever. "But I know his weakness and shall do all that is in my power to save you." Her mother's death had not been as quick as the one she had fantasized. Still, Kathleen laid it upon the shoulders of Captain Thorton. If she should ever meet with him again, she would have her revenge.

"You must tell me how you escaped," Lady Margaret prodded impatiently, jarring Kathleen's mind back to the present.

Drawing a shaking breath, Kathleen pushed the hurtful images aside. "As I stood, frozen, I was grabbed by one of the pirate crew. I fought but the man was strong. Just when I was sure I was to join my parents, Mr. Ashford appeared. He had come by way of the plank from the pirate ship. My first thought was that he was one of them. But instead of aiding my assailant, he attacked him. 'Twas then I noticed that his clothing, though bloodied and torn, were that of a gentleman and he wore shackles on his wrists, the chain of which had been broken. I learned later that his ship had been taken only a day earlier. Fighting valiantly, he freed me, and had just slain my attacker when the cry of surrender rose from the crew of my vessel. I saw the captain lying dead upon the deck and the men throwing their weapons down.

"Mr. Ashford looked at me and asked, 'Can you swim?' When I nodded in the affirmative, he said, 'We've a better chance among the sharks than remaining here.' In the next instant, he had tossed me overboard. Next he tossed a couple of barrels into the water, and then he himself followed. He aided me in using one of the barrels to keep afloat. Luckily, we were near the coast and the tide washed us up onto the beach." As an afterthought, Kathleen added, "'Twas a most harrowing experience. There are many details that remain a blank."

Lady Margaret sat back, a triumphant grin upon her face. "It will do. I especially like the business about many details remaining a blank." A malicious sparkle shown in her eyes. "I could have believed that tale myself. You are an accomplished liar."

The remembered scenes of her parents' deaths had shaken Kathleen. And she was tired. Her control slipped. "Not nearly as accomplished as you, m'lady," she replied.

Lady Margaret sat bolt upright, her demeanor that of one who had been unjustly accused. "You are a heathen," she snapped. She tilted her head as if there was a smell within the room she found offensive. "That will be the end of your lessons for this day." She waved a hand. "Get out."

Kathleen was angry with herself for allowing her temper to get the better of her, but she did not regret being freed from the enforced wooden posture. "Yes, m'lady," she said. Her control back in place, she rose and performed a polite curtsy.

"Wait," Lady Margaret ordered curtly as Kathleen started toward the door.

Kathleen groaned mentally. She had almost made it to freedom. Forcing her polite mask back in place, she turned.

Lady Margaret rose. From a table by the window, she picked up a large book that had been lying there. Approaching Kathleen, she extended it toward her. "This Bible has my family lineage inscribed within. It was a gift from my father on my wedding day," she said. "You will take it to your rooms and practice walking with it balanced upon your head. We can only hope this will improve your posture and your walk. A lady moves with grace, not like a clumsy cow."

It took every ounce of control Kathleen had, but she maintained a polite facade as she accepted the heavy tome.

"It is also my hope," Lady Margaret added, "that some of the charity described within will sink into that common brain of yours and you will see fit to do what is right by my son."

I have always and shall always try to do what is right by John, Kathleen replied to herself. She did not, however, declare this to Lady Margaret. She knew that to make such a claim to her ladyship would be futile, and Kathleen had no wish to subject herself to yet another of the woman's barbs. Aloud, she said, "Yes, m'lady," curtsied once again and quickly left.

As she entered her rooms, the urge to throw the book at the wall was strong. However, it was a Bible and she could not bring herself to show such disrespect. It was also a little large to throw, she mused, guessing it must weigh near half a stone.

Balancing it on her head, she walked across the room. "Perhaps she has decided that breaking my neck would be quicker than attempting to break my spirit," Kathleen muttered as she made a fifth trip across the room. The weight of the volume seemed to increase with each step, and she was finding it more and more difficult to keep her head up.

Deciding she had practiced enough, she seated herself and opened the Bible. Inside, as Lady Margaret had said, was her family lineage. 'Twas impressive, Kathleen had to admit, an uneasy feeling moving along her spine. As she continued down the list, she again wondered if one day John would regret aligning himself with her. "I gave him the chance to free himself," she reminded herself. Still an uneasiness lingered.

A knock on the door interrupted her thoughts. It was Nancy, coming to announce that tea was being served.

The girl's eyes rounded in surprise when she saw Kathleen sitting with the open Bible in her lap. "You can read, miss?" she asked, her voice holding a touch of awe.

Kathleen started to explain that her parents' master had been a generous and kind man who had allowed Kathleen to attend the lessons given his own daughters. Just in time, she stopped herself. Since part of her past was to be a fabrication, it would be best to reveal as little about herself as possible, she reasoned. "A bit," she answered simply.

Nancy continued to regard her skeptically. "Me mum says reading puts a harmful strain upon a woman's mind."

"It can at times," Kathleen replied, closing the volume.

Get 4 Books FREE

SEE BACK OF CARD FOR DETAILS

DETACH ALONG DOTTED LINE AND MAIL TODAY! – DETACH ALONG DOTTED LINE AND MAIL TODAY! – DETACH ALONG DOTTED LINE AND MAIL TODAY!

Chapter Eleven

By the end of the next day, Kathleen's muscles ached. Lady Margaret had again insisted on concentrating on Kathleen's sitting and walking posture. "The way a woman sits and moves is a sign of her class," she'd explained when John suggested that she should turn her attention to more practical matters, such as instructing Kathleen regarding the management of the house.

Despite his mother's claim, John had insisted that at least a few hours of Kathleen's day be devoted to learning how to run his household. Lady Margaret had conceded to this, but she had still managed to find several hours to devote to having Kathleen sit stiffly with teacup in hand or walk with the Bible upon her head.

Now, alone in her room, Kathleen sat curled in a chair in front of the fireplace. It was late. She was dressed in her shift with the shawl wrapped around her shoulders for added warmth. A soft smile played across her face as she heard the door of the music room open, and looking up, she watched John enter. But as she rose to greet him, a muscle knotted in her back and she was forced to grab on to the chair for support.

"I am beginning to wonder if you are worth the pain," she teased, straightening slowly.

"I suppose that means I must work even harder than usual to please you this night," he returned with mock disgruntlement.

In the next moment, Kathleen was being lifted in his strong arms. But as he carried her to the bed, another spasm of pain shot through her, causing her to gasp in agony.

"What is wrong?" John demanded, his voice laced with concern as he placed her upon the mattress.

"My back feels as if it's tying itself in knots," she replied through teeth clenched with pain.

"Lie upon your stomach," he ordered.

Kathleen obeyed and he began to massage her sore muscles. The heat of his touch aided his ministering. Within moments the knot was gone. "You do have very nice hands," she said, thinking that if she were a cat she would be purring.

Laughing lightly, he continued downward, gently but firmly massaging her body. The tightness of her muscles angered him. He would have a firm talk with his mother on the morrow.

Beneath his touch, Kathleen's body relaxed until she felt as if she were melting like butter on a hot day. Her mind grew groggy.

John felt her breathing becoming more and more regular. He told himself that he should allow her to sleep. But while his ministerings had relaxed her, they had not done the same for him. His hand moved upward between her legs until he found her womanly core. Gently, he stroked her and smiled when he felt her response. Leaning down, he trailed kisses along her back to her neck.

Kathleen issued a low moan of pleasure as desire flamed to life within her.

"Are you sure you are not too tired?" he asked, nipping at her ear as he read her body's signs of arousal. He did not want to offer her this opportunity to stop him, but his conscience forced it upon him. After all, it was partially his fault she was so sore.

Kathleen turned slowly onto her side, luxuriating in the tantalizing feel of his touch. "As long as you are willing to do all of the work, I'm willing to accommodate you," she replied lazily. Then, recalling their first night in this bed, she added playfully, "You do owe me a bit of pleasure for all the pain I've been through learning to be a proper lady."

John grinned. "I am a man who believes in paying his debts," he assured her. His Kate had proven to be a most enjoyable companion, he thought, as he rose from the bed and began to remove his clothing.

Kathleen watched him. Just the sight of him filled her with pleasure. Passion blazed within her. Not wanting any barriers between them, she quickly discarded her shift and pulled the warm down comforter up over her as he finished removing the remainder of his clothing.

Joining her, John ducked his head under the covering and playfully trailed the tip of his tongue over her stomach. She tasted delicious, he thought. His hand again sought a most intimate contact and he smiled. She felt delicious also.

Kathleen trembled with delight as she tried not to giggle, even though the servants and Lady Margaret should be in their beds fast asleep.

John's tasting traveled upward, exploring the firm curve of one breast, and Kathleen could not stifle a moan of pleasure as he paused to tease the hardened nipple. Impatience flowed through her. Anxious for the feel of him, she sought him and felt his need grow stronger. A womanly triumph bubbled inside of her.

John inhaled sharply as her touch sent currents of ecstasy coursing through him. He was aroused so strongly he knew he could not wait too long before possessing her. "I know you are tired and I would not want to tire you further with procrastinations," he said gruffly, rising to claim her.

"'Twould be a shame if I were to fall asleep before you paid your debt," she replied. Then she laughed lightly at the ridiculous notion that she could fall asleep. He had awakened her body until every fiber tingled with anticipation.

"'Twould be a shame," he agreed, exulting at the velvet feel of her as she welcomed his possession.

Kathleen marveled at the excitement that coursed through her as he brought her to the heights of rapture. She had been so certain that she would grow a little bored with this business of mating. Perhaps that would happen after a few more years, she thought. A few decades, she corrected, as her body ignited, and she could not hold back a small cry of bliss.

Releasing the control he had been holding over himself, John joined her, her delight adding to his pleasure and carrying him into a realm of ecstasy that left him panting for breath.

For a long while afterward, he lay quietly beside her. The urge to remain and wake with her the next morning was strong, but it would be her reputation that would suffer. With a groan of disgruntlement, he rose. "With luck, this should be the last night I must come to your bed," he said as he dressed. "Tomorrow my man should return with Reverend Vales and we shall be publicly wed. Then I will not have to go padding across cold floors in my stocking feet in the dead of night to exercise my husbandly prerogatives.''

"''Twill be nice to wake with you,'' Kathleen said softly, parroting his thoughts, as memories of the journey and their early morning lovemaking filled her mind.

"Yes," he agreed, ordering himself to leave now before he rejoined her.

Moments later, as he made his way back to his room, he admitted that the power of his attraction to her unnerved him a little. He reminded himself that, after having studied his parents' marriage, he had vowed that when he did wed, his choice would be based upon practical considerations only. And Kate is a practical choice as well as a debt of honor, he reasoned. That she pleased him so greatly was merely the luck of the draw and he should be relieved instead of uncomfortable about it. After all, it was better for a man to have a wife who sparked some interest within him, instead of one who bored him. It will make producing heirs less of a strain, he concluded.

Alone in her bed, the full meaning of John's words struck Kathleen. Tomorrow she would become mistress of Ashford Hall. A wave of uneasiness swept over her. She closed her eyes and John's image entered her mind. A gentle smile tilted the corners of her mouth. With him beside her, she could face anything. Still, the uneasiness lingered as she drifted off to sleep.

Chapter Twelve

The next morning during breakfast, John made good his promise to himself. "We will serve ourselves," he said, dismissing the servants. As soon as he, Kathleen and his mother were alone, he turned his attention to Lady Margaret. "I am satisfied with the way Kathleen sits and the way she walks. There will be no more lessons regarding her posture."

"Really—" Lady Margaret began to protest.

John held his hand up for silence. "You will instruct her as to how to run this household and nothing more."

Lady Margaret cast Kathleen a glare that implied she was certain Kathleen had complained to her son. Then a spark of malice showed in her eyes and she shrugged. "I suppose one can't train true breeding into one of lesser blood, anyway."

Kathleen's back stiffened. She felt as if she'd been issued a challenge. But just as she was about to accept it by insisting the lessons continue, a muscle in her side knotted. It would be stupid to allow pride to incite her into continuing this torture, she decided. Besides, she was confident that her posture was passable. Ignoring Lady Margaret's barb, she continued with her meal.

John scowled at his mother. She was sorely tempting his patience, he grumbled mentally. He would find a way to force her to welcome Kathleen. A sudden thought struck him. "I think it would be most kind of you to aid Kathleen and Nancy with the making of Kathleen's clothing," he said in a tone that made this more of an order than a suggestion. "Your lessons have taken a great deal of Kathleen's time during the past couple of days and I wish my wife properly clothed as quickly as possible."

Kathleen nearly choked on the bite of food she was swallowing. She had no intention of allowing Lady Margaret near her with either pin or needle in hand.

"The lessons have taken a great deal of my time as well," Lady Margaret protested, clearly appalled by this command. "And I've my canvas to finish."

John flashed his mother a warning glance, letting her know that he meant to be obeyed.

"'Tis really unnecessary for Lady Margaret to concern herself with my wardrobe," Kathleen interjected quickly.

John turned toward Kathleen and saw the protest in her eyes. Although he was still tempted to force his mother to perform this act of kindness, he could understand Kathleen's desire not to spend more time in Lady Margaret's company. Once Kathleen was officially his wife, his mother would have to accept her and this battle would end, he assured himself. "I shall leave the matter to your discretion," he replied.

Kathleen saw the flash of indignation on Lady Margaret's face. Clearly the woman was infuriated that her son would allow Kathleen even the smallest command over her. But she prudently made no comment, and Kathleen breathed a mental sigh of relief that John had been willing to give in to their wishes on this matter.

A knock sounded on the door as they returned to their meal.

"Mr. Ashford," Quinn said, entering and bowing toward John. "Jarvis has returned. He awaits you in your study."

John looked past Quinn to the door. "And the Reverend Vales? Where is he?"

"He did not come, sir," Quinn replied.

John scowled with impatient anger. "If you ladies will excuse me," he said, rising from the table.

Kathleen caught a flash of amusement in Lady Margaret's eyes as he left the room. It was as if her ladyship were having a private joke, she thought.

There was no amusement in John's eyes, however, when he strode back into the dining room only minutes later. "The Reverend claims to be ill with a fever," he said, standing at the head of the table, his gaze narrowed on his mother. "I will be leaving shortly to confirm this. If, when I reach his home, I discover this is truly the case, I shall seek a special license that will not require his presence. Upon my return, Kathleen and I will be wed, one way or the other."

Panic showed on Lady Margaret's face. "You cannot go."

"I am master here," he reminded her curtly.

Watching them and recalling the amusement she had seen in Lady Margaret's eyes, Kathleen was certain Lady Margaret had had a hand in the reverend's absence. It was also obvious to her that John guessed this was so.

"The weather," Lady Margaret protested. "Quinn tells me that Dyles is predicting a storm soon. And you know Dyles's aches that warn him of the weather are never wrong."

Kathleen, too, felt a disappointment that today was not to be her wedding day. But her concern for John was stronger. "If a storm is brewing, perhaps you should delay your trip," she suggested anxiously.

"You see, even Kathleen wishes you to wait," Lady Margaret argued.

John's gaze never left his mother. "I have made up my mind and you will abide by my decision or accept the consequences," he warned. This proclamation issued, he left the room.

Lady Margaret turned to Kathleen, her face contorted in hatred. "If anything should happen to my son, I will hold you responsible."

Kathleen was already on her feet before Lady Margaret had finished. She tossed her ladyship an impatient glance. "It's your conscience you should worry about," she snapped, her concern for John overriding her prudence.

"Impudent commoner!" Lady Margaret seethed.

But Kathleen barely heard. She was already out the door and on her way to John's rooms. "You mustn't go if there is danger," she said, bursting in without knocking.

Simon, John's valet, jerked around, nearly dropping the shirt he was folding.

"Leave us," John ordered, waving the man out. The moment they were alone, he smiled rakishly. "All this while I have been trying to be so careful and you scandalize us by barging into my rooms unannounced."

Kathleen scowled. "This is not a joking matter."

His expression became serious. "I am certain my mother is responsible for the reverend's absence. I will be back with the man within four days' time. You've no need to worry." He suddenly smiled. "But I am enjoying this show of concern." A great deal, he added to himself.

The lightness in his manner caused Kathleen to continue to frown. "I've no wish to become a widow before I am a bride."

Approaching her, John kissed her upon the tip of her nose. "I am in graver danger of catching a chill padding between our rooms than in making this journey. Before I leave, I will instruct the servants that you are to be treated with the same respect they would show the mistress of this house." His expression again became serious. "I will also instruct Mrs. Oats and Mrs. Elby to assist you in any way."

Kathleen's experience with the staff had been limited. But she did know that Mrs. Oats was the cook and Mrs. Elby the housekeeper. Clearly, John was leaving her in a position of power. While this honored her, she still did not wish to see him go. "Perhaps you should at least wait until the weather clears," she suggested.

"I shall be fine," he assured her. The urge to take her in his arms for a long final farewell was strong. But as he began to wrap his arms around her, a knock sounded on the door.

"Your horse is ready, sir," Simon said, entering at John's command.

"The sooner I am off, the sooner I shall be back," John said. He could not resist one light kiss on her lips, then he shooed her out of his room.

A little later, as she watched John riding away, an emptiness filled Kathleen. When she turned to go back into the house, a coldness swept through her. With him gone she did not feel welcome here.

Suddenly Nancy appeared at the door. "You best come in, miss, before you catch a chill," the maid ordered, her voice filled with concern.

I've at least one friend here, Kathleen thought, and her face brightened. Following the girl's advice, she went inside and together they went to her rooms and busied themselves with their sewing.

Lady Margaret paced the floor of her sitting room. Her farewell to her son had been said here in private. And it had not been friendly. Again he had warned her to treat Kathleen well. A knock sounded on her door. "Enter," she ordered.

It was Quinn.

"Has my son left?" she demanded as soon as the door was closed.

"Yes, m'lady," he replied.

"Oh, I wish Talbert were here," she fumed.

For a brief moment shock registered on Quinn's face, then his expression became staid once again. "Talbert, madam?"

Lady Margaret regarded him with an impatient scowl. "I am not naive now and I most certainly wasn't as a young girl. I know Talbert performed certain duties for my father that were neither pleasant nor legal. To be perfectly blunt, he saw that certain of my father's enemies were removed from this earth."

Coming to a halt, she faced Quinn, her mouth forming a petulant pout. "Would you be my Talbert, Quinn? 'Twould be so easy. You could slip a little hemlock in Miss James's tea. Or perhaps arrange a fall down the stairs." She frowned at this last idea. "Though she does seem to have a very sturdy neck," she muttered.

The shock returned to Quinn's face. "Really, Lady Margaret, I do believe that would be going a bit too far."

Lady Margaret shrugged off his protest. "She's a mere commoner. What harm is there in ridding the world of one of them? She is like a louse in my hair. I should not be forced to endure her.''

Quinn frowned worriedly. Out of loyalty to her and her family, he had aided and abetted his mistress in other of her schemes. But he drew the line at murder. "There comes a time, m'lady, when 'tis best to accept what cannot be changed."

Lady Margaret glared at him. "Never!"

The next two days passed slowly for Kathleen. Her one relief was that Lady Margaret remained sulking in her rooms. Worry for John had Kathleen's nerves on edge, and she was not certain she could have endured the woman's jabs with polite dignity.

Trying to divert her mind from her constant anxiety for John's safety, Kathleen realized that she would be wise to learn more about the other members of the household, especially Mrs. Oats and Mrs. Elby. Among the staff, they and Quinn held the most power. As she sat sewing with Nancy, she guided her maid into a conversation centering on the cook and the housekeeper. She learned that both were in their mid-forties.

According to Nancy, Mrs. Oats had been widowed twice. She'd been hired by the Ashfords when they'd first arrived in the colonies. Her second husband had still been alive then. He'd been good with animals and had worked in the stables. "But I ain't never seen a man so prone to accidents," Nancy said with a shake of her head. "Finally fell out of the loft one night and broke his neck. After the funeral, Mrs. Oats announced she weren't going to marry again. She said she was finished with burying husbands."

As for Mrs. Elby, Nancy explained that her husband had died before she came to the colonies. She'd been hired in London and had sailed to Virginia with the Ashfords.

"She's only been married the one time and she ain't looking for another husband, either," Nancy said. "I got the feeling her first one didn't treat her none too well."

While Nancy rattled on about the cook and the housekeeper, elaborating on how each ruled her domain with a firm hand, Kathleen worked up her courage to ask the question most important to her. Both had been polite to her but neither had been particularly friendly. And Kathleen had learned from experience that it was always wise to know who was a friend and who was a foe. Finally, when Nancy paused at the end of airing a grievance against Mrs. Elby for having scolded her because she'd missed sweeping up a "mite-sized" bit of dust in the corner of a room, Kathleen asked, "How do they feel about me?"

"They like you just fine," Nancy answered quickly.

Too quickly, Kathleen mused. Clearly, Nancy was not a very accomplished liar. "If I am to find my place here, I need to know their real feelings," she coaxed.

For a moment Nancy hesitated, then said, "They don't have nothing against you. But they're both real fond of Mr. Ashford and think he could have found a more suitable match." Nancy flushed scarlet, clearly embarrassed to have made this confession. Then her chin tightened into a firm line. "But I told them you're as good as anyone he could have found and you'll be a right more pleasant mistress than Lady Margaret. Neither of them argued that point."

Kathleen sighed. Well, she hadn't expected them to accept her immediately. At least they hadn't declared themselves her enemy.

The third day of John's absence, Kathleen awoke to discover snow had fallen. She'd heard of it, but she'd never actually seen this type of precipitation before. Her impression was that it seemed as if a lovely soft white carpet had been cast over the landscape. Then she thought of John, and the snow lost its beauty as panic for his safety swept through her.

"'Tisn't as cold as it looks," Nancy informed her, attempting to cheer her up. "The snow's already melting a bit. And Mr. John knows how to take care of himself."

Kathleen recalled John's resourcefulness during their journey and felt less frightened for him. Nancy's cheerfulness helped also. By the time she went down to the morning meal, Kathleen was still worried, but was feeling encouraged. However, as she entered the dining room, her feeling that all would go well died a quick death. Lady Margaret was there.

"If my son should perish from the cold or a riding accident caused by this storm," her ladyship said the moment Kathleen stepped into the room, "his death will be on your shoulders."

"I asked him not to go until the weather had cleared," Kathleen replied in her defense. She knew this would fall on deaf ears where Lady Margaret was concerned. But there were servants present and she refused to allow Lady Margaret to paint her as a blackguard in front of them.

Lady Margaret issued an indignant "Humph," implying that she considered Kathleen's words to be a lie. Then, as if unable to bear Kathleen's presence, she began to rise from the table. But as Quinn moved forward to aid her with the chair, the sounds of gunshots and bloodcurdling cries suddenly filled the air.

"Indians!" one of the maids shrieked.

Kathleen's stomach knotted. She raced toward the window. Outside lay the bodies of several of John's men, their blood scarlet against the snow. Cries were now coming from inside the house.

"I'll get John's sword," Kathleen said, racing toward the door. She glanced over her shoulder at Quinn. "You take care of Lady Margaret." But even as she spoke, she realized she needn't have issued that order. Quinn was already at her ladyship's side.

It occurred to Kathleen that one sword against a band of Indians would do little good, but she refused to give up without a fight. She ordered her legs to carry her faster. But with her hand on the knob of the study door, she was suddenly grabbed around the waist from behind.

She kicked and clawed at her assailant. Letting out a grunt, the Indian rammed her hard against the wall. For a moment the world went black. When Kathleen opened her eyes, she discovered a musket pointed at her chest. Through signs and grunts, her captor directed her to precede him into the kitchen. As they passed by the staircase, she saw Claire, the upstairs maid, lying dead on the steps. Her stomach knotted in fear for the others.

Her fright increased as she crossed the snow from the main house to the kitchen. Lying across the path was Ruth, the scullery maid, her hair matted with blood. Down toward the stables, Kathleen saw the slain bodies of more of John's men, clearly taken by surprise.

To her relief, when she reached the kitchen, she found Mrs. Oats, Nancy, Lady Margaret and Quinn captured but alive. Janet, one of the housemaids, and Sally, Lady Margaret's personal maid, were also there. Both were near Nancy's age. From her maid, Kathleen had learned that Janet had come to work for the Ashfords after her parents had died of the fever. As for Sally, she had joined the household to escape a stepfather who beat her. Adam, the stable master, was there, too. He was in his mid-twenties and sturdily built. Like Nancy, he'd come to the colonies as an indentured servant, bent on building a new life for himself. Janet was tying a bandage around Quinn's arm and Nancy was tying one around Adam's leg. Lady Margaret was pale and trembling and Sally was trying to comfort her. As far as Kathleen could tell the women did not appear to be injured.

"They didn't have to kill Ruth," Mrs. Oats was sobbing. "She weren't the brightest girl in the world, but she never done no one any harm."

Nancy was hugging the cook, attempting to calm her.

Kathleen caught the look of impatience in her captor's eyes. Approaching the cook, she said sternly, "Ruth is gone. If you wish to survive, you must get control of yourself."

A look of shock came over the cook's face. Blinking back her tears, she stared at Kathleen. "I cannot be so coldhearted as you," she snapped.

The words hurt. Kathleen looked to Nancy for support, only to discover her maid watching her with an expression of shock and disappointment. You cannot expect to have earned her loyalty within so short a time, she told herself. Still, she felt a sharp jab of pain that Nancy would think she could be so cruel. "I wish only to save your lives," she said in lowered tones, her voice harsh with command. "It has been my experience that if your captors think you will be trouble for them, they will kill you quick as a wink."

The disappointment left Nancy's eyes. "Miss Kathleen is right," she said.

Mrs. Oats looked past the women to the Indians. "It might be better to die now than live to face what they have in store for us," she muttered, but she stopped sobbing.

Kathleen now turned her full attention to her captors. She'd never seen an Indian up close. They looked fierce and they didn't hide their hatred. And, she confessed, she could understand their anger. John had told her of the bloodshed and broken treaties on both sides.

The big one who had captured her gave an order. A few stayed to guard the prisoners while the rest scurried away. They returned quickly, carrying blankets and bags of food. These they wrapped into bundles and began strapping them onto Kathleen and the other prisoners.

"We're to be their pack animals," Adam said grudgingly.

Kathleen told herself these savages could be no worse than Captain Thorton's pirates, but down deep she was not so certain. Still, forcing herself to stand straight and proud in spite of the heavy weight upon her back, she turned to the large Indian who appeared to be the leader. "We'll need our cloaks and coats if we're to go out into the snow." She gestured toward a number of cloaks hanging on pegs along the wall.

The Indian smiled broadly. Walking over to where the outerwear hung, he began to examine it. Then, barking out an order to his companions, he began to distribute the cloaks and coats among them. Others wrapped themselves in blankets for an even heavier covering. But the prisoners were given nothing but their loads to carry.

Smiling approvingly, the big Indian gave the signal to leave, and the Indian next to Lady Margaret motioned for her to join the others.

"I cannot possibly bear this burden," she complained, refusing to rise from the chair in which she had been sitting since her load had been strapped on her.

"I'll carry it for you, m'lady," Quinn said, starting toward her.

Laying a hand on Quinn's arm, Adam stopped him. "We're only being allowed to live because they need pack animals," he said. "If she doesn't carry her share, they'll kill her quick as you can bat an eye.'' Turning toward her ladyship, he urged, ''Please, m'lady you must try.''

Lady Margaret's jaw tightened, and tossing her captors an angry glance, she rose.

As they left the warmth of the kitchen and began to trudge through the cold snow, Kathleen wondered if she'd been born under an ill-fated star. This isn't fair, she screamed mentally. Then her moment of self-pity was over as she concentrated on surviving.

They all took turns helping Lady Margaret. When it was her turn, Kathleen could feel the woman's hate and knew it was costing Lady Margaret a great deal to accept her aid. But clearly the woman hated the thought of dying even more.

The snow, Kathleen knew, could prove to be as dangerous as the Indians. But it was also a source of hope for her. If John returned while it was still on the ground, he would be able to follow.

The Indians had two canoes waiting at the river. It took several crossings to transport all the prisoners and cargo to the northern side of the Rappahannock. All the while, Kathleen prayed John would return home quickly. Clearly, the Indians were worried about being followed. Once they were across the river, they took turns carrying the canoes overland while they forced the prisoners to maintain a rapid pace through the woods, putting distance between themselves and the plantation. By the time they stopped for the night, every muscle in Kathleen's body ached but she didn't complain. Lady Margaret was doing enough complaining for all of them.

A small fire was the prisoners' only protection against the cold. Kathleen scowled at the Indians bundled warmly in their animal skins as well as in the stolen blankets, cloaks and coats. "They're certainly a heartless lot," she muttered.

Adam frowned into the fire. "I knew it would come to this. First the traders give the Indians guns for goods so's the settlers has to worry even more about the savages. Then the Marylanders strike up a friendship with one tribe and gives that tribe guns so's they'll keep the other tribe from killing the settlers. Then the settlers make friends with the other tribe and the Indians start fighting amongst themselves for what land is left of their original territories. Then one tribe drives the other out and pretty soon you've got Indians living where they ain't never lived before, having to steal food to survive the winter and blaming all their misfortune on the settlers."

"I'm just wondering what kind they be," Janet said in a low voice. "From the tales I heard of the Doegs, we'd be better off dead. I've heard tell of them roasting prisoners alive and feeding the flesh to the other prisoners, or sticking holes in a person's flesh and putting feathers in them."

Lady Margaret let out a small wail.

"Janet, hush," Quinn ordered. "You're upsetting her ladyship."

"I was only repeating what I heard," the woman said, defending herself.

"We mustn't dwell on the evils that might befall us," Kathleen ordered. "We must devise a plan of escape."

"We must hope that my son arrives home quickly and comes to our rescue," Lady Margaret corrected curtly.

"Please keep your voice low," Kathleen cautioned. "We don't want them to know we might be followed."

Lady Margaret scowled at the reprimand. "They're heathens. They cannot know the King's English."

"Pardon me, m'lady," Adam interjected apologetically, "but Miss James could be right. Some of these heathen can understand our words."

"You should listen to your man." It was the large Indian Kathleen had decided was the leader of this band who spoke. She'd seen him approaching out of the corner of her eye and hoped he'd not overheard Lady Margaret's remark about John. "And your chattering disturbs me. I will cut out the tongue of anyone who does not remain quiet for the remainder of this night."

Kathleen saw in his eyes that he meant what he said. She knew the others had seen it, too, as a heavy silence fell among them.

The next day a bitter wind fought their every step and the sky clouded with the threat of more snow. It occurred to Kathleen that they need not worry what tortures the Indians might devise. The cold would surely kill them if they didn't reach shelter soon. But as was usual at this time of year, the weather changed suddenly, and by midday the sky had cleared and the air grew warmer. While it was still cold, they were not in such great danger of freezing to death.

They came to the edge of a marshy area, and the large Indian left his lead position to come back to speak to the prisoners. "You must follow in our footsteps exactly," he instructed. "The ground here is not solid."

By now Lady Margaret was threatening to collapse with each step. The others took turns holding her up and keeping her moving. But it wasn't easy. The path was narrow and she gave them practically no help.

While Kathleen felt no love for this woman, she could not allow her to die without a fight. "We shall have to remove her sack," she said decisively when Adam stumbled for the fourth time, trying to support his weight, Lady

Margaret's and both their burdens. "'Tis too much for one person to help her and bear the burden of their own load as well as hers."

Adam looked worriedly at the back of the big Indian. "He'll kill her."

"She'll surely die if we don't try. We can always return the sack to her," Kathleen argued. "None of us can continue to support this full load for much longer."

They'd been given no food, and their only water was that derived from eating snow as they walked. All were cold and in a weakened condition and all knew Kathleen was right.

Looking grim, Adam nodded his consent.

The Indian behind them let out a yell when the pack was removed from Lady Margaret's back, and immediately the column came to a halt. The big Indian left his lead position and came back to where the prisoners stood.

"If she cannot carry her load, then she is of no use," he said with a finality that spoke of death.

Kathleen placed herself between the Indian and Lady Margaret. She was willing to try a bluff before she returned the burden to the older woman's shoulders. "If you kill her, we will all chose to die with her. Then you'll have to carry these burdens yourselves," she said with conviction.

The Indian looked past her to her fellow prisoners. "Some might choose to die but others would not," he predicted knowingly. Then his gaze went back to Kathleen. "You would be a fool to give up your life so quickly."

"Whether I die here or a mile farther is of no concern to me," she replied. "At least I'll not have the blood of another on my hands."

The big Indian looked at Lady Margaret, who was glaring at him. "She is not so selfless. I do not hear her protesting your willingness to sacrifice yourselves,'' he pointed out cynically. "She would have all of you die for her."

Kathleen thought quickly. "She's a lady of rank," she said, forcing a deference toward Lady Margaret into her voice. "She considers it an honor for us to die for her. Clearly you're a man of rank. Would you not consider it an honor for your men to die for you?''

The Indian's gaze narrowed dangerously. She couldn't guess what he was thinking. She knew he was trying to frighten her into submitting to his will, but the threat of pain and death had hung over her before. She had learned to hide her fear then and she hid it well now.

Suddenly he smiled. "You may share your burdens as you see fit and you may attempt to keep your lady of rank alive for as long as you wish."

Watching him return to the head of the column, Kathleen knew he was enjoying watching them suffer. Her back stiffened and defiance glistened in her eyes. She'd survived Captain Thorton and his men. This Indian would not break her.

It was dusk when John and Reverend Vales approached Ashford Hall. John was tired, cold and angry. He'd arrived at the reverend's home to discover the man in excellent health. Although the reverend swore that he'd truly had a fever and had experienced a miraculous recovery, John was not convinced. Then the snow had fallen, hampering their journey. But now, finally, they were home.

Suddenly the front door was thrown open and Mrs. Elby came out onto the porch. She was carrying a pistol in one hand. "Mr. John, I'm so glad 'tis you," she cried out with relief, then ran down the path toward them.

A cold shaft of fear shot through John. Looking past her, he noticed that the house was dark, no candles had been lit. And there was a stillness about it, an emptiness. Something was very wrong.

"'Twas Indians. They attacked yesterday morning. We had no warning. Suddenly they were everywhere. I was up in the attic looking for some special linens. I hid and they didn't find me, but the others..." The housekeeper's voice trailed off. She was crying and gasping for breath as she reached him. "I've been waiting and praying for your quick return."

Kathleen's image filled John's mind. "Miss James. Where is she?" he demanded. The thought of her lying dead caused a wave of nausea and pain like none he'd ever felt before.

"Taken prisoner," Mrs. Elby replied, brushing away her tears and attempting to regain at least some of her usual composure.

John felt a shaft of hope. At least she was alive. "And what of my mother and the others?" he asked.

"Robert, Dyles, Philip, Jarvis and Claire are dead." A fresh flood of tears threatened to flow as Mrs. Elby recited the names. Fighting it back, she said, "William and David are badly wounded, but I've been doing what I can for them. Ruth had a blow to the head and she's still a bit dizzy, but she's been able to help me." A sob escaped her. "Your mother and all the others were taken prisoner. The savages ransacked the house, took all the food, blankets and weapons they could find. William was barely conscious as they passed him, but he says they loaded everything onto our people like they was pack animals."

"Was William's mind sound enough to count the number of Indians?" he asked.

"He says there were eight, maybe nine." Mrs. Elby shivered. "Seemed more like a hundred the way they came screaming and storming upon us."

John turned toward the reverend. If he had not had to fetch this man himself, he would have been here to defend his home. And he would probably be dead at the moment and his Kate would still be the Indians' prisoner, his practical side pointed out. It would do no good to cast blame. "I will follow them and you will ride for help," he ordered grimly.

The reverend nodded. "I'm sorry this happened," he said sincerely.

"'Twon't do either of you any good to go now," Mrs. Elby insisted. "'Tis almost fully dark. You'll not be able to see your hand in front of your face soon. Come inside, have something to eat and rest. Lucky for us, those savages didn't find the second storage cellar. Your father was clever to have thought of digging it." She glanced down at her hand. "They didn't find all of the weapons either." Her gaze shifted back to John. "You can start at daybreak."

John scowled at the darkness enveloping him. Every fiber of his being ached to be on his way to find his Kate, but he knew the housekeeper was right. He could not track in the dark, nor would it be safe for the reverend to find his way through this wilderness without light to guide him. It would be too easy for him to get lost. "You're right," he admitted grudgingly.

"I'll tend to the horses," the reverend said, clearly trying to be helpful.

Nodding, John dismounted and handed the man his reins. Then, leaving the housekeeper to hurry behind him, he strode briskly toward the house. Once inside, he visited with Ruth and the wounded men, reassuring them that aid would arrive soon. From William he learned what direction the Indians had taken.

After that he went in search of any weapons that had been left behind. Kate would be all right, he assured himself. She knew how to survive. She would stay alive until he could come for her.

Late that night he paced in his room, unable to sleep. He was concerned for the others, but it was Kate's image that remained foremost in his mind. "'Tis because I brought her here and promised to keep her safe," he reasoned to himself, trying to explain the intense fear he felt for her. Then he smiled cynically. "Only a fool would lie to himself and believe it," he muttered. Grudgingly, he admitted he'd done what he'd promised himself he would do with no woman... he'd fallen in love with her. "It is definitely not a practical emotion," he grumbled. But it was one he seemed to have no control over.

The next few days were some of the hardest Kathleen had ever endured. The Indians gave the prisoners only enough food for bare subsistence. For the most part, they traveled over solid ground, though periodically there were marshy areas. These Kathleen hated. If she made the slightest misstep, her foot would sink into a wet muddy hole and be chilled to the bone. Then the snow melted, adding to her discomfort. While she did not relish having frozen feet, the white blanket had given John a trail to follow. She considered leaving small pieces of her petticoats on the brambles, but knew the Indians behind them would spot the signals and remove them. She did, however, attempt to snap twigs and leave footprints wherever possible.

Finally they reached the banks of another river.

"'Tis the Potomac," Adam said. "My guess is that they be Maryland Indians."

Kathleen's spirits sank even lower. If they crossed the Potomac, any rescuers who came after them would surely never find them.

But, to Kathleen's relief, the Indians didn't cross the river. Instead they followed the southern shoreline upstream and into what Kathleen judged to be the most treacherous marshy area they had yet to encounter. For what seemed like hours they made their way carefully over the soggy ground. Late in the afternoon, Kathleen spotted smoke in the distance. Fairly soon afterward they reached a small village consisting of eight or nine huts situated on a bit of high ground completely surrounded by the marsh.

Women and children rushed out to meet them. Kathleen counted only three more males who came out to greet their fellow warriors. Guessing that they had been left behind to guard the women and children, she took heart that there were so few.

Seeing the prisoners, the children immediately picked up sticks and began hitting at them, laughing joyfully.

"Little monsters," Lady Margaret hissed.

"Be quiet," Kathleen ordered, suppressing a groan as a particularly healthy little boy hit her shin with a thrown rock.

Lady Margaret tossed her a disgruntled glance but obeyed.

The big Indian gave an order and pouts appeared on the children's faces. Frowning unhappily, as if being deprived of a particularly good time, they scurried back into their huts.

"Lay down your sacks," the large Indian ordered.

When the food and other looted goods had been laid in a pile in the middle of the village, the Indian gave another order. Immediately, Sally, Nancy, Janet and the cook were each grabbed by the arm of one of the Indians who had been on the raiding party. Even in their weakened conditions the women tried to struggle, but their captors held them easily as the rest of the village laughed at their panic.

Hiding her fear for them behind a mask of cold anger, Kathleen glared at the large Indian. "What are they going to do to them?" she demanded.

"They will be slaves," he answered. To the women, he shouted loudly, "Be quiet. Serve your mistresses and masters well and you will be cared for."

The women stopped struggling but they did not look convinced. Obviously uncertain if they should believe their captor, they turned to Kathleen for guidance.

"You may tell them that I have spoken the truth," the big Indian assured her.

She saw no alternative, at least for the moment, except to believe him. "Do as he says," she ordered the women.

As they went with their new masters, the big Indian returned his attention to Kathleen. "You and the able-bodied man will serve me."

"And what of the others?" she asked, certain, even as she spoke, that she did not want to hear what he had in mind for Lady Margaret and Quinn.

"They are useless. We have no food to maintain the useless." Nodding toward Kathleen and Adam, he said, "Come with me," and he started toward a large hut.

"Wait!" Kathleen demanded, running to get in front of him and block his way. "You cannot make people bear your burdens for days, and when their job is done, simply kill them."

"It was you and the others who bore the lady of rank's burden," the Indian reminded her.

"You are a true heathen," Kathleen snapped.

"A true heathen would torture them to death," he replied. "I shall devise a quick and easy death for them."

"You cannot!" Kathleen repeated.

The Indian gave an order, and while Kathleen watched, Lady Margaret and Quinn were led to a large tree at the edge of the camp. They were made to face the tree and then were bound to the trunk in a standing position.

As Kathleen watched in horror, the Indian continued to observe her. When his men had finished their task and left Lady Margaret and Quinn to suffer the elements in solitude, he said, "Even after days of travel, you are still strong. I will treat you well. I will take you as a wife."

Kathleen saw the lust in his eyes and balked. "I want no special attention."

The Indian scowled. "What I offer is an honor."

"To you, perhaps," she returned dryly.

The scowl on the Indian's face deepened. "Perhaps a night with your lady of rank will make you milder." He gave an order, and Kathleen was led away and tied to the tree with Quinn and Lady Margaret.

They were given no food. When Sally and Nancy tried to share what little they had been given, their Indian mistresses hit at them and ordered them back. Nancy's mistress, Kathleen noted, seemed especially brutal. She struck the girl several times when Nancy could not understand what the woman wanted her to do. Clearly these Indians were not gentle masters, Kathleen observed. Her jaw tensed. She would die attempting to escape rather than face being cruelly ruled yet again.

Night fell. After all but the sentry had entered their huts to sleep, Kathleen fought silently against her bonds. But they held securely.

"I'm afraid 'tis useless," Quinn said stoically. "I'm an old man and I knew my death would come soon. However, I had hoped to face it in more comfortable surroundings."

"You mustn't give up," Kathleen encouraged, but her voice lacked conviction. The night wind was cold. Her arms and legs were already numb and her blood was beginning to feel like ice.

Lady Margaret turned her head so she could face Kathleen. "As long as you die with us, I shall not regret my death. Your presence in my son's life has threatened to rob him of the greatness he deserves. My ghost shall dance on your grave."

"I'd hoped that, at least after what we've been through, we would not die enemies," Kathleen replied tiredly. "I've never meant to cause you or your son any unhappiness."

"Unhappiness?" Lady Margaret unleashed a harsh laugh. "Do you call robbing him of tremendous wealth and a place in court mere unhappiness?"

Kathleen felt ill. She would never rob John of a possibility of greatness. "I don't understand," she said stiffly. "I thought Ashford Hall was the extent of his inheritance. I was led to believe he could never hope for more."

"It was through marriage he would have acquired his high place," Lady Margaret explained sharply. "When he was in England, he took a fancy to Lady Andrea Clemens. She is barely twenty and strikingly beautiful. He courted her, but she was coquettish, as is the fashion, and my son is not a man who enjoys such games. They quarreled and he gave up on her. For her part, she decided to consider him a bore and let him go. But after he had sailed for the colonies, she thought better of her actions. She approached my brother and informed him that she would be interested in a marriage to John if the earl could arrange it."

Lady Margaret drew a harsh sigh. "Every moment of each day after my brother's letter arrived, I prayed for my son's safe return so that he could claim his fine future." Her expression blackened. "Then he arrived home with you and all hopes for this excellent marriage were dashed. There have been nights when I almost wish he'd perished upon that pirate ship rather than be saved only to feel honor-bound to you."

Kathleen said nothing. A numbness unrelated to the discomfort of her captivity spread through her. She hated the thought that because of a debt of honor he felt toward her, John was giving up wealth and a place among the powerful. But what was even worse was knowing there was a woman he truly desired...a beautiful young woman with wealth and station in life.

Standing there in the cold, black night, Kathleen experienced a sense of emptiness like none she'd ever known before. Even when her mother had died and left her alone on Captain Thorton's ship, she'd never felt this hollow. On the ship she'd had hope—hope for survival, hope for a life free of the captain and his pirates. But at this moment she had nothing to hope for. Even if she survived, she could not now remain with John. She'd stayed with him because she loved him and honestly thought she could make him as good a wife as any he could find in the colonies. But now that she knew the truth, remaining would be selfish. Even worse, she did not doubt for one moment that he would eventually regret his actions and learn to hate her. That she could not bear.

Standing there as the cold wind whipped about her, she no longer noticed her discomfort. For the first time in her life, she didn't care whether she lived or died.

"Miss James?" Quinn spoke her name with concern.

She started to answer, but the words choked in her throat and she suddenly realized that tears were streaming down her cheeks. Thank goodness it was dark. Her pride refused to allow either Quinn or Lady Margaret to know she'd been silently crying. She coughed to clear her throat, then said stiffly, "What is it?"

"You've not struggled against your bonds for several minutes now," he replied. "I was worried you might be giving up."

"I'm just tired," she lied. She had given up, but she was not ready to admit it aloud.

"We have all grown to depend upon your strength during these trying days," he continued in the same worried tones. An edge of embarrassment entered his voice. "Lady Margaret should not have told you about Lady Andrea, at least not at this moment."

She could handle Lady Margaret's disdain, but her pride refused to allow her to accept Quinn's pity. "I have not given up," she said firmly, then realized she meant it. She would survive these Indians. Then she would set John free and leave Ashford Hall with nary a glance back. Somewhere in this world there was a place where she truly belonged, and she would find it.

Chapter Thirteen

At first Kathleen thought the moonlight was playing tricks on her eyes. Then she saw the Indian sentry being jerked behind a tree. He did not reappear.

"Quinn, Lady Margaret, keep very quiet," she ordered. "Whatever you see, don't speak."

"What's going on?" Lady Margaret demanded, ignoring Kathleen's demand.

"I believe we're being rescued," she replied, "but if you do not keep still, you'll warn the Indians and our rescuers will be killed."

"Please, m'lady, do as she says," Quinn pleaded.

Kathleen heard a resentful hiss from Lady Margaret, but the woman fell silent.

A twig snapped behind Kathleen.

"Be very quiet," a male voice whispered.

Even without being able to see him, Kathleen knew it was John. A knife slashed her bonds and she sank to her knees as her numb legs gave way beneath her.

"Kate." John dropped to his knees beside her and took her in his arms. He had reached the encampment just before dark. When he'd first seen her tied to the tree, he'd felt a rush of relief. Now his panic had returned. "How badly have they hurt you?" he demanded gruffly.

His mere presence gave her strength. "I'm not hurt," she replied, as the heat of his body warmed her. "My legs were just numb." She wanted to stay in his arms for a little longer. This would be the last time she could allow him to hold her. But she knew the others' lives were at stake. "Help your mother and Quinn. I can feel the life coming back into my legs already."

"That's my Kate," he said with a relieved smile. Removing his cloak, he wrapped it around her. Then, after kissing her lightly on the forehead, he released the others.

Rubbing the rest of the numbness out of her legs, Kathleen watched him as he cut Quinn's bonds and then his mother's. There had been a tenderness in his voice that had touched her heart. A part of her wanted to believe he had truly learned to care for her, but she'd not lie to herself. He cared for her as he would care for any of his people, but he didn't love her. He loved an elegant lady with great wealth.

Lady Margaret collapsed with a groan into her son's arms. Moving as silently as possible, he carried her away from the village, with Quinn and Kathleen following close behind.

"Where are the other rescuers, sir?" Quinn asked when John finally came to a halt beside a tree where a lone horse was tethered.

"I'm alone," he replied, as he sat his mother on the ground. Then, taking his bedroll from his horse, he unrolled it and wrapped it around Lady Margaret. "I'm sorry I don't have any extra covering for you," he apologized.

"'Tis enough to have a last chance to fight for my freedom," Quinn replied.

"I am warmed now," Kathleen lied, removing John's cloak and extending it toward Quinn.

Quinn shook his head. "You keep it, Miss James." A warmth entered his voice. "I would not wish to see you catch a chill."

Kathleen could hardly believe her ears. Quinn was actually being kind. A little late, she mused. Still, a part of her was glad.

John heard the exchange with a sense of relief. It would seem that even Quinn had learned to like his Kate. That should make life a great deal easier, he thought. But first they must survive this adventure. Returning his attention to their present situation, he opened a saddlebag, took out a packet of food and began to pass out stale biscuits and beef jerky to the three freed prisoners.

Kathleen couldn't help noticing that even Lady Margaret took the unsavory-looking food without balking. Then she forgot about her ladyship and turned her mind to more important matters. "Is there no one else coming?"

"Perhaps, but I cannot say when," John replied. "Reverend Vales rode to gather men to help while I followed your trail as quickly as possible. I left marks along the way to guide anyone who should come."

"What will we do if they're not here by dawn?" Kathleen questioned between bites. "The moment the Indians discover we're gone, they're certain to come looking for us."

"We must flee immediately," Lady Margaret commanded, rising swiftly to her feet.

It occurred to Kathleen that her ladyship's weakness had vanished quite suddenly. But she had no time to concern herself with Lady Margaret. Anxiously, she looked back in the direction of the Indians' camp. "We can't leave Nancy and the others. The chief might decide to harm them in retribution."

"We cannot save them by ourselves," Lady Margaret argued. "Neither God nor they can blame us for fleeing from these savages."

Ignoring his mother, John turned to Kathleen. "How many able-bodied men are in the village?"

"I saw only three among the women and children when we arrived," she answered. "And I'm sure everyone who could came out to see us. There were nine who brought us here. You dealt with one, which means there are only eleven left. Also, although I don't know if 'tis a help, you should know that the chief understands the King's English."

For a long moment John was silent, then he said, "Most likely they're the remnants of one of the warring tribes. We're lucky their numbers are so few. I've a plan. 'Tis risky but it can work."

"I'm with you, sir," Quinn said.

Kathleen nodded. "I'm with you, too."

John frowned at her. He'd risk himself but he'd not risk her. "Quinn and I will try to save the others," he said tersely. "With the first rays of light, I want you and my mother to take my horse and try to reach any rescuers and bring them back here quickly."

Kathleen's jaw firmed. She'd not leave him. If she were to die trying to rescue Nancy and the others, at least it would be a noble end. "Your mother can go. I'm an expert with a knife, and with me here the odds will be only a little more than three to one."

John scowled. There were times when he wished she were a little less stubborn. "I've no time to argue. I want you where you'll be most safe."

Kathleen's mouth formed a determined line. She would not seek safety when he was in danger. "I'm helping with the rescue."

"You've all lost your wits!" Lady Margaret wailed.

"You must be quiet!" John ordered tersely. For a curt moment he studied Kathleen. "You're a hardheaded woman," he said at last. Knowing that once her mind was set, he could not change it, he added, "I don't like it, but you may stay." To his mother, he said, "Wait here until dawn, then ride for help."

"You must come with me," she insisted. "To remain is foolhardy."

Ignoring her, he turned to Quinn. His voice held no compromise. "If it looks as if my plan will fail, I want you and Kathleen to flee as quickly as possible. Hopefully you will meet with our rescuers before the Indians can find you."

"Yes, Mr. Ashford," Quinn replied. But Kathleen had learned to spot a lie and she knew Quinn had no more intention of leaving John's side than she did.

John sensed this, too. "I want your word, Quinn," he demanded.

Quinn hesitated. "I'm too old to run, sir. You must flee with Miss James."

"I'll be in no position to flee," John replied curtly. His gaze narrowed on Quinn. "I'm counting on you to obey my orders and get Miss James to safety."

"Yes, sir," Quinn replied reluctantly.

"This is madness!" Lady Margaret interjected, but no one paid her any heed.

John armed Quinn with a musket and Kathleen with a pistol and the knife he'd taken from the sentry. "We must work quickly," he said. "We'll need some torches."

While he cut several large branches, Kathleen and Quinn hunted for dry twigs. It wasn't easy finding dry kindling, but they managed to find enough. Kathleen donated her petticoats to be torn into strips and wrapped around the tops of the branches. It seemed that John was always requiring her petticoats for one purpose or another, she mused. But she made no jesting comment to him. There would be no private jokes between them again.

"I wish we had some of the bear grease the Indians are so fond of rubbing themselves with," John said in a hushed whisper as they made their way slowly back toward the village. "I'd be a lot more confident of these torches burning long enough and well enough to carry out this plan."

Kathleen looked at John's taut profile. Fear for him overwhelmed her. She was willing to risk herself, but she could not bear the thought of him dying. "Perhaps your mother is right. Perhaps we should wait," she said anxiously.

John glanced toward her. 'Twas not like his Kate to suggest prudence. "You were correct when you said that by killing the sentry, I placed the others in danger," he replied gruffly. "I'll not lay in safety while they might be harmed. But it would please me greatly if you'd go back and ride with my mother for help."

"I will not," she refused firmly.

"You do seem right at home in the thick of trouble," he muttered. He could not resist. For one brief moment, he had to hold her. Pausing, he laid aside the torches he was carrying and, his hands closing around her upper arms, he drew her to him. Her body warmed him and gave him strength. "I want you to promise me you'll flee with Quinn to safety."

She loved him too much to ever leave his side in the face of danger, but she knew he couldn't do his part well if he was worried about her. "I will," she lied.

For a moment longer he held her, studying her face. Then, kissing her lightly on the forehead, he said gruffly,

"Take care of yourself, Kate," and releasing her abruptly, he again moved toward the village.

You take care of yourself, John, she wished him silently. You have a great deal more to live for than I.

As they reached the perimeter of the village, Kathleen breathed a silent sigh of relief. All was still quiet. Clearly, the dead sentry had not been discovered.

Suddenly Kathleen's breath caught in her lungs. In the faint light cast by the thin slice of crescent moon, she saw someone leaving one of the huts. Nudging John, she pointed toward the moving silhouette and fervently prayed whoever it was would not notice the missing guard. Then she realized that the figure wore a full-skirted dress. "'Tis one of our own," she said with a relieved sigh.

As they watched, the figure made its way stealthy toward the large tree Kathleen, Lady Margaret and Quinn had been tied to.

John approached the tree also. When the figure drew near, he reached out and grabbed her, covering her mouth with his hand. "Be still," he ordered as his captive fought like a wild animal.

Immediately, the girl stilled.

"Don't say a word," he cautioned in low tones as he released her slowly.

But Nancy refused to obey. "Where's Miss James?" she demanded in a harsh whisper the moment she was free.

"I told you to be still," John growled. "'Twould seem you and Kate are definitely cut from the same cloth. Follow me." He led her to where Kathleen and Quinn waited.

"How did you get free?" Kathleen asked, giving Nancy a welcoming hug.

"They didn't bind me. My mistress just warned me with a few blows to the head that if I didn't behave, there'd be more to come. Guess they figured if I did try to run away,

I couldn't find my way back through the marsh or they'd catch me before I got too far," she answered.

"They had posted a sentry," Kathleen informed her. "Most likely, he would have stopped you the moment you tried to leave the hut if John had not taken care of him first."

"And when he did, they would have made an example of you that would have discouraged all the others," John said curtly.

"Well, I couldn't just lie there and wait to see what they was going to do to Miss Kathleen," Nancy replied self-righteously. "I had to try to help her. Friends don't desert friends." Then, looking around, she asked, "Where are the others what come to rescue us?"

Nancy's declaration of friendship warmed Kathleen and renewed her hope that she could find a place for herself where she was truly wanted. But first she must survive this night. "This is all there is," she replied. "We're hoping for help but we can't be certain when it will arrive. We must act on our own."

Nancy frowned. "I ain't real excited about facing those savages again, especially that big one what leads this band of murderers. But I'll help."

"We could use some of their bear grease," John said.

Nancy screwed up her nose in disgust. "That awful smelling stuff?"

"Do you know where we can get some?" Kathleen asked pleadingly.

Nancy nodded. "There's a pot of it in the hut I just came out of."

"Good," John said with satisfaction, then continued grimly, "We don't want them to suspect anything until we're ready. That means you'll have to return to your hut for a while. I'll follow you and bring the grease back here.

When the action begins, if you can, grab a weapon. Even if you can't get hold of one, go stand with Miss James."

"I'll find me a weapon," Nancy replied with determination. Then, very quietly, she, John and Kathleen made their way back to the village. When they reached the edge of the clearing, she stopped to give Kathleen an encouraging hug. "If we get out of this alive, I ain't never going to complain about having Lady Margaret as my mistress again," she promised solemnly. Realizing John had heard her, she gasped. "Sorry, Mr. Ashford."

"It's all right, Nancy," he assured her. "Now go. I'll follow. Just slip the grease out to me and then lay quietly until the action starts."

Kathleen prayed fervently for their safety as she watched the two silhouetted figures moving through the darkened camp. Although it seemed like a lifetime, it was only a few minutes later when John rejoined her and they made their way back to where Quinn waited.

The first rays of dawn were lighting the sky when John walked into the village under a flag of truce.

The women were just leaving their huts to build the central fire. Seeing him, they ran to the hut of their leader. Kathleen watched, keeping herself partly hidden on the edge of the village. In one hand she held a blazing torch and in the other, the pistol, cocked and ready to fire. The knife hung at her waist in its sheath.

"I've come to speak under a flag of truce," John said, addressing the large Indian in a commanding voice.

Kathleen noted that the chief was unarmed, but as the other males came out of their huts, they bore weapons.

The big Indian scanned his village. "Where is the man I left on watch?"

"He is dead," John replied.

Hatred etched itself deeply into the Indian's features. "Then you have not come in peace." He raised his hand and the other males positioned their weapons, ready to strike.

"It was a fair exchange. You killed several of my people," John replied levelly. "And if you do not want to see your village destroyed, your men killed and your women and children left to grieve and suffer, you will listen to what I have to say."

These words were the signal Kathleen had been waiting for. While the big Indian studied John narrowly, she left her sheltered position and went to stand between two of the huts, where the chief could see her. She could almost feel death brushing John's shoulder as the Indians surrounding him held their weapons at the ready. She would not let him die easily!

Ignoring all the others, John continued to regard the chief levelly. "If I fall, my men will immediately set fire to your huts, then open fire on you. The harshest portion of winter is yet to come. Your women and children will be without shelter and without men to protect them."

"I see only one woman," the chief mocked him.

"She is worth ten men," John assured him. "But she isn't the only one who stands with me." He nodded toward the far side of the village, where Quinn had moved into position. He, too, held a torch in one hand and a pistol in the other. The musket lay at his feet, primed and ready.

Kathleen saw a movement behind the hut near which she stood and her muscles tensed, prepared to do battle.

"'Tis me, Miss James," Nancy said, coming to stand beside her. "I had to knock my mistress on her head, but she deserved it. That savage tried to throw hot coals in my lap while those heathen children laughed." Apology entered her voice. "I couldn't get no weapon, though. My master keeps his snug with him."

"Those torches will be your weapon," Kathleen said, nodding toward two torches that lay ready on the ground. "Light them with mine and go stand between two huts."

Quickly, Nancy obeyed.

The big Indian scowled as he caught sight of Nancy taking her position. He shouted an order, and Janet, Sally and Mrs. Oats were grabbed by the women standing near them. Adam had seen what was happening and was trying to make his way to the edge of the village to join Quinn. But one of the savages spotted him and grabbed him, holding a knife to his throat.

"We'll slay the remaining prisoners if you do not surrender," the chief threatened.

"If we surrender, we shall all die, either during this day from torture or in the future from being worked like animals until we drop from starvation or exhaustion," John replied grimly. "We are not fools. We will not surrender, and if you harm one of the prisoners, we will set fire to your huts and kill as many of you as we can before we meet our doom. I am willing to make you a bargain. You may keep most of the food you stole. In exchange you will allow us safe passage home. We will require the return of our cloaks and coats and a small amount of food to maintain us on our journey. Also, to ensure our safe passage, I must ask you to accompany us as far as the Rappahannock. When we are safely across, you will be released."

"You speak bravely," the Indian replied with amusement. "But I do not think it necessary for me to accept your bargain. There are many more of us than there are of you. Our weapons are as deadly as yours and we can put out the fires."

"I've more men coming," John pointed out. "They should be here by midday. If they arrive and find us dead, they will surely kill all of you, including your women and children."

The chief eyed him dubiously. "If you have more men coming, why did you not wait for them?"

"It was possible that you intended to kill the three you had tied to the tree. I could not allow that to happen," John replied.

The chief scowled and shook his head. "And if I let you live, your men will come and kill us anyway. It is better to kill you now than to fight you later."

"If you spare me and my people, I will spare you and yours," John said.

The chief looked indecisive. "You would give me your word, you would not return and attack us nor send others?"

"You have my word," John replied.

"And how am I to know you are a man of your word?" the chief demanded suspiciously.

John met the savage's gaze with level assurance. "I am an honorable man. We could have, under the cover of night, burned your village and killed your men as they ran from their huts."

Looking past John, the Indian let his gaze travel over the women and children, anxiety for them showing on his face. Then his jaw hardened with decision. "You shall have your safe passage."

Kathleen breathed a sigh of relief but, in accordance with John's instructions, she and Quinn continued to stand at the ready. While it seemed as if they had won, it could be a trick. Nancy took her cue from them and also remained in position to strike.

The chief scowled. "You must tell your people to lay aside their torches," he ordered John gruffly.

"They will remain as they are until the rest of my people are freed, and we have been given our food and are ready to leave your village," John replied.

His scowl deepening, the chief gave orders, and within a very short while, the remaining captives along with the required supplies were gathered beside John.

As Adam was released, he reached toward the weapons being held by one of the nearby warriors. "I'll just have my musket and knife back," he demanded.

The Indian stepped back and prepared to fight.

"We've given you what you required," the chief addressed John with authority. "The weapons remain ours."

"I agreed only to allow you to keep the food," John replied.

The chief scowled. "We bargained for the food and the captives. There was no mention of weapons. They will remain ours."

"No." John's voice held no compromise. "You have the weapons you stole from the dead bodies of my people. That musket and knife will be returned to their owner."

The chief looked disgruntled, and Kathleen held her breath and prayed John had not gone too far. Then the Indian gave an order and the brave surrendered the weapons to Adam. Kathleen breathed a sigh of relief.

As John and the others filed out of the village, the chief in their midst, Kathleen nodded for Nancy to follow. Dropping her torches on open ground near the central fire, Nancy obeyed. Quinn nodded for Kathleen to follow. Dropping her torch near Nancy's, she walked to the edge of the village. Then, drawing the knife, she waited with pistol in one hand and knife in the other for Quinn to join her.

"Do you trust them, Miss James?" he asked as they started after the others.

"No," she answered. She knew the looks she had seen in the Indians' eyes well. "If they thought they could kill us without harming their chief, they would."

Quinn nodded. "I had the same feeling, miss."

Apparently John also did not fully trust them. "Quinn, guard the rear and keep alert," he ordered from the head of the column as the tiny band moved toward the clearing where he'd left Lady Margaret.

Her ladyship and the horse were not there. At least she had followed her instructions and gone for help, Kathleen thought with relief.

As they made their way along the path through the marsh, Kathleen studied the chief. He moved with proud dignity. Again she saw the hatred in his eyes and it frightened her. Catching up with John, she asked, "Do you think he agreed to allow us to leave merely to get us away from his village?"

"I don't know," he replied. "There was a time when an honorable agreement could be kept between the colonists and the Indians. But such truces are uncertain now. It would be best to keep a close eye on our path."

Kathleen looked around and thanked providence that it was winter. At least the underbrush was not thick and the leaves were gone from the trees. It would be difficult for the Indians to surround them without being seen.

They reached the edge of the marsh around noon. The solid ground felt good under Kathleen's feet. Still, their progress was slow. Kathleen saw her own exhaustion mirrored in the faces of her companions.

It was Mrs. Oats who finally could go no farther. Sinking onto a boulder, she said with tired apology, "I just can't make my legs move another step, Mr. Ashford."

"If you'll come just a bit farther, I'll look for a safe shelter for the night," he coaxed.

She rose, but her legs wobbled. "And where is the Reverend Vales and the men he was supposed to bring to rescue us?" she demanded, her tiredness causing her temper to flare.

"I'm sure they will reach us soon," John said encouragingly. "My mother rode ahead to hurry them along." Seeing the weakness of Mrs. Oats's limbs, he added with resignation, "We'll spend the night here."

"We should be fairly safe," Janet said, trying to sound hopeful as she glanced over her shoulder in the direction from which they had come. "After all, we do have their chief as our hostage."

Kathleen thought of her failed escape attempts from the pirates and the scars that crisscrossed her back. "It is best to stay on the alert when fleeing from an enemy," she cautioned. She saw John looking her way and knew he, too, was thinking of her past. Fighting down an embarrassed flush, she began to gather wood.

A wave of guilt washed over John as he watched her. He had failed in his promise to protect her.

Night fell and they all sat in a tight circle near the fire.

"Don't you think it might be a bit safer if you was to bind the chief's hands and feet?" Adam suggested to John, regarding the Indian distrustfully.

The chief, who had not uttered one sound since they left his camp, turned to John. "I have given my word I would remain your hostage until you have crossed the river," he said with stoic dignity.

John nodded and made no move to act on Adam's suggestion.

Kathleen could not help feeling John was perhaps behaving foolishly, but she held her tongue.

"I'll take the first watch," John said as they finished eating their meager repast.

The others gave no argument. Immediately, they each curled up and dozed, except for Kathleen and the Indian. The chief continued to sit in a grim, proud silence. Kathleen did lie down, but she couldn't sleep. Even in her exhausted state, she watched John covertly. Soon she would be parting from him forever. She told herself she was behaving foolishly. The sooner she forgot him, the better. Still, she was not willing to give up one moment's sight of him.

As if he could feel her watching him, he turned and looked toward where she lay. She started to turn away, afraid that in a moment of weakness she might allow her true feelings to show. But as she began to move, in the dimness behind him she thought she saw the silhouetted outline of a man. Then she knew she had. She sprang to her feet. But before she could let her knife fly, the chief rose and placed himself between John and the stalking shadow.

With authority, the chief called out an order in his native tongue, and the shadowy figure along with others that had been moving toward Kathleen and her sleeping companions vanished back into the woods.

"I gave my word that you would have safe passage," the Indian said simply, while Kathleen watched him mutely.

"You are a man of honor," John asserted. He breathed a tired sigh. "There is very little trust left between your people and mine. But I will not willingly fuel the fires of hatred that have begun to burn between us. I accept your word that you will cause us no harm during the remainder of our journey. You are free to go to your people."

For a long moment the chief studied John in silence. Then he said solemnly, "May your journey be swift." In the next instant, he had vanished into the woods.

"Do you think that was truly wise, Mr. Ashford?" Adam questioned.

Turning around, Kathleen discovered the rest of their party, all awake and all standing, peering out into the woods around them as if they expected the Indians to attack again at any moment. "Go back to sleep," she said simply. "We've a great deal of distance to cover tomorrow."

Still looking uncertain, they obeyed.

"With your permission I will build up the fire before I sleep," John said with a hint of amusement in his voice. The way his people obeyed her pleased him. He no longer needed to worry about her position in his home. Clearly, they would willingly accept her as their mistress.

Kathleen flushed as she realized she'd spoken as if she were in command. "You have my permission," she replied, unable to resist one final little jest between them. But as she lay back down, she felt no joy. Again, she could not resist covertly watching him. Her jaw set in a resolute line. When they reached Ashford Hall it would be her turn to do the honorable thing and set him free.

Chapter Fourteen

By noon the next day the survivors met with the band of men who had set out to aid John with their rescue. The Reverend Vales was not with them. The men informed John that they had met with Lady Margaret the day before. She had looked so exhausted and worn that, conceding to her wish, the reverend had escorted her back to Ashford Hall while the rest of their number continued in search of John and the others. "But the reverend did send a message," one of the men added. "He said to tell you that he would await your return."

John nodded with grim satisfaction while a lump formed in Kathleen's throat.

Four days later they arrived back at Ashford Hall to find Lady Margaret in command. The bodies of the dead had been buried with proper ceremony and with the help of servants on loan from the neighboring estate; the household was again functioning normally.

John ordered the rescued servants to their rooms to rest and recuperate from their adventures. "And now you will inform the reverend that Kathleen and I will be waiting for him in my study," he instructed his mother.

"Really, John, the man's exhausted. He could barely make it through the burial ceremonies," Lady Margaret argued. Her gaze raked over Kathleen. "And surely Kathleen would prefer to take a bit of time to clean herself." Admonition entered her voice as she returned her attention to her son. "And you should see that your home is back in order before all else."

"Seeing that all in my home is in order is precisely what I intend to do," he replied curtly. "Now fetch the reverend. Kathleen and I will await him in the study."

Kathleen's stomach had knotted when he'd first instructed his mother to fetch Reverend Vales. Now the knot was so tight she could hardly breathe. She'd planned to tell John as quickly as possible of her intention to leave, but she had hoped for a few more moments to rest and compose herself. However, no delay would have made this any easier. Her shoulders straightened resolutely as she preceded him into his study. She waited until the door was closed, then said, "There will be no wedding this day."

John scowled. He knew she was tired. And he guessed she would prefer to be rested and clean for her wedding, as most women would. But he was tired also and his patience was thin. "I want to lay with you, Kate, and I don't have the strength or the will to go from bed to bed tonight merely to maintain the proprieties. You are my wife. This wedding is a mere formality to avoid scandalous gossip."

She ached to have his arms around her but knew that could never be again. She faced him levelly. "I am not your wife. In my mind there was nothing legal or binding about the marriage aboard Captain Thorton's ship." She took a deep breath. The next words were the hardest she'd ever spoken. "And I do not want to be your wife."

Her words cut like a knife. Challenge flashed in his eyes. "I find that hard to believe, considering the nights we've spent together." He moved toward her, intending to prove his point.

Knowing her weakness for him, Kathleen backed away, placing the chair between them. "I do not deny that I find your lovemaking pleasurable," she admitted. "But I have spent too many years of my life in an entrapment. I will not enter another so readily. I want my freedom to go where I will, do what I please."

Anger etched itself into John's features. "You would consider marriage to me an entrapment?"

It was an entrapment, not for her but for him. "Yes," she answered honestly.

For a long moment he regarded her in silence. He felt as if she had driven a knife into him and was now twisting it. *You knew it was foolish to fall in love,* he chided himself. "And where is it you wish to go and what is it you wish to do?" he asked stiffly.

"I think I shall go to Jamestown," she said with forced enthusiasm. Lying to his face was difficult. Turning away, she wandered to a window and looked out. "I do not relish another encounter with savage Indians. I shall feel safer there. Besides, I've always thought I'd like the excitement of living in a town." Inside, she felt as if she was being ripped apart. If circumstances were different, she would have willingly lived in a cave if she could be with John. But he had an opportunity to marry a woman he would have chosen for himself and to greatly improve his position in life, and she would not stand in his way. "I shall find work there and be my own mistress." Holding herself under tight control, she turned back toward him.

The anger John was feeling grew stronger. He was furious with himself for having learned to care so deeply for her. But he could not fault her for wanting to seek a place of safety. He had failed to protect her. A coldness spread through him. He would not attempt to hold her against her will. That would only cause them both misery. *It is my* pride that is hurt the most, he assured himself. Once she is gone, she will be easily forgotten. A look of cool detachment spread over his face. "I've offered you what my honor insisted was right. If you don't wish to accept, I'll not stand in your way. When would you like to leave?"

Pain flowed through her. He showed no grief at her leaving. Grudgingly she realized she had hoped he would tell her he cared for her and beg her to stay. Fool! she chided herself. You've always known the truth. His insistence upon their marriage had always been based on his sense of duty and obligation. Clearly, he would be relieved to be rid of her. He was probably already making his plans to marry Lady Andrea Clemens. "I shall leave tomorrow," she replied.

"Fine," he agreed with no argument. "I'll arrange for an escort and have a horse readied for you."

She had known it would hurt to face the raw truth of his feelings for her, but she had not known how much. Desperate to be free of his company, she said stiffly, "Thank you," and crossing the room with dignity, she left.

Once in the hall, she quickened her steps until she reached her own rooms. She entered, locked the door behind her and stood leaning against it. "I will not cry," she told herself. "I have known all along he did not honestly care for me." But in spite of her determination, the tears began to flow. Angrily, she brushed them away. She would find a man who loved her and she would think of John Ashford no longer.

In his study, John paced the floor, calling himself the worst kind of fool. The sooner she was gone the better, he told himself. Still, he owed her a great debt. He stopped his pacing. "And as payment I shall do what I can to see that she has a good start in her new life," he swore in a low growl. His jaw firmed. "And when this duty is done, I will think of her no longer."

Kathleen forced herself to take a deep breath. Crying was a waste of time, she admonished herself. A new life awaited her. It was time to find her place in the world. Determination glistening in her eyes, she looked down at her dress. It was ripped and dirty. Discarding it, she cleaned herself. Then, dressing in a smock, she began to gather her belongings together. She would have preferred to have left with only the clothing in which she had arrived, but her pride was forced to give way to practicality. She would take a few of the clothes she and Nancy had made. After she found a job and began earning wages, she would repay John for them.

A knock sounded on her door. "I don't wish to be disturbed," she called out.

"Mr. Ashford asked me to bring these up to you, miss," an unfamiliar woman's voice called back.

Frowning, Kathleen tossed a shawl around her shoulders, then went to the door. On the other side was one of the borrowed servants holding two parchment-wrapped bundles. "He said you was to have these, miss," the girl said, entering and placing the bundles on a chair. Spotting Kathleen's much-worn shoes on the floor near the bed, the girl picked them up. "And he said I was to dispose of these."

Kathleen had been staring at the packages. She knew without opening them what they contained. Before she could pull her thoughts away, and protest about the girl taking her old shoes, the maid was gone.

For a long moment after she was alone, Kathleen continued to stare at the two packages. Then, slowly, she approached and untied them. Touching the soft leather tops of the shoes inside, she remembered the way the quill had tickled when John had outlined her foot. She also remembered the passion his touch had ignited.

"You knew your desire for him was dangerously strong," she chided herself.

She considered leaving the shoes behind, but that would be not only impractical but embarrassing. The maid had already taken her old ones, and to insist they be brought back would look foolish. They were more holes than leather. She would take one pair of the new shoes, and when she had saved enough, she would send John payment for both the clothing and the shoes.

Completing her packing, she sat down on the bed and let her gaze travel around the room. Bittersweet memories of nights spent with John flooded her mind. Stop this! she ordered herself. He never cared for you. You were simply an entertainment. Glancing at the clock, she realized it was almost time for supper. Her stomach knotted at the thought of facing him. No one would miss her if she chose to eat in her room, she decided, and ringing for the maid, asked to have her meal brought to her.

When the food came, she had no appetite but made herself eat anyway. She would need her strength. After she left Ashford Hall on the morrow, she could not be certain where her next meal would be coming from.

She had just finished eating when a knock sounded on the door. Thinking it was the maid coming to take the tray, she called, "Enter."

"I apologize for this intrusion."

Kathleen's back stiffened at the sound of Lady Margaret's voice. Pulling the shawl more closely around her, she rose and curtsied.

Lady Margaret studied Kathleen suspiciously. "My son tells me there is to be no wedding. He tells me you are leaving for Jamestown tomorrow to seek your own way in the world.''

''That is correct,'' Kathleen confirmed.

Lady Margaret regarded her coldly. ''If this is some game you are playing, it will not work. He will not come after you. I won't allow it.'' A confident smile tilted the corners of Lady Margaret's mouth. ''He is already making plans for his future and they do not include you.''

In her mind Kathleen pictured John at his desk, writing a beseeching letter to Lady Andrea Clemens and declaring his deep regard for her. Kathleen's back stiffened with pride. ''I do not expect or want him to come looking for me.'' Her words carried the strong conviction of honesty. Just the thought of seeing him again was painful. If she could do it with dignity, she would leave this house without ever setting eyes on him again.

Lady Margaret shook her head in disbelief. ''I do not understand you. You can never hope to make a better match than marrying my son.''

Kathleen's jaw tensed. ''I told you I never wanted to harm your son. Now that I know the full truth, I could never allow him to make such a sacrifice.''

Lady Margaret studied Kathleen thoughtfully. ''If that is true, I am grateful, for my son's sake,'' she said, still not looking totally convinced.

''It is not a selfless act,'' Kathleen assured her. ''I know he would eventually regret his gallantry and learn to hate our marriage. And I do not want a marriage with anger in it. I want a marriage where I will be honestly cared for.''

Lady Margaret drew a relieved breath. ''You are making the right decision, my dear,'' she said. Reaching into the small purse she carried, she drew out a bag of coins. ''I want you to have this.''

Kathleen pulled the shawl more tightly around herself. "I do not want your gold. You have given me shelter and clothing. That is enough."

"Please." Lady Margaret continued to extend the bag toward Kathleen.

"No." Kathleen refused, adding with a curt note of dismissal, "I am very tired and I want to get an early start in the morning. I would greatly appreciate it if you would leave me now."

Even Kathleen's brusqueness didn't erase the smile from Lady Margaret's face. "Yes, dear," she replied sweetly, returning the bag of coins to her purse. Glancing toward the bed, where Kathleen had bundled her clothing together with string, she said, "I shall send you up a satchel. You can at least accept that as a parting gift." Then, adding a cheerful "Good night," she left.

Going down the hall, Lady Margaret could not keep from humming. Her prayers had been answered. She could hardly believe her good fortune. Even now she was finding it difficult to believe Kathleen James was willing to give up so much. "But she has, and she will never get the chance to get it back," Lady Margaret vowed. "Once she is gone, I will see that John is never bothered by her again." Her eyes glistened with excitement. "And now I must apply myself to the matchmaking between my son and Lady Andrea. It will be so good to be in England again."

Later that night, as she crawled into bed, Kathleen experienced a strong wave of loneliness. Scowling, she said tersely to herself, "I must think of this as a new beginning, a new adventure," and closing her eyes, she fell into a restless sleep.

The next morning dawned clear and bright. Unwilling to face John over breakfast, Kathleen chose not to eat.

Instead, she dressed, then sought out Quinn and informed him she wanted to leave as soon as arrangements were completed.

"I am sorry you're leaving, miss. We here at Ashford Hall owe you a great deal," he said with sincerity. "But 'tis all for the best," he added in a knowing voice. "Sadness always follows when one marries out of one's station."

"In this instance, at least, you are quite correct," Kathleen replied, again remembering how quickly and easily John had agreed to her departure.

Returning to her room to wait, she took the knife and sheath from it's hiding place beneath her pillow and tied it to her leg. She was to be on her own again and she would need to provide her own protection.

When her horse and escort were ready, it was Janet who came to fetch her.

"Is Nancy ill?" she asked, wanting to have a moment to bid the girl goodbye.

"No, miss, she's right busy at the moment," Janet replied, adding with a note of excitement, "She's packing. As payment for her bravery in facing the Indians, the master has declared an end to her tenure. She's been freed to go her own way."

"I was hoping I might travel with you, miss, to Jamestown," Nancy said, coming up behind Janet, her own satchel in hand. "Mr. Ashford says he'll supply me with a horse if you say 'tis all right."

Kathleen suddenly didn't feel so alone. The thought that she would have a friend by her side as she set out to begin her new life lightened her heart. "Of course, you can travel with me. I would be most grateful for the company."

Nancy smiled brightly. "I'll just go wait for you outside," she said, and in the next instant she was gone.

"I'll take your bag, miss." Janet reached for Kathleen's satchel. As Kathleen gave it to her, she added, "I'm real glad Nancy will be traveling with you. I worry about her sometimes, I do."

"I shall look after her," Kathleen promised, pleased to have something other than her memories of John to occupy her mind during the journey.

"I know you will, miss," Janet replied with a friendly smile. Then, becoming businesslike, she said, "You run along now. I'll be bringing your bag down behind you."

John and Lady Margaret were standing in the entrance hall waiting to bid Kathleen a speedy journey.

As they stepped out onto the porch, John said, "I have chosen saddles for you and Nancy that may make your journey a little longer, but you will arrive in style."

Kathleen glanced toward the horses to discover that three had been saddled, two with sidesaddles. Recalling the looks of disapproval she had received upon her first adventure in riding, she nodded her consent to his choice.

"Adam will escort you and Nancy to Jamestown," John finished, explaining the presence of the third horse.

Kathleen was relieved that John had not felt duty-bound to offer his company for the journey. "Thank you for your thoughtfulness," she said.

"And I thank you for my life, Miss Kathleen James," he replied, bowing deeply before her. Again he assured himself that once she was gone she would be easily forgotten.

Kathleen wondered if he was thanking her for saving him from Joseph Yates's knife or for giving him his freedom to marry whom he chose and better himself in the process. Both, she decided. Aloud, she said with cool dignity, "I owe you my life as many times as you might feel you owe me yours."

"Then please accept this gift in memory of our adventures together," he urged with formal politeness. This would end his duty to her, he told himself, and free him from the bond that connected them.

Kathleen was having a difficult enough time facing this parting. She wanted nothing more to remember him by. But she saw Quinn standing at a respectful distance, and Janet, Nancy and Adam watching from near the two packhorses. It would be terrible manners for her to refuse, she knew. Even more, she did not want John to guess the anguish her leaving was causing her. "Thank you," she said, accepting the small package.

"May your journey take you to that which you seek the most," he said and bowed once again. She had chosen the path she wished to follow and he did hope the best for her. And now I shall return to the path I had planned to follow before Miss James entered my life, he added to himself.

Kathleen performed a quick curtsy to Lady Margaret and then to him. After which, she walked with dignity to her waiting horse. Adam had finished tying her satchel to the least loaded of the two pack animals. Now he approached her and gave her a hand into the saddle. Then, mounting his own horse, he led the way down the path away from Ashford Hall.

Against her will, Kathleen looked back, but only Quinn and Janet had remained on the porch to watch them leave. It is finished, she told herself with finality.

"What'd he give you, miss?" Nancy asked excitedly, positioning her horse beside Kathleen's.

Well, not quite finished, Kathleen corrected. She secured her reins around her wrist, then took the package from her purse. Removing the covering, she found a small, ornately carved wooden box.

Nancy's eyes danced with curiosity. "Open it, miss," she urged.

Obeying, Kathleen found a gold brooch inside. It was in the shape of a sword, with a small sapphire and two small rubies decorating the handle.

"Why, it actually pulls out," Nancy noted with glee as Kathleen started to lift the brooch by the handle and the tiny sword came out of its gold casing.

There was a note in the box also. Opening it, Kathleen read:

"Miss James,
  My father would have greatly admired you. He would have called you a first-rate soldier. I hope you find whatever it is you seek, and always remember to sleep with your shoes on when you are not certain you are among friends.

John"

"What a curious admonition," Nancy said with a puzzled frown.

Kathleen remained silent as she lifted her foot slightly. She had been too preoccupied this morning to notice anything unusual when she'd put on the new shoes. But now she realized that they were heavier than most. She knew without even looking that the heels were hollow and there was gold inside. It was his way of repaying what he considered a debt of honor, and breathing a tired sigh, she accepted it as such. If he wished to see them as two comrades in arms parting company, then so be it. She didn't like accepting his gift of gold, but at the moment she realized it would be foolish to refuse it. Someday, when she was established in her new life, she would repay him and the slate would be wiped clean once and for all.

"Well, we won't be wanting for food," Nancy was saying, her mind gone to other subjects now that her curiosity regarding the gift had been satisfied. "Mrs. Oats has sent along two right nice-sized parcels."

Kathleen could not help smiling at Nancy's enthusiasm. Again she felt grateful for the girl's company. But the smile faded as Kathleen returned the tiny bejeweled sword to it's case. There was one more duty she felt she owed John.

Nancy was rattling on about how excited she was to be going back to Jamestown. "I only got to see it a bit when I first arrived in the colonies," she was saying. "The ship what I came on docked there. But it weren't but a day after we'd reached port that the captain held an auction. And he didn't let us leave the ship aforehand, neither. Anyway, Mr. Ashford's solicitor bought my indenture in Mr. Ashford's name, and before I knew what was happening I was on my way to Ashford Hall. Didn't have hardly a moment to see what the town was like."

Kathleen let the girl talk until they were well away from Ashford Hall, then, motioning Nancy to follow, she kicked her horse into a faster gait and drew up alongside Adam. "Would you please stop for a moment?" she requested.

"Something I can do fur you, miss?" he asked politely, reining in his horse.

Kathleen fought down an embarrassed flush. "There's a favor I must ask of both you and Nancy."

"A favor?" Nancy questioned, reining her horse in next to Kathleen's.

"I think it would be best for all concerned if neither of you mentioned my connection to Mr. Ashford," Kathleen explained evenly. "Neither he nor I enjoy being the brunt of gossip, and any mention of our broken engage-

ment would surely bring that upon us. So I would ask you
to remain totally discreet about the matter.''

"Lady Margaret done told all of us what serves her and
Mr. Ashford the same thing," Adam said, while Nancy
nodded in the affirmative. "You can count on us, miss.
Discreet is what we'll be."

Kathleen rewarded them with a grateful smile before her
jaw tensed. She didn't like the next request she was going
to make, but she felt it had to be done. She wanted to take
no chance of bringing scandal to John's name. He had
done the honorable thing by her and she would do the
honorable thing by him. She felt confident Lady Margaret would control the gossip along the Rappahannock
and among John's friends who might have learned of the
engagement. People who crossed her ladyship discovered
quickly it could be very uncomfortable, but even more,
John was well liked, and those who knew him would not
want to cause him any grief.

For her part, Kathleen was determined not to carry the
gossip to Jamestown. "I hate to ask you to lie for me. But
I feel it would be best for Mr. Ashford and myself if you
simply didn't mention that I'd been at Ashford Hall at all.
If it was known I was there, people would want to know
why, and that would only lead to a barrage of questions.
If anyone should ask about my origins, you could say you
met me along the road and invited me to ride with your
party."

Adam looked a bit confused, but he nodded in the affirmative. "Yes, ma'am, if that's what you'd like. Nancy
and me feels we owe our lives to you, miss. And it ain't
exactly a lie. You did join us along the road—it were just
at the beginning of our journey and not in the middle."

Kathleen breathed a sigh of relief. "Thank you."

Acknowledging her words with a nod, Adam flicked his reins, and leading the packhorses, he again started them moving toward Jamestown.

Kathleen paced her animal to give the pack animals plenty of room.

Again drawing her horse up beside Kathleen's, Nancy studied her former mistress with a frown. "I'll do as you ask, miss, but I don't really understand any of this."

"I am merely trying to keep scandal from touching either Mr. Ashford or myself," Kathleen explained tightly. "You know how people talk. If they found out I had been engaged to Mr. Ashford, they would spend hours speculating as to why the engagement was broken."

But Nancy continued to frown. "What I really don't understand, miss, is why you broke your engagement. I know you care for Mr. Ashford. I've seen the way you look at him when you think no one is noticing. And while he's a bit overbearing for my taste, he made a good match for you."

"You are making too much of a few glances," Kathleen admonished curtly.

Nancy shook her head. "It still don't make any sense to me. He was a fine match."

"I did what had to be done and I don't wish to discuss this matter any further," Kathleen said with finality.

"I never thought you'd be one to give in to Lady Margaret," Nancy persisted, with a sad shake of her head.

Kathleen ignored this remark. She had no intention of letting Nancy goad her into divulging anything she did not wish to divulge. Falling silent, she concentrated on the road ahead. This should feel like a welcome adventure, she told herself, angry that she could not work up some enthusiasm. John had been glad to see her go. Pride demanded that she should be equally happy. At least I won't have to endure Lady Margaret as a mother-in-law, she reasoned.

"I didn't mean to offend you, miss," Nancy apologized worriedly. "I know I can be a real trial sometimes. I can never seem to control my curiosity."

"I'm not offended," Kathleen replied, adding, "And, please, you must call me Kathleen. We're on equal footing now and I'd like to think of you as my friend as well as a traveling companion."

"I'd like that too, miss," Nancy replied brightly.

The journey to Jamestown took several days. The roads, which were not good in the best of weather, were at their worst during these winter months. There were no public lodgings along the major portion of their route. For the most part, they were forced to seek shelter and food at private residences.

John had given Adam enough gold to see that they were always welcomed, housed and fed. And upon opening her satchel for the first time, Kathleen also discovered that it now contained all of the clothing that had been made for her and the second pair of shoes. A part of her wanted to think that this had been done out of kindness, but another part couldn't help feeling that it had been done because the master and mistress of Ashford Hall wanted nothing to remind them of her presence in their home. If this was so, she couldn't blame them. She had come very near to ruining John's life.

The journey also gave Kathleen the opportunity to formulate a story as to her history, and Nancy and Adam time to adapt to it. In determining what she would say, Kathleen decided she could not mention Captain Thorton's ship. That would surely connect her with John. And in truth, she did not relish admitting to having spent so many years in the pirate's company. Many, she knew, would think as Lady Margaret had, that Kathleen had been sorely used. Thus, while they might pity her, her reputation would be blemished. This was to be a new beginning, she reminded herself. And had she not suffered enough? Did she not deserve a truly fresh start? Concluding that she did, she devised a new past for herself, keeping it as simple as possible.

The only truth Kathleen felt comfortable allowing herself to admit was that her parents had been killed by pirates. However, she chose to claim that she and they had been living in a cabin in an isolated area of Carolina, and that her parents' deaths had occurred during a shore raid. To explain her survival, she decided to say that she'd been out for a walk. She had heard gunfire and raced back, but had stopped abruptly at the edge of the clearing. From there she had seen her parents lying dead and the pirates looting their cabin, taking what food and other possessions interested them. Realizing she could do nothing, she'd hidden in the woods. When the pirates left, she'd buried her parents, packed what she could carry and fled north, going inland as far as possible because she so feared seeing pirates again. But inland she learned of the Indians and decided that she would feel safest in a town. She had been making her way to Jamestown in hopes of finding work when Nancy and Adam had been kind enough to offer her their companionship. Finally, to provide herself with a way of escaping having to produce more exact details of her journey or her parents, she chose to say that she found it all too difficult to speak of at any great length.

It was a cold, overcast day when they finally arrived in Jamestown. Rain mingled with sleet intermittently.

"Me mum used to say it was good luck to arrive at a place in the rain," Nancy said, as usual trying to find a bright side even to bad weather. "I wonder if that counts when you arrive the second time, if you wasn't in the place long the first time."

"I'm sure it does," Kathleen replied, feeling suddenly very nervous as Adam brought them to a halt in front of a small brick house near the edge of town. Her new life was actually beginning, and she hoped fervently the fates would smile upon her this time.

"This must be Mistress McGee's place," Nancy said. "Mr. Ashford said I should stay here. He says the rooms are clean and she don't serve rotten meat. If you'd like, we could share a room. Mr. Ashford gave me some money to see me through 'til I find work. If you don't have any coin of your own, I could loan you a bit until you find work, too."

"I'd enjoy sharing a room with you," Kathleen replied, adding, "and I've a bit of money, so I can pay my own way."

Nancy smiled with pleasure and the two women dismounted and entered Mistress McGee's boardinghouse together.

Adam unloaded the packhorses and carried their belongings inside. Then, bidding them a fond but polite farewell, he headed toward the inn where he would spend the night before beginning his journey back.

Late that night, lying in bed in the small room that was now their new home, Kathleen looked out the window at the midnight sky. The weather had cleared and the waxing moon was dimming the brightest stars. Except for the money she planned to pay back to him someday, all of her ties with Jonathan Ashford were now severed. Ever since this journey had begun, she had willed herself not to think of him, yet as she lay there, she found herself longing for him.

Stupid fool! she berated herself. He certainly wasn't lying in his bed longing for her. No doubt he was thinking of Lady Andrea Clemens and feeling impatient to be back in England.

Angrily she shoved him from her mind. This was a new beginning and all that was past was gone forever. On the morrow she would find work, and a new and wonderful future would open up for her. With this thought firmly in mind, she closed her eyes and went to sleep.

Chapter Fifteen

By the end of her first week in Jamestown, Kathleen was ready to believe in Nancy's mother's prediction of luck. Nancy had found work with Mistress Osburn, a seamstress, and Kathleen had found work as a serving maid in one of the nicer taverns. Her new life was going very well, indeed.

After delivering two tankards of ale to the table by the fire, Kathleen paused and glanced around the room to see if any of her other customers required her immediate service. From his table in the corner, Mr. Dermot waved her over. He was about John's age and build. His hair, like John's, was brown and hung in rich, full waves. But that was where the similarity ended. His eyes were blue and he was a quiet, solemn man who rarely smiled or showed a sense of humor. From others at the tavern, she knew he'd come to Jamestown five years earlier with a young bride and had opened a blacksmith shop. His wife had died of a fever only months after their arrival. Since then, he'd lived alone. He was considered a fine craftsman and was well respected in the community. "I'd like another dish of stew and a fresh pint of ale," he requested when she approached his table.

He is either very brave or has lost his sense of taste, Kathleen thought as she picked up his bowl and mug and carried them toward the kitchen. The cook had fallen ill that morning and Mistress Neils, the tavern owner's wife, had taken over the kitchen. While Mrs. Neils was a pleasant person and skillful in many ways, it was rumored that Mr. Neils had gone into the tavern business to escape her cooking. From the smell of the meal tonight, Kathleen believed it. Several customers had asked her if she thought the cook would be well on the morrow, leaving the distinct impression they'd not be returning until Mrs. Neils was once again out of the kitchen. But Mr. Dermot was actually ordering a second plate.

"That lad must have a stomach of iron," Mr. Neils said, watching his wife refill Mr. Dermot's plate.

Mrs. Neils glanced toward him haughtily, then gave Kathleen a warm smile. "'Tis love, I'm thinking. You didn't mind my cookin' when you was courting me, Mr. Neils, and Mr. Dermot ain't never been a regular customer here 'til Kathleen come to work fur us. I'm thinking he's not even tastin' his food."

Mr. Neils laughed and gave his wife a playful pat on her bottom. "Could be you've got a point there, me love."

Mrs. Neils flushed with pleasure as she gave her husband a coquettish smile. Then, turning to Kathleen, she said, "Mr. Dermot ain't a bad match. He'd be a right good provider. People say he turns out the best nails around and he does a fine latch and hinge."

"He's right good with any bit of ironwork what needs making," Mr. Neils interjected.

Mrs. Neils nodded vigorously, then added in a motherly tone, "I know he seems a bit boring, but he's a good man with high standing in the church."

Kathleen accepted this bit of matchmaking with a friendly but noncommittal smile. She knew she should make an effort to be interested in other men, but every time she did, John's image would come into her mind.

"Best get Mr. Dermot to pay for this second serving before he eats it," Mr. Neils suggested with a laugh as she started toward the door. "We might have to cart him off to the doctor afterward."

"You look healthy enough," Mrs. Neils remarked, retaliating by giving him a swat on the arm with a wooden spoon.

"I've a mind to show you just how healthy I am, too," Kathleen heard Mr. Neils saying as she left the kitchen. Mrs. Neils answered with a playful laugh, and memories of John's lovemaking suddenly washed over Kathleen. Her legs weakened and a burning ache filled her.

"Damn!" she muttered angrily under her breath. She had to get Jonathan Ashford out of her system. Approaching Mr. Dermot's table, she took a closer look at the man. If Mrs. Neils was correct about his reason for frequenting this tavern, she knew she should feel flattered. Mr. Dermot was certainly a suitable catch for any woman of her station in life. But then Mrs. Neils was a matchmaker at heart, and she'd suggested the same about every new male customer who'd come into the tavern since Kathleen's arrival. Of course, Mr. Dermot had become a nightly customer and he did always leave a nice gratuity.

If he was interested in her, then she would develop an interest in him, she promised herself firmly.

That night Kathleen slept restlessly. John's image wove itself into her dreams more strongly than ever. Still feeling nearly as exhausted as when she had first lain down, Kathleen groaned unhappily when Nancy shook her awake the next morning. "Just let me sleep a little longer," she pleaded, pulling her pillow over her head.

"Kathleen James, you've got to get up now!" Nancy insisted with urgent demand. "'Tis Sunday. We have to get to church or we'll be fined. They is right strict here in Jamestown. They collect their fines quick if you don't have good reason for missing the service. Even worse, we'll make a bad impression."

Lifting her pillow away, Kathleen opened her eyes and peered at her friend. She saw the glimmer in Nancy's eyes and wondered who the girl was worried about making a bad impression upon. Since their arrival in town, three different gentlemen had walked Nancy home from work. Kathleen, who was already at work at the tavern when Nancy arrived back at Mistress McGee's boardinghouse each evening, had never seen any of them. She had, however, heard about each and every one of them in detail from both Nancy and Mistress McGee.

"I'm going down to have a bit of breakfast so my stomach won't growl and embarrass me. You best hurry if you want anything to eat before we leave," Nancy admonished.

Left alone in the room, Kathleen dragged herself out of bed and splashed cold water from the basin on her face. Dressing as quickly as possible, she went down to breakfast. Although she had no young man she wanted to impress, she didn't want to begin her life in Jamestown by being fined.

"I hear tell Mistress and Mr. Holme is to be doing penance this day," Mistress McGee was telling Nancy as Kathleen joined them at the table. "That couple has fought like cats and dogs ever since they was married and most people have got used to it. But last Sunday they got into a shoutin' match. Not only was they heard cursing and making the most disrespectful accusations against one another, they was arguing so loudly they kept their neighbors from their devotions."

But when Kathleen entered the church a little later, she had to stifle a gasp of shock. Mrs. McGee's warning had not prepared her for the sight that greeted her. Inside near the front, wrapped in white sheets and holding white wands, was the miserable couple. To add to their discomfort, they were required to stand on benches so that the whole congregation could view their penance, and during the service they were several times required to respond to words directed to them by the Reverend Howard.

"I'm sure going to mind me manners," Nancy said as she and Kathleen walked back to the boardinghouse after the service. Because Mrs. McGee had wanted to stay and speak to a few friends, they were alone. Still, Nancy kept her voice lowered as if afraid of being overheard as she added, "I heard tell of such things as what we saw today, but I ain't never seen it before."

Kathleen nodded her agreement.

Suddenly a young soldier approached them. From the twinkle that suddenly appeared in Nancy's eyes, Kathleen guessed this must be the lieutenant who had walked Nancy home two evenings before. He had garnered a two-hour description, whereas Nancy's other escorts had received only one.

"I was wondering if I might see you ladies home," he said, performing a deep, polite bow in front of Nancy.

"I'm sure we'd be most pleased," the girl replied brightly, then, remembering her manners, quickly curtsied.

The soldier then turned to Kathleen and bowed. "Lieutenant George Harley at your service."

"Kathleen James," she introduced herself, as she curtsied.

"Is there some trouble, Miss James?" a familiar male voice asked from behind Kathleen.

Turning, she found that Mr. Dermot had approached them. "No," she assured him. "Lieutenant Harley was simply offering to escort us back to our lodgings."

"I see." For a moment Mr. Dermot looked indecisive, then, removing his hat and bowing low, he said, "Perhaps I could walk along with you also."

The determination to put John totally out of her mind filled Kathleen. "Yes, of course," she replied, then quickly performed the necessary introductions.

As the four of them resumed walking toward Mistress McGee's boardinghouse, Nancy and her soldier moved slightly ahead, leaving Kathleen alone with Mr. Dermot. Uncertain of the proper decorum, Kathleen spoke of the weather, feeling that would be a safe topic of conversation. Mr. Dermot responded with a dissertation on the present weather as compared to that of the spring, summer and fall, plus a very thorough comparison of the present winter with that of the past two winters.

Kathleen's smile felt wooden when he left her at Mistress McGee's porch. She could not remember ever being so bored. John's image flashed into her mind. There had never been anything boring about the time they spent together. Angrily she shoved these thoughts from her head. Mr. Dermot was a kind, polite man who was spending time with her because he wanted to, not because he felt bound by a debt of honor. Entering the house, she went into the kitchen to check on the stew Mistress McGee had left simmering over the hot coals of the fireplace.

"Right pleasant-looking fellow, your Mr. Dermot," Nancy said, joining her a few minutes later.

"Yes," Kathleen agreed with what she hoped sounded like enthusiasm. But the thought of talking about Mr. Dermot left her cold. Hoping to turn the conversation away from herself and him, she said, "I thought your soldier was quite handsome."

Nancy's face lit up. "He is right special."

"You both seem to have made the acquaintance of some very nice young men," Mrs. McGee said, entering the room at that moment. "Perhaps we'll be having some weddings to plan soon."

"Perhaps," Nancy agreed with a giggle.

Kathleen merely smiled. As much as she wanted to deny it, and as many times as she had denied it to him, deep within she felt married to John. It's idiotic to think that way, she admonished herself, but the feeling refused to go away. Determinedly, she ignored it.

The next night after work, she found Mr. Dermot waiting for her at the entrance to the tavern. "You should not have to walk home alone at this time of the night," he said, offering her his arm.

It felt nice to have someone who wanted to protect her, and Kathleen rewarded him with a smile as she accepted his company.

After that, each night when she came out, she found him waiting. He was never improper. Even after walking her home for nearly a full month, he did not try to kiss her or make any forward advances.

She grew accustomed to his company and comfortable in it. It wasn't like being with John. Giles Dermot wasn't exciting. He talked of his work and would spend hours describing exactly how to determine if the metal was just right. He was a very shy man and a very intense one. But unlike John, Kathleen knew he wanted to be with her.

January turned to February. Then one afternoon, as March drew near, Mr. Dermot found the courage to kiss her. He'd come by Mrs. McGee's to deliver some hinges and a new latch he had made for the proprietress. Kathleen had not yet gone to work and he took the opportunity to do a bit of courting. They'd gone into the parlor, and he was describing to her the ironwork for a gate he would be beginning that afternoon when he suddenly leaned toward her and, taking her hand, placed a light kiss upon her lips.

For several days she'd been waiting for this. In fact, she was beginning to think his shyness was going to prevent him from ever kissing her. But now that it had happened she felt a sudden strong guilt, as if she were betraying John. Well, I'm not, she told herself curtly, reminding herself of Lady Andrea Clemens. No doubt John would very soon be enjoying kissing that particular lady and he would feel no guilt.

Mr. Dermot was about to kiss her again, and this time she was prepared to kiss him back, when Nancy burst into the room, her cheeks flushed. "Some men don't know what they have 'til it's lost to them," she said as tears began to flow like rivers down her cheeks.

"It would appear your friend needs solace," Mr. Dermot said, rising hurriedly, as if he'd been caught in a most improper act.

"Oh, I'm so embarrassed," Nancy wailed, just then realizing that Mr. Dermot was present. "Please, don't leave on my account." Whirling around, she fled from the parlor.

Kathleen frowned worriedly as she heard her hurrying up the stairs. Nancy was such a cheerful spirit, it hurt Kathleen to see her so upset.

"You must see to your friend," Mr. Dermot said, looking concerned about Nancy also.

"Yes, I must," Kathleen agreed.

"And I hope you'll not think I've been too forward," he added quickly, a flush beginning to build from his neck upward as if he'd just then realized the extent of his actions.

"No," she replied, forcing an encouraging smile. While she wanted Mr. Dermot to continue his courting, she was disappointed by the effect of his kiss. She had not expected to feel the fire she'd felt with John, but she had hoped for a few embers or at least a tiny spark. But there had been nothing. It's better this way, she told herself. With Mr. Dermot she felt an easy peace, and that was what she wanted. She'd had enough adventure for two lifetimes.

"Then I shall call upon you again tomorrow," he promised and left.

Going upstairs, Kathleen found Nancy flung across the bed sobbing. "Do tell me what has happened," she pleaded sympathetically.

"I never want to see Lieutenant Harley again," Nancy choked out between sobs.

Kathleen studied her friend anxiously. She knew how fond Nancy had grown of the soldier and she'd thought the lieutenant was equally fond of Nancy. Apparently she had been wrong. This goes to prove that I am right in my attitude toward Mr. Dermot, she told herself. Love only leads to pain. Aloud she said, "If he has hurt you, he isn't worthy of you."

"He has humiliated me!" Behind her tears, Nancy's eyes flashed with anger. Sitting up, she brushed at her cheeks. "His attentions caused me to believe he honestly cared for me. Then today..." Her words caught in her throat as a fresh flood of tears rolled down her cheeks. Brushing them away, she continued, "Today a boat arrived from Philadelphia. Mistress Osburn was expecting some cloth and she sent me to fetch it. I was walking down the street when I saw George—" Nancy's jaw tightened and she corrected herself "—Mr. Harley helping a beautiful young woman disembark. Then, right there in front of everyone, he—he—he hugged her." Nancy broke into another fit of sobbing.

"And what did you do?" Kathleen asked worriedly. Knowing Nancy's unpredictable temperament, she wasn't certain if the girl had reacted with decorum. Without any great difficulty, she could picture Nancy having to stand in church wrapped in white on the coming Sabbath.

"I turned and walked straight back here. I just couldn't face anyone," Nancy replied. "And I *never* want to see *him* again."

Kathleen breathed a sigh of relief. "I'll go fetch the bolts of cloth for Mistress Osburn and tell her you've been taken ill with a headache."

"Yes, please." Clutching her pillow, Nancy sat up, her eyes still filled with tears. "And tell Mrs. McGee I won't be down for dinner. She's bound to ask me about the lieutenant and I couldn't answer. Not tonight."

Kathleen gave her a hug and went out to do the errands she'd promised. But as she stepped out onto the porch, she nearly ran into Lieutenant Harley. "I must see Miss Peters," he said when Kathleen greeted him with a cold stare.

"She does not want to see you," she informed him curtly.

"But I must explain," he pleaded. "She has misunderstood."

Kathleen saw the anguish in the man's eyes. It was the kind of anguish she had hoped she would see in John's eyes when she'd told him she was leaving. Well, at least Nancy's lieutenant cared for her.

"I know she'll forgive me, if only she will listen," the man continued.

Kathleen drew a shaky breath as she shoved the image of John's cool countenance from her mind. If Nancy had a chance for true love, she would not let her throw it away. "I'll speak to her on your behalf. Please wait in the parlor," she said, then retraced her steps back up the stairs.

Nancy was brushing her hair vigorously when Kathleen entered the room. "I'm glad you came back. I've decided that I'll not hide here and lick my wounds," the girl said with proud dignity. "As soon as I've rewound my hair and splashed some cold water on my face, I'll go fetch the cloth myself. And if I should see Lieutenant Harley, I shall pass him with my chin held high."

"You'll not have to go far to see him," Kathleen said. "He is down in the parlor."

"In the parlor!" Dropping the brush, Nancy rose, her complexion ashen. "I told you I never wanted to speak to him again. How could you allow him in?" she demanded in an accusing voice.

"He looked so unhappy," Kathleen replied. "I just know he cares for you. He says he can explain."

Pride glistened in Nancy's eyes. "I won't play the fool for him. I know what I saw. There can be no explanation." Her jaw tightened. "I wonder where his lady friend is now and what she would think if she knew he was here. He probably thinks he can string us both along with his fancy lies."

Kathleen frowned thoughtfully. "He's never seemed like the kind of man who would lie."

"Me mum told me all men would lie if it suited their purpose," Nancy spat back. Then, as another flood of tears threatened, she added weakly, "But I did think Lieutenant Harley was not like that." Her chin trembled. "I trusted him."

Approaching her friend, Kathleen hugged the girl tightly. She knew the kind of pain Nancy was feeling. But in Nancy's case she could not help but think it was unnecessary. The anguish she had seen in the lieutenant's eyes had been real. "Please speak to him," she urged.

Nancy's back stiffened. "Perhaps you're right," she conceded. "At least this will give me a chance to tell him what I think of his brutish behavior."

Again Kathleen worried about Nancy's decorum. "But do it with dignity," she cautioned. "You don't wish to spend Sunday wearing the white."

Nancy's shoulders straightened even more. "I'll maintain control of myself," she promised.

"And I'll chaperon," Kathleen said firmly, anxiously wondering if she had acted wrongly and was going to bring more disaster down upon her friend.

As they entered the parlor, Nancy closed the door. "I know 'tis not exactly proper, but while I don't mind you hearing what must be said, I'll allow no others," she whispered in response to Kathleen's raised eyebrow.

Kathleen couldn't blame her for wanting privacy. She felt like an intruder herself. But Nancy was sure to stand in the white if she met with the lieutenant in the parlor alone with the door closed.

Lieutenant Harley had been standing by the window. Now he turned and walked toward Nancy, his expression solemn.

She raised her hand to signal him to stop. "Do not come any closer," she ordered.

Kathleen saw Nancy's chin begin to tremble and hoped she had not made a mistake in speaking for the lieutenant.

"I pray you'll listen to my explanation," Lieutenant Harley beseeched Nancy.

Kathleen saw her friend's determined anger waver at the remorse in the lieutenant's eyes. Then Nancy's jaw stiffened and she said curtly, "I do not see how there can be any explanation."

"The woman you saw me with is my sister," he replied.

Nancy flushed scarlet. "I've made a complete fool of myself," she gasped, her hands going to her face as if to hide her shame.

But Kathleen saw the love in the lieutenant's eyes and knew Nancy was mistaken.

"No," he said gruffly, approaching Nancy and taking her hands in his. "'Tis I who am the fool. I should have asked you for your hand in marriage long ago. But I wanted to be certain of the depth of my feelings, so I hesitated. Today when I thought you might never speak to me again, I was in a panic. Nancy... Miss Peters, you bring a joy into my life I do not want to live without. Will you do me the honor of becoming my wife?"

Tears were again running down Nancy's cheeks, but this time they were tears of joy.

Discreetly, Kathleen slipped out of the room. Standing in the entrance hall, she fought back her own tears as she found herself again thinking of John and wishing he'd said those words to her. But he never will, she chided herself. And she was a fool to still let him enter her thoughts! Taking several deep breaths, she again pushed him out of her mind.

Standing guard outside the parlor door, she was watching the front walk through the window when she heard the kitchen door squeak. Thank goodness that hinge was never oiled properly, she thought frantically as she knocked firmly on the parlor door, then entered. The lieutenant released Nancy and took two steps back to put proper distance between them.

"My, my, what's going on here?" Mistress McGee demanded suspiciously, coming up behind Kathleen. She frowned censoriously. "I run a decent establishment here."

"I've asked Miss Peters to be my wife and she has accepted," Lieutenant Harley replied, performing a deep bow toward Mistress McGee.

"How wonderful!" Mistress McGee exclaimed. "And when will this wedding take place?"

"As soon as possible," the lieutenant replied, "if that's amenable to Miss Peters."

"Yes, quite amenable," Nancy agreed, her eyes resting upon him with total devotion.

Mistress McGee smiled excitedly. "Then we must make plans."

While she was happy for her friend, Kathleen felt the need to escape. "And I'll go fetch that cloth you were to fetch for Mistress Osburn," she said.

"First you must agree to be my maid of honor," Nancy insisted.

"Yes," the lieutenant seconded. Bowing low before Kathleen, he added sincerely, "I owe my happiness to you. I will forever be in your debt."

"Yes, of course, I'll be honored to be in your wedding," Kathleen agreed. Then, curtsying to them all, she left.

As she passed the blacksmith's shop, Mr. Dermot came out to speak to her.

"How is your friend?" he inquired politely.

"She is quite happy now," Kathleen replied. "She's engaged to Lieutenant Harley and they're at this moment planning their wedding."

"'Tis a good time for a wedding," he remarked thoughtfully.

Kathleen knew without a doubt that he was thinking of marriage to her and the thought left her cold. Aloud, she said, "I must make haste. Mistress Osburn is waiting for some cloth she'd sent Nancy to fetch and then I must be getting to the tavern." Curtsying quickly, she hurried away.

For the next three weeks, Kathleen's emotions flip-flopped between excitement for her friend and feeling that once again she would be alone in the world. But she wouldn't really be alone, she comforted herself. Nancy and Lieutenant Harley would be living in town and she could visit.

Finally the day of the wedding came and went.

"'Twas a charming ceremony," Mr. Dermot said as he and Kathleen and the other guests waved Nancy and her lieutenant on their way.

The couple would not, however, be going far, Kathleen knew. The lieutenant had not been able to get any leave time, thus he and Nancy would be spending their honeymoon in their new home on the edge of town. But Kathleen was certain this did not bother either of them. All they wanted was to be together.

"Yes," Kathleen agreed. It really had been lovely, and Mistress McGee had outdone herself preparing a reception feast that was enjoyed by all. But as happy as she was for Nancy, a sudden emptiness filled her. "I'd best get inside and help with the dishes," she said, looking to escape this sudden burst of melancholy by busying herself.

"Please, wait one moment," Mr. Dermot requested. He glanced around to make certain all the other guests had left and they were alone in front of the house, then he said, "I know this might not be the best time, but I'm not good at choosing my times and I want to say this while I have the courage. I care deeply for you, Miss James, and I'd be honored if you'd marry me."

Kathleen had been having a running debate with herself for the past weeks about what she would say if Mr. Dermot actually did gain the courage to ask for her hand. There were many good and practical reasons for her to say yes. And, although she didn't love him, she did care for him as a friend. That was a reasonable emotion on which to base a lifetime together, she told herself. They would be comfortable. An acceptance formed in her mind, but first she felt she must be honest with him. She wouldn't tell him about John; that was her secret to keep forever. But she would tell him of the time she had spent aboard the pirate ship. "Before I answer, there are some things about my past you should know," she said evenly.

He held up his hand to silence her. "I know speaking of your past brings you great sadness and I don't wish to cause you any distress. Tell me only that you have not acted in any way which good and rational people would consider dishonorable and I require no more."

"I have not behaved dishonorably," she replied. She did not consider allowing John Ashford to make love to her dishonorable because despite the many times she had claimed their marriage was invalid, in her heart she had felt she was his wife. But she had freed him and thus freed herself. Now she would marry whom she pleased.

"Then I'll ask you again, Miss James," Mr. Dermot said with a formal bow. "Will you do me the honor of becoming my wife?"

Kathleen chewed on her bottom lip for a moment, then, her jaw stiffening with resolve, she said, "Yes."

Smiling broadly, Mr. Dermot lifted her hand to his lips, while Kathleen reassured herself firmly that she had done the right thing.

But during the next week, while Mrs. McGee and Nancy happily planned Kathleen's wedding, the small nagging doubts in Kathleen's mind taunted her until they became very large nagging doubts. She even thought she saw John on the street one day. She knew he and his mother would most likely come to Jamestown to board their ship bound for England, and she'd carefully braced herself for a chance meeting. But for that moment when she mistook a stranger for him, she'd felt a terrible pain and weakness. Her breath had caught in her throat and her knees had threatened to buckle.

She began to sleep badly. Finally, as she tossed restlessly late one night, exhausted and yet unable to escape into the abyss of sleep, she forced herself to think about her wedding night and realized that she could never give herself to Mr. Dermot. In her heart and in her soul she was still Jonathan Ashford's wife. "Maybe someday I'll find a man who can erase him from my mind, but Mr. Dermot is not that man," she admitted resignedly. Promising herself that she would seek Mr. Dermot out early the next day and break their engagement, she finally fell into a restless sleep.

Chapter Sixteen

A sharp knocking on Kathleen's door awakened her. Opening her eyes slowly, she looked toward the window. Dawn had barely broken. The knocking sounded again. Rising and pulling a shawl around her shoulders, Kathleen answered the summons.

Mistress McGee stood on the other side of the door, looking anxious and a bit frightened. "Lieutenant Harley is here to see you, miss."

"Has something happened to Nancy?" Kathleen asked, suddenly terrified that some horrible catastrophe had befallen her friend.

"He wouldn't say why he's here, miss," Mistress McGee replied. "But he looks very grim."

"I'll be down quickly," Kathleen said, closing the door as she spoke.

In less than ten minutes she was dressed. Hurrying down the stairs, she found Lieutenant Harley standing stiffly in the parlor. "Has something happened to Nancy?" she questioned urgently.

"If you'll just come with me, Miss James," He requested, indicating with a wave of his arm that he would like for her to precede him out the door.

Kathleen felt her knees weakening. "Something so terrible has happened you're afraid to tell me," she said in a voice barely above a whisper.

"Something terrible has happened," he confirmed.

"Oh, my." Mistress McGee had been standing behind Kathleen and now began to cry. "I'll get my cloak and come with you."

"No." It was a command. "Miss James must come alone."

"I don't understand any of this." Mistress McGee shook her head in confusion. "If something so terrible has happened to Nancy, she'll be needing the both of us."

"Nothing has happened to Nancy," he assured her. His expression grew grimmer. Turning to Kathleen, he said coldly, "As a member of the king's military sent to Virginia to protect the good and decent citizenry, on orders from Sir William Berkeley, Governor of Virginia, I've come to arrest Miss James on charges of piracy and murder. We've apparently all been fools to her true self. I shudder to think that my Nancy befriended her so readily. But then Nancy is a much too trusting soul."

"That can't be," Mistress McGee gasped, while Kathleen stood dumbfounded.

"Two seamen who were aboard the *Erica Anne* when she was attacked by Captain Thorton and his band of pirates some two years ago arrived in Jamestown yesterday. I don't know if you remember, Mistress McGee, but the majority of the crew of that vessel was killed as well as the good captain. Last night, these two survivors went to the tavern where Miss James works. There they saw her, and they are ready to swear she was a willing member of Captain Thorton's band of pirates," the lieutenant explained. Facing Kathleen, he demanded, "Can you deny these charges?"

"Yes," she replied, finally finding her voice. "I was aboard Captain Thorton's ship, but as a prisoner, not as a member of his crew."

"If you were a prisoner, how did these men come to see you aboard their ship?" he questioned sharply.

"The captain allowed me to board the captured vessels in order to aid the wounded of both crews," she explained. A sinking feeling in the pit of her stomach warned her that no one was going to believe her story, especially after she had lied about her past already.

"'Tis not Captain Thorton's reputation to show compassion even to his own men," he challenged.

"My situation was unique," she replied. Quietly, she told him her story, carefully leaving out the portion involving Jonathan Ashford, and claiming that she'd escaped alone. But even as she spoke, she could see on his face that he didn't believe her.

"'Tis not for me to judge. You will have to face the governor and his council," he said sharply when she'd finished. "I've merely come to arrest you."

Kathleen turned to say goodbye to Mistress McGee, but seeing the terror in the woman's eyes, she didn't approach her. As she pulled on her cloak, she knew from the landlady's expression that Mistress McGee was saying a silent prayer of thanks that Kathleen had not murdered her in her bed.

When they reached the street, several other soldiers joined them, and Kathleen realized the lieutenant's men had been surrounding the house in case she tried to bolt. Clearly they believed her to be a very dangerous woman.

The day was now beginning, and some of the citizens of Jamestown were leaving their homes on their way to their fields or shops. Kathleen fought down an embarrassed flush as they stopped and stared at her and her soldier escort. She was innocent and she would be freed, she told herself, but she didn't really believe it. Lieutenant Harley hadn't believed her, so why should the governor and his council, who didn't even know her?

As they passed the blacksmith shop, Mr. Dermot came hurrying out. Looking from Kathleen to the soldiers and back again, he frowned in confusion. "What has happened?"

"Miss James is being arrested on charges of piracy and murder," Lieutenant Harley replied in an official voice. A hint of pity for Mr. Dermot entered his eyes as he added, "We've two witnesses who will swear she was a member of Captain Thorton's pirate band."

Mr. Dermot paled. "This cannot be," he stammered, but Kathleen saw the suspicion in his eyes. Then anger etched itself into his features and he faced her accusingly. "You told me you'd done nothing dishonorable and I believed you. Clearly you are a clever liar and a truly evil-hearted woman."

Kathleen's jaw tensed. He'd not even asked her if she was innocent. He was willing to accept the word of two strangers that she was guilty of the most atrocious crimes. "I spoke the truth," she said, her head held high. "But I am glad of one thing. I see now how shallow your pledge of love is."

"Piracy and murder," Mr. Dermot muttered. "'Tis no wonder you were so private about your past." Shaking his head, he backed into his shop as if he found the sight of her horrifying.

It didn't help her case any when the Captain of Guards' wife searched Kathleen for weapons and found the sheathed knife tied to her leg. Kathleen started to explain that she hadn't even realized she'd tied it on; that wearing it was a habit, a source of security to her. But she knew they wouldn't understand and so she kept silent.

Even her whip marks were used as proof she'd been an active member of the pirate crew.

"If she'd been a prisoner," the Captain of the Guard reasoned when his wife told him of the scars, "they'd have bedded her or killed her or both, but they'd not have punished her as such. No, 'tis obvious they treated her as one of their own kind, and she was whipped for disobeying the captain, as any pirate is apt to be once in a while, undisciplined lot that they are."

As she entered her cell and the door closed behind her, dread filled her. The pile of straw on the floor that was to serve as her bed smelled old and musty, and in the dim sunlight allowed in through the tiny barred window, she was certain she could see vermin crawling happily around in it. A mouse played in one corner. Her only solace was that she had the cell to herself.

Noon came and a guard brought her a mug of water and a piece of plain brown bread. She wasn't hungry. She tossed a piece of the crust to the mouse and nibbled on the rest. Many times she'd faced thoughts of her death, but she had never imagined she would die on a gallows.

Fear threatened to overwhelm her. While she tried to hold on to hope, in her heart she knew she was doomed. She could not blame people for believing the worst. She had been secretive about her past, and even John had not at first believed it was possible for her to survive aboard the pirate ship for eleven years without submitting to the crew and their ways.

"But I shall die with my dignity intact," she promised herself.

She recognized the guard who brought her dinner. He was one of the soldiers who frequented the tavern. He drank a bit too much and had made some very unsavory advances toward her. Once Mr. Neils had even had to throw him out.

"Pretended you was too good for the likes of me and me buddies, you did," he chided her laughingly. "Got yourself hooked up with the right proper Mr. Dermot. Guess he's wishing he'd left you to us, he is. Been taking a bit of ribbing, so I hears tell. Some is saying he's right lucky he didn't find himself dead in his wedding bed and you, the merry widow, gone with all his money and personal belongings back to your pirate friends."

"I have no friends among those cutthroats," she informed him curtly.

He gave a particularly nasty guffaw. "They all claims to be innocent what come in here." Then, still laughing, he handed her the bread and water and left.

Night came. No light was provided her and she found herself enveloped in a world of murky darkness. Though she could see nothing, she could hear small rodents and other tiny beasties moving around in the blackness. Sitting huddled in a corner, her skirt tucked tightly around her ankles, she was afraid to sleep for fear of what might attack or bite at her should she let down her guard. Resting her head on her knees, she prayed the night would not last too long.

"I cannot believe you would allow her to be put in such a place," a female voice reprimanded in a harsh whisper.

Kathleen raised her head. She saw a light in the corridor coming her way. As it approached her cell, she saw three small furry bodies scampering toward the darker corners. She wondered if they always came to this cell or if, because she had fed one at noon, the others had come to join her for dinner. They'll get no more from me, she decided. They looked much too healthy as it was.

The light reached her cell and she saw Lieutenant Harley with Nancy at his side.

"I just can't believe people would believe the stories your accusers are telling," Nancy said as Kathleen rose and moved toward the barred door.

As glad as she was to see her friend, Kathleen feared for her. "You shouldn't have come," she said worriedly. Then turning toward Nancy's husband, she added curtly, "You should not have let her come."

"I couldn't keep her away," he replied grimly, and Kathleen knew from the tone of his voice they'd fought hard about this.

"I owe you my life, Kathleen. I don't know if I could've stood up to those heathen Indians without your lead," Nancy said, reaching for her friend's hand through the small barred window on the door. "I know you're a brave soul who wouldn't hurt no one save in self-defense. You'd never lead the life of a pirate."

"I didn't," Kathleen said simply, Nancy's loyalty causing hot tears to burn at the back of her eyes.

"And Mr. Ashford knows that, too. He was aboard Captain Thorton's ship. He knows you were a prisoner like himself or else he wouldn't have brought you to his home," Nancy added.

Kathleen's tears suddenly turned to ice at the mention of John's name. "You promised me you would never mention Mr. Ashford."

"I know," Nancy admitted. A plea of understanding entered her voice. "But I had to tell George about Mr. Ashford to try to convince him of your innocence."

Kathleen met the lieutenant's cool gaze. "But you did not convince him," she pointed out curtly.

Nancy frowned worriedly. "He had some difficulty when the story you told him didn't match the one you and

Mr. Ashford told when you returned. But I figured you and Mr. Ashford only lied to save you the embarrassment of having to admit to all those years aboard the pirate ship. That would've raised quite a few eyebrows. And I know you left Mr. Ashford's name out of your story when you told George about your adventures because you didn't want him involved." Nancy scowled at the lieutenant. "My husband is a hardheaded man at times, but I'll make him believe in your innocence and help you."

In spite of Nancy's confident words, Kathleen read her fate on the lieutenant's face. He would never believe in her innocence, nor would the governor or his council. "It means a great deal to me to know you believe in my innocence," she said to Nancy. Then, knowing how people had turned against her so quickly, she added, "But I think it would be best if you didn't come again. People remember trouble for a long time and you might suffer for having your name linked with mine."

"You've got truth on your side," Nancy replied, as if this fact could save Kathleen. "And I'll pray for you every minute of every day. The court has to believe you. I had George collect your things from Mistress McGee and bring them to our home. They'll be there waiting when you're freed."

Kathleen's jaw trembled at the strength of Nancy's loyalty. "That was kind of you. If I'm not released I want you to have what is mine."

Nancy shook her head. "I'll hear no talk like that. It would be murder if they was to convict you."

Kathleen gave her friend's hand a squeeze. "I would like to believe that the truth will prevail, but that doesn't always happen. It will be only my word against my accusers."

"What of Mr. Ashford?" Nancy demanded. "He was there with you. He could speak for you."

Kathleen paled. She had almost ruined John's life once. She would not bring him into this scandal. "No," she said sharply and without compromise. Her gaze burned into Nancy's. "You must promise me you will keep his name out of this." Turning her attention toward the lieutenant, she pleaded, "Please, do not allow him to be brought into this."

"You must allow Mr. Ashford to be summoned to speak for you," Nancy pleaded.

"No," Kathleen said again, this time without the anger but with a decisive firmness. She turned to Lieutenant Harley. "It's clear that, even knowing about Mr. Ashford, your husband still thinks I am guilty. For Mr. Ashford to speak on my behalf would only expose him to scandal, and no good will come from it. The kindest folk will think he was misled by me. Most people have so readily believed I'm a murderess and a pirate, they'll surely believe I'm cunning enough to have fooled him. No, I will not allow it."

"You're being much too morbid," Nancy argued. "Mr. Ashford is a gentleman with honor and standing. He'll make them believe him."

"I'm being practical." Kathleen turned her gaze toward Nancy's husband. "Am I not, Lieutenant Harley? Even after hearing the truth from your own wife's lips, you aren't willing to concede that there is even a small chance I may be innocent, are you?"

"The accusations against you were made by men with friends who will attest to their honesty," Lieutenant Harley replied stiffly. "And it could be that you don't want Mr. Ashford to testify because what he has to say will do you more injury than good."

Nancy glanced toward her husband angrily. "You are truly a bullheaded man!" Turning back to Kathleen, she said tersely, "You cannot give up without a fight."

"I will fight by telling the truth." Kathleen's jaw hardened with resolve. "But I will not expose Mr. Ashford to scandal, and I don't want you risking yourself by coming here again." Nancy's visit meant a great deal to her, but she knew what she had to do for her friend's sake. Turning to Lieutenant Harley, she said, "You will see that she doesn't come again."

"I'll come as I please," Nancy interjected.

Kathleen held her friend's hands tightly. "You mustn't. If not for your sake, then for your husband's and for the children you'll have."

"We may not have any if he doesn't stop being so stubborn and distrusting of my judgment," Nancy said, casting a threatening glance toward the lieutenant.

"You mustn't judge him so harshly," Kathleen pleaded tiredly. "The fabric of lies I have woven around myself to avoid gossip and scandal has placed me in a precarious position. But it is my own doing and what is done is done. I will not have you risk your happiness because of me. You must think of your husband's career and his future. Just knowing you still believe in me is enough." Turning back to the lieutenant, she said, "You must take her away now."

He nodded. "We must leave," he ordered Nancy.

Ignoring him, Nancy peered into the shadows behind Kathleen. "We cannot leave her alone in this vermin-infested hole."

"You must go," Kathleen insisted.

"Yes, we must." Lieutenant Harley captured his wife's arm in an iron grip and began leading her away.

"Don't give up hope," she urged Kathleen over her shoulder.

Kathleen watched them leave with a sinking heart. She heard the heavy door close behind them and she was in darkness again. It was ironic, she thought bitterly. Held prisoner among the pirates, she'd never lost hope. But here, imprisoned unjustly, waiting to be tried by good people, she knew she was doomed.

Sinking back onto the floor, she again wrapped her skirts tightly around her legs. Drawing her knees up, she rested her head on them and prayed morning would come soon.

In spite of her uneasiness, she was dozing when the sound of the key being turned in the lock woke her. Looking up, she saw Lieutenant Harley entering with one of the soldiers under his command. The vermin again ran for the safety of the dark shadows as the interior of the cell was lighted by the lamp the lieutenant carried.

"I'll guard her while you work," Lieutenant Harley said authoritatively. "Now clean out that old straw."

Kathleen saw the pistol the lieutenant held at the ready and found herself remembering the day he'd declared himself indebted to her for life. The temptation to laugh was strong. But realizing it was more from hysteria than humor, she swallowed it back.

"Shouldn't she be shackled, sir?" the soldier questioned, watching Kathleen guardedly. "I hear tell how she'd sooner slit a man's throat than eat a good meal."

"I'll protect you from her," the lieutenant promised dryly.

Kathleen sat silently watching as the soldier shoveled the old straw into a wheelbarrow, all the time keeping an eye on his back as if he feared at any moment she would overpower the lieutenant and then attack him. Her gaze shifted to Lieutenant Harley and she wondered if he honestly thought she would kill him and his man if given the opportunity. It was only two nights ago she had sat at his table and jested and laughed with him and Nancy.

"And now give the floor a quick sweep," Lieutenant Harley ordered when the man had finished with the bedding.

The soldier obeyed with haste. Clearly he wanted to be free of Kathleen's company as quickly as possible.

"Now go fetch the bundle," the lieutenant ordered, as the man finished and pushed the wheelbarrow out of the cell. Even when they were alone he continued to stand with the pistol leveled at Kathleen and she had the answer to her question—he did think she was capable of murdering him and his man. This hurt deeply. But knowing it would be futile to again protest her innocence, she remained silent.

The soldier returned quickly and handed the lieutenant a bundle. Lieutenant Harley dismissed him, then tossed the bundle to her. "Here is your bedroll. I will see that fresh straw is provided you in the morning," he said grimly.

"Thank you," she replied, catching the bundle and holding it close. He thought her guilty but he had shown kindness. Gratefully, she added, "And thank you for having my cell cleaned."

"'Tis Nancy you have to thank," he replied stiffly. "She wouldn't allow me in our bed until she knew you were as comfortable as possible."

"Then thank her for me," Kathleen said, adding beseechingly, "And do not be angry with her. She may not always act wisely, but that is because she has such a large heart."

As if he felt he needed to defend his position, Lieutenant Harley squared his shoulders. "Even Nancy was momentarily shocked to learn just how long your sojourn with the pirates was. But her loyalty to her friends is strong and I cannot love her less for that."

Kathleen nodded to let him know she understood his position.

For a long moment the lieutenant continued to regard her hesitantly, then he said curtly, "There was a brooch, a very valuable brooch, hidden in a box in the bottom of your satchel. Nancy told me it was a gift to you from Mr. Ashford. She said she actually saw him give it to you." His gaze narrowed on her. "Why would he give you such a gift?"

"We survived many ordeals together," she replied simply. Then, her jaw tightening, she said, "I would ask, as a favor for him, never to link our names together again. Forget where the brooch came from. If I am not freed, then Nancy may do with it as she pleases."

Again he studied her for a long moment, then turned briskly on his heels and left.

After he was gone, it took her eyes a few moments to readjust to the dark. Then, in the dim moonlight that managed to make its way in through the tiny window, she unrolled the blanket. Inside she found candles and flint and, wrapped carefully so as not to soil the bedding, some bread and freshly roasted meat.

Kathleen ate, then slept.

The next day she was informed that her trial was to be held in a week's time.

That night Lieutenant Harley brought her a bowl of Nancy's stew.

"I don't want either her or you to be tainted by an acquaintance with me," she said, refusing the food. "Take it back and tell her I wouldn't accept it."

"Then she'll come herself," he replied curtly. "You must take it." In less hostile tones, he added, "It'll do her no harm that she shows kindness to you. She's well liked and considered by most to be a bit naive. They look upon her loyalty to you as bad judgment but not a sin.''

"She has told no one else of Mr. Ashford or my time at Ashford Hall?" Kathleen questioned worriedly.

"She has told no one," he assured her.

"I hope Mr. Neils's business has not suffered because of me," Kathleen said as she began to eat. "He and his wife were both kind to me."

"On the contrary." Lieutenant Harley smiled cynically. "His business has doubled. Everyone wants to see where the female pirate worked. Old Tom Payton even tried to claim you'd picked his pocket to explain to his wife where his weekly wages had gone. 'Course everyone knew he'd lost the money playing cards." The lieutenant shook his head as if amazed by human nature. "Even Mistress McGee has profited. She's started charging for people to come see the room you and Nancy shared."

It was clear the town had already judged her. As good as Nancy's stew was, it lost its flavor for her. Kathleen handed him back the bowl with only half its contents eaten.

The next days passed slowly. On the morning of the trial she did what she could to make herself presentable, but it was not easy considering her living conditions.

Catching a glimpse of herself in a mirror that hung by the jailer's desk, her chin trembled. Nancy had sent a clean dress for her to wear, but although she had washed her face and arms, there were still streaks of dirt on them and the dress was already mussed. As for her hair, she had worked hard to make it look presentable, but it, too, was dirty and had refused order. In spite of her efforts, she looked unkempt. She was, in fact, the picture of a pirate wench.

Still, she stood with dignity as the charges were read. After entering her plea of not guilty, she glanced surreptitiously toward the audience filling the courthouse.

Nancy was there, looking hopeful. Mistress McGee was also present, and even Mr. Dermot was there, looking angry and aggrieved. With bitter humor she recalled how a mere two weeks earlier he had pledged his heart to her and begged for her hand in marriage. The Neilses were there, too. She'd hoped to see a bit of support in their eyes or at least a touch of sympathy, but there was only condemnation. Clearly, they too had already judged her as guilty.

At least Mistress Neils won't be cooking for the customers today, Kathleen thought wryly as the first witness against her took the stand.

The man was a sailor. Vaguely Kathleen recalled having seen him in the tavern.

"I were sailing on the *Erica Anne* about two years ago," he said, watching Kathleen with distaste. "When we was attacked by Captain Lawrence Thorton. We was a merchant vessel sailing with few armaments, and his pirates quickly took us. When the battle was over and we was waitin' to hear what our fate was to be, I seen her." He pointed an accusing finger at Kathleen. "She was going amongst the bodies. At first I wasn't certain what she was up to, then I saw her approach one of our wealthy passengers what had been struck down in battle. The man weren't quite dead, so she pulls out her dagger and slits his throat." The sailor paused to draw his finger across his own throat in graphic demonstration. "Then she proceeds to cut off all his gold buttons."

Horrified by this lie, Kathleen gripped the wooden rail in front of her for support. "That's not true," she cried out.

The sailor raised his head high. "I seen it with me own eyes and I'll swear as such on a stack of Bibles."

Watching the faces of the governor and the council, Kathleen felt her fate being sealed.

The second sailor told the same story, only embellished it further by claiming he saw her in the thick of the battle. "Our captain were struggling with one of the cutthroats and she sneaks up behind him and stabs him in the back, killing the good man without him ever having a chance to defend himself against her," he said with the assurance of one telling God's truth.

Unable to stop herself, Kathleen glanced toward Nancy, wondering if even her friend now questioned her innocence. But Nancy met her glance with unwavering support. What Nancy thought would make no difference in the outcome of this trial, she knew, but it gave her courage.

When it was finally her turn to tell her story, she spoke with conviction and dignity. Leaving out any reference to Jonathan Ashford, she told of her life on board the pirate ship. Her explanation that she had boarded the captured ships merely to help the wounded was greeted by jeers.

"Help them to the other side so's you could steal from them," a man in the galley yelled, and others voiced their agreement with loud "ayes."

When she told of escaping in the midst of a storm and making her way overland to Virginia, someone among the viewers suggested loudly that she had grown too cold-blooded even for her pirate comrades and they had cast her overboard.

The governor called for order in the sternest manner after each of these outbursts, but Kathleen saw in his eyes that his sentiments were the same as those being expressed. It was the sailors the court believed.

She stood with her shoulders squared and her chin held firm as the sentence was pronounced upon her.

"You have been fairly judged and found guilty of piracy and murder," Sir William Berkeley, Governor of Virginia, said in a voice filled with authority. "In one week's time you shall be hanged by the neck until dead as payment for these crimes."

A wave of nausea swept over Kathleen. Swallowing back the bile that rose in her throat, she faced him with proud dignity. "You shall be hanging an innocent woman."

His features hardened into an expression of assured self-righteousness. "Take the prisoner away," he ordered.

"Aye, she's getting what she deserves," Kathleen heard several people saying. "Look at her," another demanded of his companions. "She don't show one bit of remorse."

Kathleen wanted to scream at them that she was innocent but she knew it would do no good. She saw the sailors who had testified against her being led off as heroes. Tonight they were sure to get drunk on the free ale provided them to toast their courage.

They're no better than Captain Thorton's pirates, she thought bitterly.

Back in her cell, a coldness came over her and she began to shiver. She wrapped her blanket around herself, but still her blood felt like ice. She knew it was fear but she refused to give in to it.

"I will die with dignity," she announced to the emptiness around her. But late that night, sitting in the dark when no one could see her, she cried silent angry tears.

About midmorning of the next day, Reverend Howard came to call upon her.

"'Tis time to repent your sins, my child," he admonished her. "I'm here to cleanse your soul."

"It is the hangman's soul you must cleanse," she replied. "When he kills me, he will be murdering an innocent victim of the most malicious slander."

"My child, you must not die with this lie upon your tongue," he cautioned.

"I will not confess to that of which I am innocent," she replied.

Shaking his head as if greatly saddened by her obstinacy, the reverend departed.

Her next visitor was Lieutenant Harley. "Nancy still believes in you," he said stiffly.

Kathleen stood before him, her chin held high. "And you think she is a fool."

The frown on his face deepened. "The evidence is against you. What motives would those sailors have to bear false witness?" he challenged.

"None, that I know of," she admitted.

He nodded as if this proved his point. Then, drawing an impatient breath, he said, "However, Nancy has been very forward about reminding me that you interceded on my behalf when she wished never to speak to me again. For that action on your part, I'm grateful. I will make your final days as comfortable as possible."

"I am innocent," she said for what had to be the hundredth time.

"For Nancy's sake, I wish I could believe you," he replied. "But even then I doubt if I could do anything to save you. The court has ruled and 'tis my duty to abide by that ruling."

When he had gone, Kathleen paced the floor of her cell. She had not given up when Captain Thorton wanted her dead. She would not give up easily for the "good" citizens of Jamestown. Carefully, she considered plans for escape. But none seemed workable. She was well guarded.

During the next few days, she studied the guards' routines, looking for some breach of security. Finally she was forced to admit that a miracle would be required for her to escape.

That night, fear again threatened to overwhelm her. She was not ready to die. It was not fair. She'd barely had time to live. A desperate, angry scream built up inside of her. Determinedly, she fought to hold it back.

Seeking an escape if only in her mind, she allowed herself to do what she had promised she would never knowingly do again. She allowed herself to think of John. Huddled tightly, with her blanket around her and her arms wrapped around her legs, she let herself, in her mind's eye, see him as she'd first seen him, fighting gallantly against Captain Thorton's pirates to save the ship upon which he sailed.

During the next days and nights, very slowly, savoring each memory, she let herself retrace each moment of their time together. Periodically she would sleep and nightmares of the hangman would taunt her. She would awaken trembling with tears of terror in her eyes. Then she would again think of John, and her thoughts would take her out of the darkness and into the light.

Chapter Seventeen

"Kathleen, wake up."

It was John's voice, as clear and real as if he were in the cell with her. She'd again fallen asleep, only this time providence had been kind and allowed her to dream of him. Now she was awakening to his voice. Fear has driven me so insane I'm hallucinating, she mused, unwilling to open her eyes and find herself alone.

"Kate, come along," the voice ordered with terse impatience.

She smiled. He'd used that tone a lot with her. "I was a trial for him," she murmured.

"Forget about the trial," the voice said gruffly. "You'll not hang. You're to go free."

She felt herself being lifted up by two strong arms. Her imagination was not that good! Her eyes opened and she saw the taut profile of John's jaw. "You're real!" she gasped.

"You must think very little of me to believe that I would prefer to sit idly by and allow you to die for crimes of which you are innocent," he growled angrily.

"I didn't want to bring scandal to your name," she replied in her defense.

He looked down at her then. There was rage in his eyes. "But you would bring dishonor upon me by dying because of my silence."

Her jaw trembled. "I didn't think of it that way."

"'Tis a good thing Nancy summoned me as quickly as she did. As it was I barely made it here in time." His jaw hardened into a rigid line and he lapsed into a cold silence.

With Kathleen still in his arms, John strode out of the jail, Lieutenant Harley at his side, and down the street toward Nancy's home. Dawn was breaking and Kathleen blinked against the light. There was a slight chill in the air, but the sky was clear. A joy filled her. It would be a bright, sunny day and she would live to see the sunset. But as quickly as it had come, the joy faded. She could feel a barrier between herself and John. It was as solid as any physical wall. She knew he was there only because of his deep sense of duty, and she was equally certain that he did not want to be there. "Thank you for coming," she said tightly. "I'm sorry I continue to be such a burden to you."

John was too angry to respond. But the anger was directed at himself, not at her. When she had left Ashford Hall, he had determinedly pushed her from his mind. Once in a while she had managed to sneak back in. But at those times, he'd reminded himself that she didn't wish to be there and he'd shoved her out. It had become his desire never to see her again. But when word had reached him of her sentence, he'd ridden like a madman to get here, crazed with fear that he would arrive too late. Even now, he was still badly shaken by her close brush with death. How could he allow a woman who wanted no place in his life to continue to have such a hold over him? Bitterly he scoffed at himself.

Kathleen took his silence as acquiescence to her description of herself and her back stiffened. "I can walk, if you'll just put me down."

"Quiet, Kate," he ordered curtly. "This is neither the time nor the place for you to make an exhibition of your stubbornness."

Townspeople were coming out of their homes, and they stopped in amazement at the sight of the convicted pirate and murderess being carried away from the jail.

Kathleen heard hammering. Looking over John's shoulder, she saw a notice being nailed to the prison door. Standing beside it, the town crier was proclaiming loudly, "By the order of Sir William Berkeley, Governor of Virginia, on this the tenth day of March in the year of the Lord 1674, Miss Kathleen James is declared innocent of all charges brought against her."

The people in the streets looked confused and angry. Lieutenant Harley motioned for some soldiers standing nearby to join him and John.

Nancy was waiting for them when they reached her home. It was a small one-room cabin on the edge of town, but Nancy had added feminine touches that gave it a soft, homey feel.

"Delouse her," John ordered, setting Kathleen on the floor. "Lieutenant Harley and I will stand guard outside."

"I'm so glad to see you, I could hug you," Nancy said, but as she started to move forward, she stopped. She wrinkled her nose as her gaze traveled over Kathleen and she added, "Almost." Then, shaking her head at her friend's disheveled appearance, she motioned toward the fire. "I've a tub and some hot water and soap waiting."

Her scars now public knowledge, Kathleen made no pretense of modesty in front of her friend. Stripping off her clothing, she threw the garments into the fire. "Never in a hundred years could you get the bugs out," she said by way of an explanation. Then she stepped into the tub and scrubbed until her skin was raw. Suddenly something John had said finally registered in her mind. Pausing abruptly, she turned toward her friend. "While it was against my wishes, I owe you a debt of gratitude for sending for Mr. Ashford."

Nancy breathed a sigh of relief. "I'm glad you're not angry. I had no choice but to contact Mr. Ashford. Although you're my very best friend, I was sworn to let him know if you was ever in any trouble. He made me promise I would. Besides, I couldn't let them hang you without trying to help."

As the full impact of Nancy's words sank in, Kathleen frowned with disbelief. "Are you saying that he released you from your indenture so you could come with me and keep an eye on me?"

"That was the bargain," Nancy admitted sheepishly.

Kathleen shook her head. "The man does have a deep sense of honor."

Nancy nodded her head vehemently. "He's always been that way. Mrs. Oats says he takes after his father. There weren't never more honorable nor brave a man than Martin Ashford save his son, according to her. They'd die for their honor before they'd betray it."

Or chance ruining their future, Kathleen mused tiredly, wondering what Lady Andrea Clemens would think of this. Then she pictured John in her mind. If her ladyship wouldn't forgive him, the woman was a fool. No woman could hope for more in life than to have a man such as Jonathan Ashford as a true and loving husband.

"You should've seen Mr. Ashford," Nancy was saying as she poured more water into the kettle on the fire. "He arrived here in the middle of the night, half-dead from lack of sleep. At his insistence and my begging, Lieutenant Harley had the two witnesses against you brought here, and all of them went to see the governor. My lieutenant says Mr. Ashford was so insistent that the governor actually left his bed to hear him out. Then Mr. Ashford told of what he'd seen aboard the *English Wench*. He told how the captain was right cruel toward you and said that from his own ears and eyes he could swear the story you told was the truth.

"Then he turned on the two witnesses. My lieutenant said he's never seen a look so dark with rage as that in Mr. Ashford's eyes. Then Mr. Ashford commanded the two men to speak the truth as to what they had seen. George says the men looked terrified and began to babble about how they might've been mistaken.

"By the time it was finished, they'd admitted that after a few drinks at the tavern they'd begun to embellish their story about the attack on their ship. Then, before they realized the consequences, you'd been arrested and they was afraid to back down. 'Twas then that the governor declared you innocent and warned the men to get out of Virginia and never show their faces in his colony again." Nancy paused and drew a wistful breath. "I do wish I could've been there to see it."

Kathleen pictured the proceedings in her mind's eye as she oiled her hair to kill the lice, then scrubbed it until it felt soft and clean. One thing was clear—John hadn't mentioned their marriage. She was happy for him that he obviously felt free of it and hoped that one day she could rid herself from this feeling of being bound to him.

Resolutely rebuilding the barrier around her emotions, she dressed herself in the clean clothing Nancy had laid out for her. Then, seating herself on the hearth near the fire, she began to dry her hair.

"I best be getting the men in and feeding them," Nancy said, walking toward the door. "They've been so busy freeing you, they've not had a bite of breakfast."

"Miss James." Immediately upon entering, Lieutenant Harley approached Kathleen. His expression grim with remorse, he bowed low. "I hope you'll be so forgiving as to accept my apologies."

"You were kind to me even when you thought I was guilty of the most horrendous of crimes," she replied. "For that I shall always be grateful. And because we both care for Nancy, your friendship would mean a great deal to me."

"'Tis yours," he replied solemnly.

Glancing covertly toward the table, Kathleen saw John seating himself. She had been in such a state of shock when he'd rescued her from the gallows she hadn't see him clearly. Now she noticed the lines of exhaustion etched deeply into his features. She felt his weariness as if it were her own and hated the strength of the feelings she still held for him.

He ate only a little, then declared he had to rest.

"You must use the bed," Nancy insisted when he started toward his bedroll.

He did not give her any argument, but before he lay down, he approached Kathleen. "I want your word that you'll be here when I awaken."

The longing she felt for him was so intense it was a physical pain. Afraid he might read what she was feeling in her eyes, she continued to look into the fire as she said evenly, "I've a life I must get back to."

Crouching down so that his gaze was level with hers, he caught her chin in his hand and forced her to face him.

"At this moment you have no life in Jamestown. The governor has enemies who might try to injure him by claiming that his pardon of you was bought and that you are truly guilty, as the court declared. To cause as little dissension as possible, I've promised him that I would return to Ashford Hall as quickly as possible with you by my side. This will give credence to my faith in your innocence. Now for my sake, Nancy's sake, the lieutenant's sake and the governor's sake, I want your word that you'll remain here."

What she wanted was to put as much distance between herself and Jonathan Ashford as possible, but she could not risk the reputations of those who had helped to save her. "You have my word," she replied stiffly.

Satisfied, he rose and continued toward the bed.

The lieutenant left soon afterward to make his daily rounds. Kathleen helped Nancy with the dishes, but her eyes continually traveled to the bed where John slept. It took all of her strength not to go over and touch his face gently. She couldn't go back to Ashford Hall and be subjected to his plans of marriage to Lady Andrea Clemens. She would leave town with him, but somewhere along the way she would convince him they must part company.

A little past midday he rose and left, saying he had business in town.

He was no sooner gone than Mistress McGee came knocking on Nancy's door.

"I'm so glad the truth was found out in time, my dear," she said, giving Kathleen a hug.

Kathleen was tempted to mention the good fortune her bad luck had brought Mistress McGee, but held her tongue. It was best to let this incident be forgotten.

"I saw the very handsome Mr. Ashford on my way here," the woman continued, her eyes dancing with ex-

:itement. "It was so heroic of him to ride all this way to save Miss James's life in payment for her having saved his." Then, her gaze narrowing on Kathleen, she said with a puzzled frown, "What I don't understand is why you never mentioned Mr. Ashford before."

"She didn't want his name mixed up in this scandalous mess if it was at all possible because she's an honorable woman what don't like to bring no harm to others," Nancy answered before Kathleen could speak.

Mistress McGee flushed self-consciously. "Her being an honorable woman and all brings me to another reason for my visit." She glanced over her shoulder toward the door, as if she felt someone watching her, then turned back to Kathleen. "Mr. Dermot has asked me to ask you if you would see him. He's waiting outside."

Kathleen had wondered if the man would have the courage to show his face. "I'll speak to him," she consented coolly. Before Mistress McGee could move, Kathleen brushed past her and out the door.

Seeing her, Mr. Dermot approached and bowed low. "I've come to beg your forgiveness," he said as he straightened.

"It is given," she replied, choosing to be magnanimous.

He smiled and took her hand. "I've instructed Mistress McGee to proceed with the plans for the wedding."

Kathleen pulled her hand free. "Then you must find another bride, for I surely will not marry you. No woman could want a man who would so quickly turn against her in the face of adversity."

Mr. Dermot's back straightened. "Your name is not without blemish in the eyes of many. You'll not find another man who'll be so generous as to honor a commitment to a woman who was so near to ending her days on

the gallows. There are even some who are suggesting tha
your pardon was bought as payment for a duty Mr. Ash
ford felt he owed you.''

''Then you should be relieved not to have a wife who i
whispered about behind her back,'' she replied icily, add
ing with curt dismissal, ''Good day, Mr. Dermot.''

''Good day, Miss James,'' he replied sharply and, bow
ing once again, turned and walked away.

''Well said.''

Startled, Kathleen whirled around to find John stand
ing behind her. ''It isn't polite to eavesdrop,'' she admon
ished curtly.

Ignoring her admonition, he studied her narrowly
''You've made the right decision. You're better off with
out a man who would not stand by you. I realize it's dif
ficult now, but your heart will mend.''

He thought she was in love with Mr. Dermot! Well
perhaps that was best, she decided. At least he would no
guess her feelings toward him. ''I'm sure you're right,'' sh
said, turning away from him and going back into the
house.

John watched her go. When he had first learned of he
engagement, he had felt a rush of anger that another mar
was to be given the privilege of touching her. Then he'c
chided himself for that moment of jealousy. He should be
happy for her. Kathleen had wanted her own life and she
had found it. Still, he could not deny that he was pleased
she would not be marrying Mr. Dermot. The man was no
the right choice for her, he told himself. A woman like hi
Kate needed a husband with a firmer hand and a stoute
heart. John's jaw tensed. ''She is not *my* Kate,'' he
growled under his breath.

* * *

Mrs. Neils came by for a short visit that evening while Kathleen and Nancy were alone in the cabin preparing supper.

"I brung a pudding," the woman said, handing the dish to Nancy. "Mr. Neils said I should tell you the cook made it," she added with a chuckle.

Both Kathleen and Nancy breathed a sigh of relief.

"I have to admit I was hoping to get a real good look at Mr. Ashford," Mrs. Neils said with a touch of disappointment, glancing around as if he might be lurking in one of the corners of the cabin and she just hadn't noticed.

"He and Lieutenant Harley are having a walk around town," Nancy informed her.

Mrs. Neils's disappointment vanished as she turned to Kathleen and smiled widely. "'Twas a wonderful thing Mr. Ashford did, coming to your rescue. There be a great many others who would not have risked their reputations to speak for you." She continually nodded her head as she spoke, to add emphasis to her words.

"Mr. Ashford is a man of honor," Kathleen replied.

"And speaking of men..." Mrs. Neils's eyes gleamed with interest as she stopped nodding and fastened her gaze intently upon Kathleen. "I understand you've freed Mr. Dermot from any obligation to you."

Kathleen faced her proudly. "He was very quick to turn against me. A woman needs better than that in a husband."

"Aye," Mrs. Neils agreed, nodding her head again, this time freeing a lock of hair that bobbed with her. Refastening the wayward strand, she again fixed her gaze on Kathleen. "'Tis probably best you don't stay in Jamestown at the moment anyways. There's certain to be bad memories for you here. I hears Mr. Ashford is taking you back to his home for a rest."

"He does seem to have appointed himself Miss James's guardian," Nancy interjected with a sly smile toward Kathleen.

"He is merely paying back a debt of honor," Kathleen responded tersely. She had already placed John's name in grave danger of scandal. She would not risk his chances further by allowing unfounded rumors to spread about a possible romantic attachment he might feel toward her. There were none and she knew it.

"Well, I do hope you'll be stopping by to see me when you pass through on your way to England," Mrs. Neils said, looking disappointed that Kathleen had squelched a juicy bit of gossip.

"England?" Kathleen and Nancy questioned in unison.

"Why, yes," Mrs. Neils replied, her face suddenly brightening as she realized she knew something neither of the other two women knew. "Mr. Jacob Mattery was in the tavern just this afternoon telling as how Mr. Ashford had asked him to arrange for passage for three to England on a good and sound ship."

John was planning to sail for England as soon as possible! As often as she'd told herself there was no place for her in his life, Kathleen felt a hard knot form in her stomach. Furious, she told herself she was happy for him. Aloud she said evenly, "I've no intention of going to England. I'm sure the passage he booked was for himself, his mother and a servant for Lady Margaret."

"I does understand Lady Margaret is sister to the Earl of Wheaton. Right fancy company that is," Mrs. Neils said, nodding her head again and freeing the lock of hair once more. "I suppose Mr. Ashford will be seeking a right suitable wife whilst he's there."

It was clear to Kathleen that now that Mrs. Neils had come back to reality and realized John's place in the world, she recognized how preposterous it was to think he would be interested in marrying the very ordinary Miss James. "I'm certain he will," Kathleen replied with schooled evenness.

"I'll wager he'll not be short on prospects, either," Nancy mused, watching her friend closely.

Kathleen saw the concern in Nancy's eyes and realized her friend still harbored thoughts of a romance between Kathleen and John. "I shall pray he finds a suitable match that pleases him," she said with conviction. "He is a good man and deserves what his heart desires." For an instant every fiber of her being ached with the wish that his desire could be for her, then, angry with herself for even thinking such nonsense, she busied herself with setting the table.

But late that night the thought of him with another woman came to taunt her. At both Kathleen's and John's insistence, Nancy and her lieutenant slept in their bed while Kathleen and John slept in their bedrolls on the floor in front of the hearth. They had laid them out a discreet distance apart, but she had been as aware of him as if they were sharing the same pallet.

She had slept restlessly and awakened in the small hours of the morning with a chill. Carefully laying a fresh log on the smoldering embers, she watched until it began to flame. Her back was stiff from trying not to look at John, but as she lay back down, her weakness won and she turned toward him. In the light cast by the fire, she watched him sleeping and longed to have him hold her. He was so near and yet she knew there was a distance between them she could never overcome. "I do hope you're happy with your fine lady," she murmured and, turning over, fell again into a restless sleep.

Chapter Eighteen

The next morning, as they left for Ashford Hall, Kathleen noticed several makeshift stands on the outskirts of town. It looked as if preparations were being made for a fair.

"Your hanging was to have been quite a party," John said, noticing the direction of her gaze.

Kathleen shivered as she pictured a huge gathering of men, women and children all gleefully waiting to watch her die. She kicked her horse into a trot to put Jamestown behind her more quickly.

But putting Jamestown behind her did not free her from her ordeal. As dusk fell, they stopped at a cabin to seek shelter for the night.

"You be the lady pirate." A man near John's age watched her cautiously as he stood in his doorway, his musket resting across his arm. "We traveled into town to see your hanging." There was an edge of disappointment in his voice.

Kathleen saw John's jaw harden in anger, but his voice was calm as he said, "Then you know she was declared unjustly accused by the governor."

"I don't mean to be impolite, Mr. Ashford." A woman with two small children clinging to her skirt and a baby in her arms, peered around the man's shoulder. "But many a man's had his good sense turned wrong by a pretty face and a bit of tear."

Putting herself in the woman's place, Kathleen couldn't blame her for wanting to protect her children. "We'll not bother you further," she said, and giving her horse rein, rode away.

John was furious with the couple. Had not Kate suffered enough? He cast them a scowling glance, then gave his horse a nudge and rode to catch up with her. "They meant no harm. It simply takes time for fears to fade," he said with apology, pacing his animal beside hers.

"I know," she replied honestly. Then, glancing toward the sky, she added, "We're in luck. The night should be clear."

"A fine night to spend under the stars," he agreed, covertly studying her rigid profile. He knew she was hurting and he wanted to take her in his arms and comfort her. But she would not want that, he reminded himself. And it was better for him to keep his distance.

They found a high piece of ground not far from the trail and set up their camp. Darkness had closed in around them by the time they started their fire. Kathleen watched the flames dance on the logs as she ate some of the bread and cheese Nancy had sent. Pulling her mind away from the fire, she turned toward John. This was as good a time as any to tell him of her plans, she decided. "I won't be stopping at Ashford Hall," she said with resolve. "I intend to continue across the Potomac into Maryland and then make my way to Pennsylvania."

John wanted to let her go. But until he was satisfied that her health had been restored, he could not. "You will spend some time at Ashford Hall," he said with firm resolve. "You look like you've been through hell. You need to rest and recuperate from your ordeal. Also, I gave the governor my word I would watch over you."

"As long as I'm out of Virginia, I cannot believe the governor will care what becomes of me," she countered, adding tersely, "And I don't require anyone to look after me."

"That," he remarked dryly, "is a matter for debate."

She tossed him a haughty stare. "There'll be no debate. My mind is set."

For a long moment he studied her in silence. Abruptly, a thought entered his mind that caused a sharp jab of discomfort. "Is this determination to flee Virginia because of Mr. Dermot?" he demanded, then heard himself add reprovingly, "Surely you've more pride than to allow a man of his weak character to cause you such pain that you feel you must put a border between you?" The moment he'd said this, he regretted it. Her heart was not his concern.

While Kathleen had chosen to hide behind the misconception that she had fallen in love with Mr. Dermot, her pride wouldn't allow her to let anyone believe he could send her fleeing from Virginia. "Mr. Dermot has nothing to do with my decision," she assured him. "I'm merely attempting to free you from an obligation that I'm certain you don't want and is really not necessary. When you return to Ashford Hall you'll be much too busy preparing for your journey to England to be bothered with a houseguest."

He frowned thoughtfully. He had been certain that his movements were of no concern to her. "And how do you know of my purchase of passage to England?"

A momentary fear that her knowledge of his activities might cause him to see behind her facade of indifference swept over her. Then, calming herself, she said with cool nonchalance, ''Your activities whilst you were in James-town were well documented.''

''I suppose they were,'' he conceded, calling himself a fool for thinking she had truly been interested in his plans. Again he wished he could allow her to go her own way immediately. But despite her protests, she looked exhausted and undernourished. It is my duty to see her fit and healthy, he told himself. And he would use her knowledge of his activities to gain this end. ''Since you know of my plans,'' he continued in reasonable tones, ''then you must surely understand my desire to have you stay at Ashford Hall. I've appointed myself your guardian, whether this suits you or not. Knowing you're securely housed in a safe place, I shall be able to travel with a much freer mind. Once you've regained your full strength and allowed some time for this unfortunate adventure to be put behind you, then you may go where you will. I'll give Adam instructions that he's to see you're well prepared for whatever journey you wish to take. May I have your word that you'll come to Ashford Hall and stay long enough to ease my mind?''

Kathleen wanted to refuse him more than she'd ever wanted anything in her life, but she knew she was trapped. His argument was well stated and his reasoning sane. Not only would it be impolite to refuse him this request, even more, he might become suspicious and guess the truth of her feelings. I'll have to stick it through, she decided unhappily. ''If you insist, then,'' she replied with schooled detachment. ''Of course, I cannot refuse your hospitality.''

The next night they found shelter with an old man. His one-room cabin was small but clean. He'd outlived his wife and children and now he tilled his fields and whittled small animals out of wood to pass the time until he joined them.

"Hear tell a woman of your description and name was ried for piracy and murder," he said as he, Kathleen and John sat around his table near the hearth.

"She holds a paper from the governor declaring her innocent of the charges brought against her," John informed him sharply.

"If our presence here bothers you," Kathleen interjected, rising as she spoke, "we will leave." She had her pride and she wouldn't remain where she wasn't wanted.

"No, no, please stay." The old man motioned for her to be seated. "I meant no harm. You was probably convicted on a drunken sailor's testimony, I bet you was." He shook his head. "The law here in the colonies ain't no better for a poor man nor woman than it were in England. You was lucky you had a man of prominence who was willing to speak for you or that pretty neck would be well stretched by now."

Kathleen shivered as she was once again reminded how close she had come to meeting a very unseemly death.

The next morning as they prepared to leave, the old man gave Kathleen a carving of an owl. "They's those who believe in one thing and those that believe in another," he said. "But it were an owl's hoot what woke me in the middle of the night once when a critter were about to pounce on me whilst I was sleeping in the wild. May this carving bring you the same such luck during your journey."

Kathleen thanked him and John placed a bit of gold in the old man's hand. Their host smiled brightly and waved them farewell.

That night they were again without shelter. They had traveled into the wilder section of Virginia, where homesteaders were few and far between. Sitting around the fire, Kathleen held the owl in her hand as she studied its crafts-

manship. She could certainly use a bit of luck. Suddenl
her back stiffened. She had the strangest sensation of be
ing watched. She turned and peered into the woods be
hind her and then on either side.

"What is it?" John demanded.

"I had the strangest feeling we were being watched. Bu
the woods look empty." She shrugged a shoulder. "It mus
have been my imagination."

"I'll take a quick look around," John said, already ris
ing. "A bit of caution is always wise."

Kathleen slipped her hand under her skirt to seek the
handle of her knife. If there was any danger, she would be
ready to help.

John moved silently around the perimeter of their camp
his gaze penetrating into the dark shadows beyond. "I saw
nothing," he said as he reseated himself by the fire. "You
ordeal most likely still has your nerves on edge."

"Most likely," she conceded. Still, an uneasy feeling
lingered. Attempting to ignore it, she returned her attention to the owl. Her luck, she decided, had balanced out
as well as that of many others. Although evils had befallen her, she'd survived them. And one day I shall find a
place where I belong and a man who will love me and
whom I shall love in return, she told herself firmly. After
rubbing the owl with the tip of her finger for good luck,
she spread out her bedroll and lay down.

She had just begun to doze when the snapping of a twig
behind her caused her to start. She opened her eyes to see
John rising and unsheathing his sword in one smooth motion. Then she heard a familiar laugh and her blood ran
cold. Rolling over, she saw Mr. Barrows coming toward
her with a cocked pistol in his hand.

"Ye didn't think ye could escape from me so easily, did
ye, lass?" he asked.

Frantic, she turned back toward John, only to see a large form looming behind him. "Behind you," she screamed in warning.

"Now that weren't nice," Mr. Barrows reprimanded as John swung around just in time to save himself from Joseph Yates's sword.

Her wits coming quickly back to her, Kathleen reached for her knife.

"Now you be behavin', girl," Mr. Barrows ordered. Grabbing a corner of her bedroll, he gave it a yank, nearly sending her into the fire. Again she tried to reach her knife, but he grabbed her by the arm. Jerking her roughly to her feet in front of him, he nestled the barrel of his pistol in her side. "Just stand calm," he hissed in her ear, "and we'll see what short work Joseph makes of your fancy husband."

The sound of steel clanging against steel filled the night air as John and Joseph battled one another. John was quicker, but Joseph's blows were those of a strong man bent on vengeance.

"I cannot believe you left the sea to search for us," she said incredulously, her mind moving with John, willing him to keep free from Joseph's blade.

"It weren't exactly like that," Mr. Barrows replied. "It were more a stroke of luck." He groaned slightly as John's sword caught Joseph's arm and left a gash. "Yates be strong as an ox but none too agile," he muttered. For a moment he watched the fight in silence, then, satisfied that Yates was not badly injured, he gave a small laugh.

"That storm done destroyed the *English Wench*. She went down near the outer islands, taking the captain and most of the crew with her. Mr. Yates and I managed to make it to shore. It were a rough winter. We was about to meet the devil when we come across some friendly Indians. They helped us get across to Carolina. There we found this nice little cabin. Once we'd done away with the man of the house, the woman kept us right comfortable." He laughed. "It weren't her choice, but I've always liked a woman who puts up a bit of a struggle."

Kathleen felt a surge of sympathy for the woman and wondered if they'd left her dead or alive.

"But she'd lost her fight and most of her mind, and Joseph and me was thinking of moving on to find us a ship when we heard tell of a female pirate being hanged," he continued with an evil chuckle. "When they said she'd sailed with Captain Thorton, we had to have a look, and bless my soul if it weren't our long-lost Kathleen."

"Your soul will never be blessed!" Kathleen hissed, attempting to pull free.

"Now you just stand straight, lass," he ordered, jabbing the gun even harder into her side.

Joseph Yates let out a roar of anger as he lunged toward John and nearly lost his footing.

"He fights like an ox," Mr. Barrows commented, with a shake of his head. "Too bad you had to let out that warning yell. Joseph would've hacked yer man's head off in one blow and then you and I could've had some fun. Now we'll have to wait."

Kathleen saw John glance her way. "Don't worry about me," she yelled. "Defend yourself."

"He'll not live to see the morrow," Joseph promised with a snarl. "He escaped me once, but this time I'll have my revenge." Again he lunged toward John with all his might.

Kathleen barely breathed as she watched John evade the mighty swing of Yates's sword.

"Enough of this," Mr. Barrows ordered. "Step back and shoot him."

Clearly Joseph was beginning to weary. Nodding, he stepped away from John and reached for the pistol in his belt. But John moved quickly. In an instant, the belt was slashed and the pistol fell to the ground.

"Be damned!" Joseph yelled in a rage, and again lunged toward John. As John sidestepped him, he tried to turn awkwardly and, this time fully losing his footing, fell hard upon the ground. In the next instant, John's foot was on Joseph's sword hand and his blade at Joseph's throat.

"Release Miss James or I shall kill your friend this instant," John demanded.

Mr. Barrows merely laughed. "You release Joseph, or as much as I'd hate to miss the bit o' fun I've got planned, I'll put a ball into your lady friend."

Kathleen saw John's hesitation. It was as if they'd come full circle. The day they'd met she'd risked everything to save him from Joseph Yates, and here they were, facing the same enemies yet again.

"You'll not die because of me," she promised, driving an elbow into Mr. Barrows's side.

Letting out a surprised yell, he tightened his hold on her. But she paid no heed. Struggling with all her might, she kicked and clawed at him. The pistol fired and burning pain shot through her abdomen.

Kathleen saw the look of horror on John's face. For a moment his position over Yates weakened and she saw Yates tense to take advantage of John's distraction. His free hand grasped John's ankle, but as he jerked down, John shifted his sword and drove it though the pirate's heart.

Kathleen felt her strength ebbing as pain racked her body. Mr. Barrows released her and she crumpled to the ground. Her hand went to her side and she felt the wetness.

Looking up, she saw Mr. Barrows. He had moved toward the dead body of his friend and was aiming the second barrel of his gun at John's chest. If it took her last ounce of strength she would not let John die. Her hand groped along her leg and she drew the knife from its casing. Willing strength into her arm, she let the blade fly.

Mr. Barrows staggered. The sound of a pistol shot filled the night air as the pirate fell forward onto the ground.

Frantic, Kathleen looked toward John. He stood uninjured.

In the next instant he was kneeling by her side. Her head felt light and her body cold. Reaching up, she touched the hard line of his jaw. "Perhaps this is the way it was always meant to be," she murmured. Then blackness closed in around her and she felt nothing more.

Vaguely, Kathleen became aware of voices around her. Every breath she took sent spasms of pain coursing through her. "I didn't think death was supposed to hurt," she muttered. "I thought one left one's mortal body and found some sort of peace."

"You're not dead and you're not going to die," she heard John scold her gruffly. He sounded determined to keep her alive by the sheer power of his will, if that were necessary.

Kathleen opened her eyes a slit and saw him. Behind him stood a man and woman who looked to be in their early thirties, their clothes clean but ragged. Then, out of the corner of her eye, she saw several children peering around the legs of the adults. Vaguely she realized she was in a cabin.

"She's lost a lot of blood and the bullet's still lodged within her," the man was saying, his expression grim.

John's expression was equally grim. "I have to remove it and stop the bleeding or she'll surely die," he replied.

The pain was so intense Kathleen could scarcely breathe. "Please, just let me die in peace," she pleaded, wanting only to be free of this agony.

"I will not let you die without a fight," John growled. Turning to the others, he said, "You must help hold her. She cannot be allowed to move."

Very gently he stroked her cheek. His own stomach was knotted with pain at the sight of her anguish. Again he promised himself that he would not allow her to die. "This will hurt but 'tis necessary," he said with deep apology. Then, his face becoming stern, he walked over to the fire and heated his knife in the flames.

"Hold her," she heard him order, and she felt hands close around her legs and arms. "Tightly," he commanded.

Kathleen felt him cutting the fabric of her dress around the wound.

"Be strong, Kate," he ordered.

She screamed as his knife felt its way into her, and with her screams echoing in her head, she again escaped into the blackness.

The next time she awoke it was to John's urging. "You must eat," he was saying determinedly.

Weakly she shook her head, then wished she hadn't as a wild dizziness overtook her.

"Kate, you've got to eat. You've lost a lot of blood. You have to rebuild your strength," he urged.

Her mouth felt too dry to speak, still she had to try. But when she opened it, suddenly there was liquid being poured very slowly into it. She swallowed as best she could but some of the broth went down her windpipe and she coughed. Pain like none she'd ever known pierced her and, once more, she lost consciousness.

The next time she awoke, John was there again. He looked tired and haggard. "You must eat," he ordered. "I'll not let my surgery go for naught."

This time she didn't fight him and managed to get down several sips.

The next couple of days were vague in Kathleen's mind. Her temperature rose, the pain grew worse, and she felt herself slipping into a state of delirium.

"I'm taking you to Ashford Hall," John told her. "Mrs. Oats has worked miracles and we need one at the moment."

Chapter Nineteen

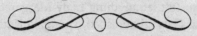

Almost as if it were happening to someone else, Kathleen was aware of riding cradled in John's arms. The journey seemed endless. Intermittently she would feel warm sunlight on her face, then she would open her eyes and see the stars. But always, there was John's jaw, set in a hard, determined line.

When she thought she could endure no more, she awoke to the sound of familiar voices around her. She was back in her room. Her dress and bandages had been removed and Mrs. Oats was there with Janet. They were placing warm poultices on her abdomen.

"We've drained the wound and if this don't suck out the rest of that poison, I don't know what will," Mrs. Oats was saying.

"It's a miracle she's survived this long," Janet replied worriedly.

Suddenly the door burst open. "I can't believe this woman is back under my roof!" Lady Margaret shrieked, striding toward the bed as if she intended to pick Kathleen up bodily and throw her out. "She is like a curse upon us! My son insists on risking scandal to save her from her un-

savory past, and now we must heal her. Will we never b
rid of her?''

"Get out!" It was John's voice coming from some
where on the far side of the room. Kathleen heard the rus
tling of a skirt and the door being slammed.

"I bring him nothing but trouble," she muttered.

"You mustn't let anything Lady Margaret says bother
you," Mrs. Oats admonished, sponging Kathleen's brow
with a cool cloth. "The rest of us is real pleased to have
you back. We all missed you. And Mr. Ashford wants you
here. He wouldn't have brung you otherwise. Now you just
concentrate on getting well."

He brought me here because he promised the governor
he would, Kathleen corrected silently. Aloud she said only
"I feel so tired."

"You must take some nourishment before you sleep,"
Janet insisted, seating herself next to the bed. Picking up
a cup of broth, she began spooning it into Kathleen's
mouth.

Afterward, Kathleen slept. Late in the night she awoke.
There was a full moon out and its light was streaming in
through the window, illuminating the room. Janet was
asleep in a chair beside the fire, while John sat in the chair
beside the bed. There was an angry, brooding look on his
face.

He's regretting having ever crossed my path, she mused,
and her chin tightened with pride. "I'm sorry to be an intrusion on your life once again," she said stiffly.

John blinked his eyes as if coming out of deep thought.
"I've never considered you an intrusion," he said gruffly.
"It is I who should be apologizing to you for always
seeming to put your life in danger."

Kathleen scowled. "This was not your fault. It was because of me they found the both of us."

"It doesn't matter how they found us." His voice took on a gentle, soothing quality as his hand stroked her brow. "What matters is that they can harm us no longer. Now you must concentrate on getting well." Worry creased his brow. "Your fever is still high."

The depth of concern in his eyes threatened to take her breath away and his touch caused her to forget her pain. Suddenly afraid that in her weakened state she would reveal what she most wanted to keep hidden, she said, "I'm very tired." And closing her eyes, she went back to sleep.

As John watched her sleep, the brooding look returned to his face. He promised himself that if she survived, he would do all in his power to see that she found happiness.

The next day Kathleen's fever rose dramatically. Janet and Mrs. Oats continued to change the poultice every hour. But it was John who never left her bedside. It was he Kathleen saw each time she opened her eyes.

"The poultices are coming off cleaner," she heard Mrs. Oats telling him anxiously. "But her fever don't seem to want to break."

Kathleen's mind began to wander. At times she thought she was back on the pirate ship, and once she thought she was back in her cell, awaiting the gallows. But each time when she came back to reality, John was there, and just seeing him gave her comfort.

But even his presence was not enough. Her strength began to fail her. As the sun set and the moon rose, from the shadowy places in the room and the darkness beyond the window she saw vague ghostly images beckoning her to rise and come with them. She was tired and the peace they offered was inviting.

"I'm so frightened," she murmured weakly.

"You've nothing to fear here," John assured her.

"They're beckoning me. They want me to come wit them," she tried to explain, her eyes wide as she looke beyond him.

Mrs. Oats crossed herself. "She be seeing the callers o death, Mr. Ashford."

"They'll not have her," he declared. Setting on the bed he gathered Kathleen in his arms and held her tightl against him. "I won't let them have you, Kate," he snarle in her ear.

Her hands closed on the fabric of his shirt. In spite o her pain, in his arms she felt comfort and safety. No harn could reach her here. She buried her face in the soft fabri of his shirt and the musky smell of him filled her senses His strength seemed to flow into her. Her body began t tremble.

"No!" he growled. "I will not allow you to leave me Kate." His arms tightened around her like bands of iron.

The possessiveness in his voice sent a surge of fir through her, then a cold sweat broke out on her brow. Sh clung to him as darkness once again filled her mind.

When she awoke again, Kathleen actually felt hungry The sun was high in the sky and Janet was smiling dow at her. "Mrs. Oats says you're going to live," she in formed her brightly. "It were Mr. Ashford what kept yo with us. It were as if he was holding off death by the shee power of his will." She continued to regard Kathleen wit friendly interest. "Even after your fever broke, he re fused to leave your bedside until dawn. Then Mrs. Oat insisted that he get some rest. He hasn't spend a night in hi own bed since he brung you here."

Lying quietly, Kathleen remembered how possessively he'd held her. But that afternoon when he came in, although he was polite and spoke kindly, there was an air of detachment about him. He might go so far as to consider me his friend, she mused, but I'll never be more than that to him.

Four days later, when Janet carried Kathleen's luncheon tray in to her, she was in a huff. "I swear if her ladyship don't get off to Jamestown to board her ship for England soon, we'll all go mad."

Kathleen forced a smile. She'd known the time would come for John to leave. She'd even told herself she was looking forward to it. With him gone, it would be much easier to put him out of her mind, she assured herself. Especially knowing he was on his way to wed someone else. "I'm feeling strong enough to feed myself," she insisted as Janet sat down and began to spoon the broth to her lips. "You run along and help speed the party on its way."

"Thank you, miss," the maid said gratefully, and she hurried away.

Left alone in the room, Kathleen had no appetite. Looking around, she felt John's presence everywhere. You're lying if you think it will be any easier being here with him gone, she chided herself. Picking up the spoon, she began to eat. The sooner she had her health back, the sooner she could leave.

That evening when he came to call upon her, her mask of polite indifference was firmly in place, but John was in an unusual mood. There was an indecisiveness about him that Kathleen had never seen before. As usual he inquired about her health, and she assured him she was feeling much better. During the past few days it had been their routine that she would then ask about the crops. He would

say a few words, then leave. But tonight after answering
her polite inquiry, he wandered over to the window and fell
into a pensive silence.

He has appointed himself my guardian and feels as if
he's deserting me, she thought glumly. "I understand you
and Lady Margaret will be sailing for England soon," she
said with forced cheerfulness. "I want to wish you a safe
and swift journey."

"My mother is sailing for England. I am not," he replied stiffly, continuing to stare into the darkness beyond
the window. "She'll be taking Quinn and her maid, Sally,
with her as companions. They'll see she's well cared for."

It's his damn sense of duty again! Kathleen cursed
mentally. He feels he cannot leave me in this state of
health. "There is no reason for you to cancel your plans on
my account. I'm much better and will be up soon, leaving
to start my own life once again."

He turned toward her then, a dark frown upon his face.
"I had no plans to sail for England. This is my home and
it is where I shall stay."

Kathleen looked at him in confusion. "But you said—"

"I know what I said," he interrupted curtly. "It was
merely a ploy to get you here without argument. I didn't
enjoy the thought of spending our journey in an endless
discussion. I had promised the governor I would bring you
here and bring you here was what I intended to do. I
wanted to be certain you recovered from your ordeal in a
safe haven. I apologize for the lie, but I felt it was necessary." Before she could speak, he strode out of the room.

Lying back in bed, she stared up at the canopy and
frowned. If he was not going to England, then he had no
intention of marrying Lady Andrea Clemens. But it also
became very clear during the next several days that he had

no intention of asking Kathleen to remain with him. While he was always polite and called upon her each day, there remained a coolness between them.

Determined to be away as quickly as possible, Kathleen began to leave her bed and walk around her room. At first her legs were wobbly, but it did not take long for their strength to increase. She was fully on her way to recovery, and with each day she felt much stronger than the day before. Very soon she was insisting on dressing and going downstairs for her meals.

Then one sunny summer day, about midmorning, John knocked on the door to her room. "I have a surprise for you," he said, offering her his arm. He had braced himself for this moment, still this was one of the most difficult things he had ever done in his life. It would be easier to face a hostile band of Indians, he thought, as he walked her down the stairs and out into the garden.

"You could give me a hint," Kathleen coaxed, trying not to think of the warmth spreading through her from the feel of his arm beneath her hand.

"Then it would not be a surprise," John replied, coming to a halt at the beginning of the boxwood maze. "You'll find the answer at the center." Leaving her, he strode back toward the house. He had arranged the surprise but he had no wish to observe her reaction.

In confusion, she watched him go. Then, frowning dubiously, she entered the maze and began making her way along the path between the carefully manicured walls of shrubbery. The air smelled warm and sweet. Rounding the final bend that led to the center, she came to an abrupt halt and stood staring in shock.

"I'm so glad to see you again, my dear Kathleen," Mr. Dermot said with the enthusiasm of an ardent lover. Rising from the bench on which he'd been sitting, he bowed low as he presented her with a bouquet of flowers. "I've thought of you constantly since your departure from Jamestown. You've tormented my dreams and destroyed my sleep. I cannot tell you what delight I felt when Mr Ashford sent word that I should come if I were still interested in having you as my wife. My heart fairly leapt in my chest to think there might be a chance you could be persuaded to forgive my brutish behavior." He fell to his knees before her. "I swear I'll never leave your side again. And, I shall challenge any man who would say one word against you."

For a moment longer, Kathleen stared at him in stunned silence. Then, finding her voice, she said dryly, "I cannot ask so great a boon from you. I'm certain there are still those who would speak against me, and I'll not bring such upheaval to your life."

"I care nothing about the upheaval," he protested, taking her hands in his. "My heart is yours. Bid me do any deed to prove myself and I will comply."

John had played matchmaker for her! Clearly he was anxious to be rid of her. Tears of anger burned in the back of Kathleen's eyes. "I cannot marry you," she stated simply but firmly.

"I know you must be worried about returning to Jamestown, but you've no need," he assured her. "On her way through, Lady Margaret painted such a picture of you as a true heroine, you will be welcomed back with honor."

Again Kathleen stared at him in stunned silence. Then, recovering from the shock of this news, she told herself that she shouldn't be surprised by Lady Margaret's actions. John had connected himself publicly with her, so for his sake and the sake of the Ashford family name and position, Lady Margaret would naturally try to make Kathleen as socially acceptable as possible. Her gaze narrowed on Mr. Dermot. Cynically, she wondered if he would have come if Lady Margaret hadn't spoken for her. "It would seem that my marrying you would cause you no great upheaval after all," she noted. Jerking her hands free, she added with finality, "I shall never marry you and wish you to be gone from my life as quickly as possible."

"You must give me a chance to prove myself to you," he pleaded. "We could have a wonderful future together. Mr. Ashford has even offered a dowry as a gesture of his gratitude to you for having saved his life."

A dowry! John was actually willing to pay to have her taken off his hands. That was the last straw! "No!" she snapped and stalked out of the maze.

Entering the house, she went straight to her room and began to pack. She would leave here before the end of the day.

A knock sounded on her door. "Go away," she ordered, continuing to throw her things haphazardly into her satchel.

John scowled at her command. It hadn't been easy, but he'd tried to do what he thought would please her. She had not, however, reacted as he had expected. But then he had never been particularly successful at predicting Kate's reactions in any given situation. Ignoring her order, he entered the room. Seeing the half-filled satchel, he frowned in confusion. "You are packing?" he demanded. "Mr. Dermot has told me you rejected him." A cynical edge entered his voice as his gazed narrowed on her. "Or was that merely a feminine ploy to make him suffer a bit more for his disloyalty?"

"'Twas no ploy," she replied sharply. Pausing, she glared at him. "If you wanted me gone, you had only to say so and I would have left in an instant. There was no need to go search me out a husband." Her cheeks reddened with indignation. "And there was certainly no need for you to offer to provide a dowry. I will not be sold to any man!"

John scowled. He had not meant to offend her. "The dowry was offered as a gift of gratitude, nothing more," he said stiffly. "And I was not searching you out a husband. I was merely trying to undo a wrong I felt I had done."

Kathleen stared at him in angry confusion. "A wrong?"

Sending her into another man's arms was difficult enough. He could not face her while he did it. Turning away from her, he paced across the room. Coming to a halt in front of the window, he looked out at the world beyond. "I spoke against Mr. Dermot when you were first freed. But during the past weeks I've had much time for thought. Love is a very difficult commodity to come by and I did not want you to lose it because of my callous remarks." He turned back toward her, his expression grim. "Mr. Dermot is waiting in the downstairs parlor. I suggest you forget your pride and go to him."

His anxiousness to see her married to Mr. Dermot cut like a knife. "He may sit until he rots," she snapped, continuing with her packing.

John's jaw tensed. She was surely the most stubborn woman in all of Virginia, perhaps even in all of the colonies, he decided. But he had promised himself that he would fight for her happiness no matter how bitter the words tasted in his mouth. "You must have loved him greatly once to have agreed to marry him. I would not want to see you make a mistake you will regret for the rest of your life."

His pleading on Mr. Dermot's behalf was more than Kathleen could bear. "I was never in love with Mr. Dermot, nor will I ever be!" The moment the words were out, she wished she'd bitten her tongue. A flush began to creep up her neck. What did it matter if he knew the truth? she reasoned in an attempt to ignore her embarrassment. He cared nothing for her. Avoiding looking at him, she picked up a dress, rolled it into a ball and shoved it into the satchel.

John stood regarding her in frozen silence as anger flowed through him. A question rose in his mind that demanded an answer. He was not certain he would like what he heard, but perhaps it would free him of her once and for all. Reaching her in three long strides, he captured her by the arm and jerked her around to face him. "If you were willing to marry Mr. Dermot when you did not love him, why were you not willing to marry me?"

Kathleen's chin threatened to tremble but she held it firm. "A gentleman would never ask a lady such a question," she retorted, trying to pull away from him.

She was right, but his need to know her true thoughts about him so that he could be rid of this hold she had over him was too great. His free hand closed around her other arm and he held her firmly in front of him. "Look me in the eye, Kate," he ordered. "I want an answer. And I want the truth."

She saw the cold fury in his eyes and knew that she had wounded his pride and injured his self-esteem with her lies. He would never forgive her. However, it was time to tell the truth. He was a good man and he deserved to have his pride repaired before she left. "It was not that I did not want to marry you," she confessed. "And for a short while I thought I could be as good a wife to you as any woman. Then I learned of your courtship of Lady Andrea Clemens and realized how many doors of opportunity you had open to you without me in your life. I knew it was only honor that bound you to me. I could not remain and ruin your chances to better yourself." Swallowing down the lump this admission had brought to her throat, she firmed her jaw. "As for Mr. Dermot," she continued tersely, "I knew I was as good a wife as he could seek."

John drew a terse breath. She had wanted to be married to him! The urge to shake her for lying to him was close to overwhelming, and yet at the same time he wanted to pull her into his arms and kiss her. He was amazed that it was possible to be so angry with someone and yet so happy at the same time. "Lady Andrea Clemens is a spoiled brat. I've no desire for a wife such as she," he growled. "As for my sense of honor, I had none where you were concerned. If I were an honorable man I would have allowed you your freedom from the beginning. Instead, I seduced you and insisted on calling you my wife against your wishes. I told myself I was being unfair, but I argued that I could give you as good a life as any man. I wanted you beside me always."

Kathleen stared at him incredulously. "I thought it was only pity and duty you felt toward me."

"I have felt a great many things toward you, but pity and duty were not high amongst them," he replied huskily. "It was as if a part of me was ripped away when I allowed you to leave after we'd escaped the Indians. But when you called marriage to me an entrapment, I was forced to face my selfishness. I loved you too much to bind you to a life you did not truly want."

Kathleen looked up into the dark depths of his eyes. The anger was gone, replaced by a heat that sent a current of warmth racing through her. "I thought you were relieved to be free of me," she said, her voice carrying a note of awe that he had actually used the word *love* in describing his feelings toward her.

"I paced my room for nights unable to sleep," he confessed gruffly. "When I did sleep, I dreamed of you."

She wanted to believe all he said. Still… "If you feel so strongly toward me, why did you send for Mr. Dermot?" she forced herself to ask.

John read the anguish in her eyes and knew she had suffered as greatly as he. "During those long hours when I feared you might die, I promised myself that I would do all that was in my power to make you happy. Of your own free will you had agreed to marry Mr. Dermot, and by your own words you had led me to believe you loved him." His jaw tensed as he recalled the torment these thoughts had caused him. "Sending for him was the hardest thing I have ever done," he continued grimly. "But I knew I'd behaved jealously and I didn't want anything I'd done to stand in the way of your happiness."

Tentatively, as if still afraid to believe he could care for her as deeply as he professed, Kathleen touched the line of his jaw. "During the night, before the morning I was arrested, I had decided that I must tell Mr. Dermot I could never marry him. In my heart and in my soul I was still your wife."

John issued a low growl of satisfaction. Drawing her into his arms, he found her mouth in a hungry, demanding kiss.

Kathleen's heart soared. She could no longer doubt that he honestly cared for her. As their lips parted and she trailed light kisses down his neck, she asked huskily, "And now will you send Mr. Dermot on his way?"

"In a moment." Releasing her completely, his manner became formal. Taking a step back, he took her hands in his. "First I must ask you a very important question. Will you marry me, Miss Kathleen James, officially in the eyes of the government of Virginia on this very morning?"

Kathleen smiled happily. "I will marry you any time and any place you choose, but I don't understand how we can officially wed this very day."

A sheepishness came over his features. "The Reverend Vales is in my study. I was determined to speed you on your way to happiness as quickly as possible." The grimness returned to his face. "I had hoped that knowing you were happily wed would free me of you and give me back my heart."

"For me to be happily wed will not provide you or your heart freedom," she replied, rising on tiptoe to kiss him. He tasted so very good. She ran her hands over his chest and up onto his shoulders. "I have greatly missed your company," she said with a sigh.

He saw the passion in her eyes and smiled. "This time you will have to make an honest man of me first," he stipulated, catching her hands as she began to unfasten the buttons of his waistcoat.

Her mouth formed a mischievous pout. "It has been a very long time," she reminded him coaxingly. She knew she was behaving wantonly, but her desire for him was too strong to resist.

"A very long time," he agreed gruffly, as she kissed the hands that held her wrists captive, enticing them to release her. He ached to give in to her seduction, but he was determined that the next time he took her to bed it would be as his legal wife.

"And it's going to feel like years if you leave me now," she pointed out, kissing him lightly between words. "First you must offer Mr. Dermot some luncheon before he leaves and then you must find two witnesses."

Feeling his resolve weakening, he released her abruptly and stepped back from her touch. "You forget, Kate, I'm a man of action," he reminded her. "Wait here," he ordered.

Kathleen wanted to rush after him the moment he left. But this time she obeyed his command.

Within a few minutes, he returned with the Reverend Vales, Adam and Mrs. Elby. All three looked somewhat confused, especially the reverend. Still, Adam and Mrs. Elby were smiling brightly with approval.

In front of the cook and the new butler of Ashford Hall, John and Kathleen pledged themselves to one another through trouble and strife, through good and bad.

"And I will always love you and always stand by your side," John finished solemnly as tears of joy filled Kathleen's eyes.

"And I will always love you and always stand by your side," she promised. "For that is clearly where I belong."

"Clearly," he agreed, taking her in his arms and kissing her as the reverend pronounced them husband and wife.

Releasing her, John turned his attention to the document lying on the table. "You will observe that I am signing this paper of my own free will, not because there is a gun pointed to my head," he whispered in her ear as he opened the inkwell. "And I will expect you to respect it and not burn it," he added. Then, with the expression of a man with a purpose, he placed his signature upon their marriage contract.

"This one I shall lock away in your safe," she assured him as she inscribed her name upon the document.

Finally Adam and Mrs. Elby added their marks and the reverend his name, making it official.

When the last signature was finished, John cupped Kathleen's face in his hands. "The deed is done and this time it can never be undone. You are now and forever my wife."

"Now and forever," she conceded solemnly.

"'Twas so beautiful," Mrs. Elby sobbed quietly.

"'Twas a privilege to witness such an occasion," Adam agreed with a broad smile. Suddenly a solemn expression came over his features. Bowing low toward Kathleen, he said with deference, "'Twill be an honor to serve the new mistress of Ashford Hall."

"An honor indeed," Mrs. Elby agreed, curtsying deeply in front of Kathleen.

As she was addressed by her new name, Kathleen flushed with happiness. She had finally found the home she had sought for so many years.

Adam coughed lightly, clearly a habit he'd picked up from Quinn. "What is it?" John asked, glancing toward him.

"What shall we do with Mr. Dermot?" he asked.

"Offer him some sustenance and tell him I've decided to save the price of a dowry and marry Miss James myself," John replied with a mischievous grin.

"You do have a wicked sense of humor," Kathleen muttered as they ushered the Reverend Vales, Adam and Mrs. Elby from the room, chuckling under their breath. "I've half a mind to—"

Closing the door, John turned and stopped her playful tirade with a kiss.

Lifting her head away from his, she gently stroked his jaw. "I have missed you so very much," she confessed again. "It was only thoughts of you that kept me sane when I was certain I was doomed."

"I shall provide you with more than thoughts this day," he promised, beginning to unfasten her dress.

Kathleen gasped with delight as he nipped her bared shoulder, sending currents of desire coursing through her. "You do have a most exciting touch," she murmured.

Grinning, he continued to rid her of her clothing as he said in a poetic rhythm,

"There was a young woman named Kate,
Who tried to deny her fate.
But today she shall learn how hot passion can burn
Held in the arms of her mate."

Laughing softly, Kathleen began to unfasten his clothing. "'Tis a good thing your lovemaking is better than your poetry."

His hands trailed fire as they followed the naked curves of her body. "A wife should have more respect for her husband's creative abilities."

Discarding his shirt, she kissed the hollow of his neck. "I've great respect for your creative abilities," she admitted huskily, reaching for the fastenings of his breeches. "Just not as a poet."

Laughing softly, he allowed her to finish undressing him, then, lifting her in his arms, he carried her to the bed.

Lying beside her, with his hands and his lips he teased her body until she craved his possession with every fiber of

her being. But as she arched against him, inviting him t
own her, he drew back.

Lifting his head, he looked into her passion-darkenec
eyes. "Who are you, Kate?" he questioned demandingly.

She knew what answer he wanted. "Your wife," she replied, running her hand along the firm, taut muscles of his
thigh.

"And you will never try to deny that again?" he demanded gruffly.

"Never," she promised, moving against him with urgent invitation.

"Never?" he demanded once again.

"Never," she promised even more firmly.

"'Tis about time you admitted to it," he growled, accepting her invitation.

* * * * *

COMING NEXT MONTH

#131 TEXAS HEALER—Ruth Langan
Morning Light, sister of a great Comanche chief, had vowed
never to trust a white man. But Dr. Dan Conway's soothing
touch soon healed her bitter, lonely heart.

#132 FORTUNE HUNTER—Deborah Simmons
Socialite Melissa Hampton and impoverished Leighton Somerset
both profited from their marriage. Yet, was Lord Somerset the
one plotting Melissa's demise—or had he truly fallen in love
with her?

#133 DANGEROUS CHARADE—Madeline Harper
Beautiful Margaret Hanson had told Steven Peyton a pack
of lies. Why should he believe her now, when she claimed
he was a missing prince and begged him to save his tiny
European country?

#134 TEMPTATION'S PRICE—Dallas Schulze
Years ago Matt Prescott chose adventure over the girl
he'd been forced to wed. Now he was back—and one look at
sweet Liberty told him that *this* time, she wouldn't be so easy
to dismiss....

AVAILABLE NOW:

**#127   THE LADY AND THE
LAIRD**
Maura Seger

#128 SWEET SUSPICIONS
Julie Tetel

#129   THE CLAIM
Lucy Elliot

#130 PIRATE BRIDE
Elizabeth August

HARLEQUIN

Romance®

Harlequin's Ruth Jean Dale brings you THE TAGGARTS OF TEXAS!

Those Taggart men—strong, sexy and hard to resist . . .

There's Jesse James Taggart in **FIREWORKS!**
Harlequin Romance #3205 (July 1992)

And Trey Smith—he's **THE RED-BLOODED YANKEE!**
Harlequin Temptation #413 (October 1992)

Then there's Daniel Boone Taggart in **SHOWDOWN!**
Harlequin Romance #3242 (January 1993)

And finally the Taggarts who started it all—in **LEGEND!**
Harlequin Historical #168 (April 1993)

Read all the Taggart romances!
Meet all the Taggart men!

Available wherever Harlequin books are sold.   DALE-R

COMING IN JULY
FROM HARLEQUIN HISTORICALS

TEMPTATION'S PRICE
by Dallas Schulze

Dallas Schulze's sensuous, sparkling love stories have made her a favorite of both Harlequin American Romance and Silhouette Intimate Moments readers. Now she has created some of her most memorable characters ever for Harlequin Historicals. . . .

Liberty Ballard. . . who traveled across America's Great Plains to start a new life.

Matt Prescott. . . a man of the Wild West, tamed only by his love for Liberty.

Would they have to pay the price of giving in to temptation?

AVAILABLE IN JULY WHEREVER HARLEQUIN BOOKS ARE SOLD

Take 4 bestsell[ing]
love stories FRE[E]

Plus get a FREE surprise gift